I0720820

HUNTER'S CHOICE

TIMBER PHILIPS

COPYRIGHT

Text Copyright © 2014 by A.J. Downey DBA Timber Philips

All rights reserved.

No part of this book may be reproduced in any form or by any electronic or mechanical means, including information storage and retrieval systems, without written permission from the author, except for the use of brief quotations in a book review.

This is a work of fiction. The names, characters, businesses, places, events, and incidents are either the products of the author's imagination or used in a fictitious manner and are not to be construed as real except where noted and authorized. Any resemblance to persons, living or dead, or actual events are entirely coincidental. Any trademarks, service marks, product names, or names featured are assumed to be the property of their respective owner, and are used only for reference. There is no implied endorsement if any of these terms are used.

The author acknowledges the trademarked status and trademark owners of various products referenced in this work, which have been used without permission. The publication/use of these trademarks is not authorized, associated with, or sponsored by the trademark owners.

~

ISBN: 978-1-950222-19-3

Edited by Barbara J. Bailey

Book design by Maggie Kern

Cover art by Clarissa Yeo of Yocla Designs

DEDICATION

To my wonderful and loving fiancé. You give me inspiration daily; I don't know what I would do without you.

PROLOGUE

*H*unter

Sharp grinding pain caused my eyes to water. My left leg and wing were useless to me. I was trapped, unable to do anything for myself, too weak to make anything other than a piteous call that would likely go unheeded.

I closed my eyes and lay still and waited for death. Thousands of years of living and this is how I would go: in the middle of a stretch of asphalt, the cold rain pattering down on me while heartless humans passed me by in their nice warm cars, 'tsk'ing under their breath at the poor bundle of floundering feathers in the road.

Idiot.

I was an idiot, pure and simple.

I wailed my frustration as my heart pounded against my delicate ribs, each beat sending a fresh lance of pain through my broken wing, a sympathetic sharp pang echoing in my leg.

Who would have thought I would die like this? It was shameful. Ridiculous even. A being as old as I, so intent on their prey, as to be unaware of his surroundings. It was the mistake of a youngling, not of my kind.

A sharp sound, footsteps, I swiveled my head to take in a pair of worn brown work boots jogging across the highway. Gentle hands in thick leather closed around me and I screeched. As much pain as I was in, I couldn't help it. I was turned, and as I was, I looked into the most beautiful eyes, deep and soulful, the color of the sea meeting a storm-swept horizon. They were surrounded by pale milky skin and wisps of hair I swore was spun copper.

For a moment I thought it was Bébinn, come to fetch me to Annwn, but the pain she had wrought when she plucked me from the grit of the modern highway told me otherwise. I fought her; I couldn't help myself, but she took me from the road and got into a vehicle and that was all I could remember for some time...

CHAPTER ONE

*J*essamine

"You name this one yet?" Charlie asked me, and I shook my head.

The barred owl had been under my care for a couple of months. His left wing and left leg had been broken, but thankfully, both had been simple fractures. He was on the mend and due for release, as soon as I could get his atrophied muscles built back up.

I couldn't bear to name him, it wasn't so simple... he wasn't like the other owls under my care. He was different, somehow. Big for a barred owl, for one, and the way he watched me move through the old barn we used as an aerie, well, it bespoke an intelligence far beyond any ordinary owl.

No, I just couldn't name this one.

"Well, now, maybe that just means you're finally growing up, Jessamine!" He winked at me and I gave an indelicate snort, wrinkling my nose in distaste at the idea, and shook my head violently, strawberry blonde bangs flopping into my eyes, ponytail dragging against the rugged green canvas material of my Carhartt jacket.

"N...n...n...n...nnnnever!" My stutter was horrible but I forced the word out through it anyway.

Most of the time I chose to remain silent. I carried a notepad and pen on a string around my neck for when communication was absolutely required.

Charlie had fashioned a cover out of leather, made so that I could replace the notepad in it whenever I needed to. He'd spent so much time on it, tooling a barn owl into its medium-brown leather surface by hand. The loop that held the pen was sturdy.

It was a parting gift when I'd gone off to veterinary college. That had been when I was eighteen. Now, I worked full time at a veterinary hospital in Port Angeles, about thirty minutes from my owl-rehab facility. I'd worn it every day since he'd gifted it to me.

I'd lived here with my aunt and uncle; well, my mom's aunt and uncle, she didn't have any siblings, since I was seven. The old farm was my property now, for all intents and purposes, just not in name. They wanted it to be, but I had refused such a generous gift. They had in their wills that it would go to me, but I wasn't sure if I would be ready to really own it, even though I had been operating it for years.

Aunt Margie and Uncle Dave had recently retired to Arizona and a warmer climate. Even though Charlie was about the same age as them, he'd never do the same. Not him. Nope, he would live and die around these parts and his tribe, the Quilleute of the Olympic Peninsula in Washington State.

Moonchild's Owl Haven had started when I was nine, with a sick spotted owl my uncle and I had found while mushroom hunting. We had no idea what to do, but we couldn't just leave the poor thing. So, we took it to the vet, and insisted on learning.

A local bird sanctuary, the Northwest Raptor and Wildlife Center, took us on as volunteers. We had done things almost all wrong with the spotted owl, who, by the grace of some higher power and Jaye Moore, the director of the Raptor Center, had lived. Despite, or maybe because of, our bungling the initial care of Hootie back then, I had fallen in love with the cause almost instantly and my uncle and I had been willing pupils under Jaye. We had learned everything there was to learn about caring for all types of birds from her, but for me, it had always been about the owls. I'm not sure why.

My uncle and I had spent every summer from the time I was nine to when I was thirteen renovating the old barn on the property, to get it ready to house any injured owls. When I was thirteen, my uncle and I applied for the necessary permits to become a wildlife rehabilitation facility. We won the permits, and had rehabilitated quite a few owls in the fifteen years between then and now. In that time, only three had become fixtures, their injuries necessitating a permanent residency under my care.

I went around the large open interior of the old barn, cleaning cages, feeding my charges and checking on the newer birds.

When I came to the back wall of the barn, I looked up at the almost-life-sized tree artfully burned into its raw wood surface. Leaves bearing the burned-in name of every owl we had ever helped hung on brass hooks from the many branches. It was a project my uncle and I had started on day one.

"What're you going to put on his tag, if you don't name him?" Charlie asked as I looked over the tree. I shrugged my shoulder and turned; he was watching the bird with a curious look on his face. The bird, though? He was watching me.

He was more brown than white, his patterning dappled and streaked in such a way as to remind me of the light falling through the trees. His beak was the color of bone, not yellow like a lot of the barred owls around. His eyes, though; they were limpid pools of darkness, large and oddly expressive, and followed me as a man's would, drinking me in as I moved about the barn. There was something there, something I couldn't place, but he, he was like no other owl; be it barred, barn, spotted, or any other species I had housed under my roof.

"Odd feller, ain'tcha?" Charlie asked absently. The bird turned and looked Charlie in the eye and Charlie shuddered as if he'd gotten a sudden chill.

I clapped twice and Charlie looked at me. I signed out that I was cleaning up and calling it a day out here and that he should do the same.

Throughout my childhood, Charlie, my uncle and I had developed a series of hand signals for me to let them know what I was up to. My aunt had never grasped it, but it was like our own sign language.

I had never bothered learning ASL, American Sign Language; what was the point out here where my world was as small as it was? Where no one else spoke it? I didn't venture to the city very often, and my notepad and pointing sufficed, more often than not.

Was I lonely?

Yes, sometimes, but that was my lot in life. Besides, I had Charlie, and my owls. They were like my feathered children and I loved each one, choosing a name, growing attached, and crying with a sense of loss at every release. Some would call me masochistic, and to some degree I suppose that was true, but you can't do what I do and not feel. That would simply be barbaric.

I stopped in front of my unnamed barred owl's cage, Charlie ducked out of the barn and into the ever-present light drizzle outside. I considered the owl, who cooed softly at me, another odd occurrence. I looked around to make sure that Charlie was good and gone from hearing range.

"W-what's your n-n-n-n-ame, fella?" I asked, softly.

When it was just me and the owls, away from human judgment, my stutter was much less. Psychogenic they called it, as opposed to neurogenic. It meant that there was nothing neurologically wrong with me or my brain to cause the stutter. No, mine was all in my head on a psychological level due to trauma. Not something I liked to think about or talk about.

The owl cocked its head almost all the way 'round upside down, like they do sometimes, and considered me. It gave a familiar broken call and I smiled. That was where my initial love of owls had come from.

When my aunt and uncle had plucked me out of the temporary state custody I'd been in, I'd already been self-conscious of my speech. Aunt Margie and Uncle Dave were a childless couple by fate, not design. So when Uncle Dave's niece, my mom had gotten into... trouble... and could no longer take care of me, Aunt Margie had insisted that she and Uncle Dave come to the rescue. It was the kind of people they were, and I loved them for it.

Unfortunately for me, going from life in the city to life here on the Olympic Peninsula was a lesson in culture shock. It was so quiet here at night, and the animal sounds from out there in the dark were terrifying at first.

That is, they were until Uncle Dave told me the broken hooting I was hearing was an owl, and he pointed out a ghost of a bird in one of our trees.

He told me that there was nothing to be afraid of, that the owl was just saying 'Welcome to the neighborhood,' and that she just had a stutter, like me. I think it was his attempt at telling me not to let my stutter get me down, that the animals didn't, but I was way beyond a small pep talk at that point.

The big barred owl hooted at me questioningly and I smiled. He was just so *odd*. It made me wonder about him even more. I pursed my lips in thought and rejected the notion of going into his enclosure for now. As human as his mannerisms were, he was still a bird of prey and as such, pretty dangerous and unpredictable. I smiled at him and backed away. He ruffled his feathers and hunkered down on his perch, blinked, and watched me go. He would be ready for release as soon as I could get him back into flying form, so, a month or more down the road.

I slipped out into the mist-like rain, shutting and securing the old barn door behind me. I looked out over my small side yard at the two story cedar-shake-sided house that had been lovingly built, by my uncle, for my aunt. I had taken over the master bedroom on the second story when they had cleared out. A small deck jutted out from the floor-to-ceiling windows on either side of the French doors.

I traipsed across the gravel drive and mounted the steps to the small deck two at a time. I wiped my boots carefully on the mat before letting myself in to my bedroom.

I took off my boots just inside the doors on the slate entryway, before it transitioned into carpet. I took pains to keep the outdoors where they belonged, and not in my house. I stepped into my rubber-soled sheepskin slippers and padded across the floor to the bedroom door. My bedroom was, technically, on the side of the house, rather than the back or front. I took off my coat as I went down the stairs, hanging it carelessly on the banister as I passed into the kitchen. I set about making myself and Charlie some dinner, boiling water for hot tea.

After a time, he came in through the back door. I scowled and pointed at his boots. He laughed and took them off. I scowled again at his holey sock where his big toe poked through as he took a seat at the marble kitchen counter.

"That big barred bastard is about ready to go into an aviary," he grunted, and I smiled. I'd imagine being Quilleute, hell, being Native, gave Charlie a stronger opinion than most about the subject, and rightfully so. In Charlie's world, barred owls were interlopers, forcing the native spotted owls from their rightful territory. The barred owl wasn't exactly native to the Pacific Northwest and was forcing out the much rarer, and endangered, northern spotted owl, both by killing the slightly smaller owl and by interbreeding with it. To quote the villain of the movie Braveheart, "If we can't get them out, we'll breed them out."

Still, Charlie was like me, a firm believer that every creature great and small deserved to live as pain-free an existence as possible. The world was harsh enough without us adding to it.

That's not to say we were vegetarians, or anything close. We *did* have a deep respect for what we ate and after I dished up the salmon steaks and green beans, we bowed our heads in a moment of silence, paying our respects to the creature we were about to consume.

"Gotta mend the south aviary tomorrow if you're gonna start working that big barred, getting him ready to fly." He spoke around a mouthful of food, and I rolled my eyes while simultaneously giving him a thumbs-up. He laughed, knowing exactly what it was I meant. He didn't apologize for talking with his mouth full, he just shoveled more into his maw and chewed with gusto.

I cooked, he cleaned. That was the deal around here. I poured us some steaming mugs of blackberry tea and added a generous amount of honey to both while he rinsed dishes and loaded the dishwasher. He'd be heading home in his big old Ford pickup soon. I'd told him he should just move into the downstairs room but he'd have none of it, swearing he'd live on the res and die on the res, which was a good forty minutes away.

I sighed and went into the living room, adding logs to the ravenous potbellied stove in the corner.

"Well, Jessa-my-girl, it's time for me to haul my old bones back to the res." Charlie stretched and dropped into one of the seats at the little dining nook. He laboriously began pulling on his old boots.

"You going into town tomorrow?" he asked. I swiped across my neck once, our sign for 'No'. It was my day off, but he already knew that.

"All right then, sweetheart, you going to help an old man get that aviary up and running?" I shrugged and raised three fingers and pumped my fist up and down twice, holding imaginary jesses. He raised an eyebrow. Right now we had five birds, three of which needed exercise, which is what I'd just told him.

"Well, when you're done, you know where to find me at," he grumbled and I smiled sweetly. I went over and gave him a hug. He went out the back door and around the house, boots crunching on the gravel drive. I closed the door and a moment later I heard his old Ford rumble to life.

I sighed wearily and doused the lights on the first floor, after setting the coffee pot timer for the morning.

Sometimes there weren't enough hours in a day. Today had been no exception. Still, the birds and Charlie were fed, and tomorrow was a new day.

I shuffled up the stairs, leaving my coat behind, and put myself squarely into a hot shower. As I climbed into bed, I could hear the big barred owl all the way from the barn, his call clear and loud. Scientists call it the "Who cooks for you! Who cooks for you all?" which I thought was funny. It didn't sound like that to me.

To me it sounded like all was right in my world.

CHAPTER TWO

Jessamine

My alarm went off before sunrise and I pretty much beat it into submission, or at the very least, silence. I flopped onto my back under my plush and warm microfiber comforter and huffed out an irritated breath. Damn it, I felt like I hadn't slept at all. I got up and cursed, silently, of course. I could hear the rain sloshing in the gutters and down the drainpipe outside. I was used to it. It came with the territory, living in a temperate rainforest; I wasn't lucky enough to live inside the rain shadow.

I went about dressing both warmly and as waterproof as possible for the day, in long underwear and jeans with thick wool socks. I had one of those white waffle-pattern thermal shirts on under my flannel button-down. It was a green-and-gray plaid pattern that brought out the blue in my eyes. I had rolled the sleeves of the flannel shirt up to my elbows but left the sleeves of the thermal hugging my wrists.

I picked up my boots and padded downstairs in my stocking feet.

I went into the kitchen and dropped the boots on the slate entryway before the hardwood took over. The rich smell of coffee permeated the space and I gravitated in the direction of the pot. My favorite mug was standing by to do its duty. I poured myself a generous cup and praised the man who invented coffee pots that ran on a timer. I added some flavored creamer from my fridge and enjoyed my sugary caffeinated jolt while I set about making myself some peanut butter toast.

The light of false dawn was just beginning to show by the time I finished my toast and coffee, and I went and got my jacket off the banister at the foot of my stairs. After I shrugged into my Carhartt I went back into the kitchen to pull on my boots, lacing them up tight and double-knotting them to keep them from getting untied.

I was as ready as I was going to get.

I went out the back door and bolted through the rain and into the barn, slipping inside. It was warmer by a little, and much drier. I went up the steps to the old hayloft, which we had painstakingly remodeled into an examination area and kitchen of sorts.

I went about getting our guests' breakfast ready; it consisted of beef liver supplemented with liquid calcium to aid in healing any broken bones. I looked up at the whiteboard and brought out enough for those that needed it. I alternated the beef liver with live or dead mice, but typically left them in the enclosures at night. Most of our residents would only eat the mice when no one was looking, and to tell you the truth, I was fine with that.

One of our newest residents, a northern pygmy owl I'd named Rosie, was so ill I needed to feed her with a tube. It was awful and stressful for her, so I tried to make quick work of it. She was my top priority of late, so I set everything up and went back down the stairs, tugging on some flexible leather gloves that went halfway up my wrists. She just wasn't that big, only about the size of a sparrow. I wouldn't need any more protection.

I stopped at the bottom step. One of the yellow legal pads we kept notes on was resting up against the big, unnamed barred owl's cage.

I frowned; I could have sworn I was the last one out of the barn last night. I approached the pad with some trepidation, looking around to make sure there wasn't anyone hiding, though they would have to be a fool to hide in an enclosure with one of the birds.

There was no one that I could see. I stooped down in front of the cage and tugged off the gloves. Thick black writing done in Sharpie pen swirled across the pad in a calligraphic font. It was handwritten and said "My name is Hunter." I blinked and looked up into the soulful, dark eyes of the barred owl. He stretched his wings, which was all the enclosure would allow for and folded them against his back. He adjusted his feet on the perch, first one, and then the other, and blinked back at me as if to say, *Well, say something!*

I wondered if Charlie was messing with me. I stood and put the pad on top of the cage and resumed what I had been doing. I pulled my gloves back on and went to the stacked kennel-like cages, small and restrictive, where we housed the new patients.

I opened Rosie's cage and smiled, letting out a breath I hadn't realized I'd been holding when she blinked her big yellow-orange eyes at me. Her eyes reminded me of the color of rose gold, set in her dark brown feathers spotted with tan and white, which is where I picked her name from. I reached in carefully and captured her between my gloved hands. She didn't even try to put up a fight, and I felt a pang of panic mixed with concern. The only time an owl behaves even remotely tame is when they are at death's door, or imprinted on a human, meaning too used to humans to be released into captivity.

I took Rosie upstairs and fed her some wet cat food pureed a little smoother with water through a syringe. I didn't have to force the cannula down her gullet, which was a good sign. Rather, I just carefully introduced small amounts into her beak and let her swallow on her own, which she did. It was encouraging. She didn't fight too much, which was both good and bad. I gave her the medicines she needed and stroked her feathered head with my finger. We weren't out of the woods yet, so to speak. I was still afraid we might lose her.

I'd lost some throughout the years and it was never fun. We had a small pet cemetery complete with headstones on the far end of the property. The leaves burned with the names of our little lost ones were piled in a drift at the base of the tree on the barn's back wall. Thankfully, there were a lot fewer than what graced the branches. I would just have to wait and see when it came to it, where little Rosie's leaf would end up.

I put her back in her cage just as a light rap came at the barn door.

I went over to it and opened it up, expecting Charlie, but wondering why on earth he would knock.

"Jessamine! I thought you might be back here." I stepped back to allow the officers' entry into the barn. One of them I knew, he was an officer with the Washington State Department of Fish and Wildlife. I smiled up at Officer Baker and gave a little wave. He was familiar with my speech problems.

The man behind him was also an officer but he didn't wear the familiar dark green uniform of the Fish and Wildlife department. No, his uniform was the deep tan of the Clallam County Sheriff's Department. I stepped back and let them both in.

I pulled a handheld whiteboard off its Velcro mounting against one of the cages and wiped out the name and information of the bird that had been on it. I hastily scrawled along its surface with the blue dry-erase pen tied to it.

What's wrong? I flashed at them. The big barred owl clacked his beak in warning at the two men as they drew closer.

"Nothing! Nothing!" John Baker exclaimed.

"Hi, Ms. Connors... I'm Deputy Ron Caruthers. John, here, brought me out to see you; there's been a rash of thefts, appears to be drug-related and the thieves are getting bolder as time goes on. There've been several home invasion robberies over the last few weeks. We wanted to come out and just touch base with you, see if you'd seen or heard anything?"

The man smiled.

He was older, probably late fifties, early sixties. He had twinkling blue eyes the color of winter skies, over a thick salt-and-pepper mustache. He looked more like a friendly park ranger rather than a Sheriff's deputy with his Smokey the Bear hat. I wiped out the message on the board with the side of my hand.

I haven't seen or heard anything. Have they been near here? I watched as they read over the message; John's expression darkened a little, while Ron's remained smiling.

"Yes, your neighbors, about a mile up the road were robbed two nights ago. Mr. Jenkins is still in the hospital with a head injury." The Jenkins were an older couple; Mrs. Jenkins baked me lavender Madeline cookies, from scratch, from some of the lavender from the nearby farms. She was always a bit frail, on account of her heart.

I scribbled furiously at the whiteboard. *What about Mrs. Jenkins, is she okay? She has a bad heart.* I watched the two men apprehensively.

"Mrs. Jenkins is just fine. The two young men gave her quite a fright, but when Mr. Jenkins got between them and what they were after, they hit him in the head with a bat. He'll be all right in a day or so. The hospital is just keeping him for observation." John answered me.

"Still, it seems these two have been camping in the park and you're out here all alone, so we thought we'd come check on you."

John winced. The barred owl was putting up his warning call and clacking his beak menacingly. I put up a finger and motioned for the two men to follow. I wrote as I climbed the stairs into the converted loft.

Camping close to here? I asked, handing John the board.

He was an okay guy. We'd gone to high school together. He was stocky, with a wide breadth of shoulders tapering down to an almost-too-narrow waist. He had sandy blonde hair and brown eyes and, I suppose, was good-looking by the general standard. I'd just never been attracted to him, myself.

I picked up the metal mixing bowl of beef liver soaking in liquid calcium and a pair of forceps. I waved my hand at the two men, a clear indication to keep talking. John smiled. He knew to keep things to a simple yes and no when my hands were busy.

"So you haven't seen anything, then?" he asked.

I shook my head no. I handed the bowl to the Sheriff Deputy who took it with surprise. I propped the forceps along the edge and pulled on my leather gloves. I huffed a sigh at the big barred owl and opened up his enclosure. Firmly, but gently, gripping him by his ankles and cradling his back, I extracted him from the cage and held him. I jutted my chin at the bowl and then at John.

"Putting us to work, eh?" he asked and laughed.

I nodded. He plucked a bit of liver with the forceps and brought it to the bird's beak. The bird snatched it warily and I smiled down at him. We continued to feed him as we talked.

"You have someone that can stay with you for the time being?" the Sheriff asked.

I raised a shoulder in a half-shrug.

"Can Charlie stay with you?" John asked.

Again, I half-shrugged, I would have to ask him.

"Will you ask him?" John was searching my face.

I nodded.

"H-h-h-ow-w-w-w f-f-f-f-far?" I forced out, and the Sheriff raised his eyebrows in surprise.

"How far were they camped?" John asked.

I nodded.

"About a half-mile from here," he grunted.

"If you see anything, you really should call 9-1-1 immediately. We're pretty sure these guys are on something. They've already proven themselves dangerous." Ron was scowling.

"Hey, Jess! Everything alright in here? Looks like a damn doughnut convention in the driveway." Charlie came into the barn.

I nodded. He took in the Sheriff Deputy and John's presence.

"Nothin' wrong with our permits," he grunted.

"No, nothing like that Charlie," John placated him. "We were just stopping by to check on Jessamine, here. Bad element in the area..."

It was of some concern that there were a couple of drug -addled idiots causing problems in the area, especially for the Jenkins, who were such a nice couple. But I was watching the barred owl in my hands. He was eating from the forceps that John was holding, but he was watching me. I smiled down at him and let the men talk.

The owl finished his meal, and I carefully bounced him to get him to spread his wings. He did so without so much as a sound, and flapped them pretty well; he would be ready for the aviary in a day or two. I put him back in his enclosure and he stretched his wings, folding them back down against his back with a few disgruntled clicks of his beak. I pulled off the gloves and hung them on their hook. I thought that was the last time he'd be getting the liver. It would be mice, from then on.

The men were still talking about the Jenkins, filling Charlie in. I took the bowl from the Deputy and set it on a side table, and plucked down the yellow pad of paper from the top of the big barred's cage. I held it out to Charlie and raised an eyebrow in silent question.

"Whatcha got there?" he asked, and I held it out so he could read it.

"Who's Hunter?" he asked me, and all three men looked at me.

I pointed to the barred owl.

"So you named him, eh?" he asked.

I shook my head and took back my whiteboard.

I found that propped on his cage. I thought you did it. I held it up so they could see.

"Wasn't me." Charlie looked as confused as I felt.

"Was anyone else out here last night?" John asked.

Charlie and I both shook our heads.

I wiped the board clean and hastily scrawled out *I was the last one out. Charlie and I had been talking about Hunter's name, and this morning I found that.*

"Wasn't me, Jess!" Charlie repeated.

Ron got on his radio and walked out of the barn. John was looking at me with some concern.

"Somebody left it," he said.

I doubt it was the boys your Sheriff friend is after. Doesn't seem like something two violent druggies robbing people would do.

Charlie barked a laugh. John frowned, and Ron stepped back into the barn.

Somebody's just having a bit of fun at my expense. Nothing is missing and nothing else is out of place.

"I've ordered a step-up in patrols, just to be safe," Ron said, catching sight of my sign. John came over and took me by the elbow, guiding me to the back of the barn, out of earshot of Charlie and Ron.

"Jess, you know, I'd be happy to come by, spend a little extra time out here with you," he said gently.

That won't be needed. I'm perfectly fine, honest. A flicker of something crossed his face, I winced inwardly and hastily added

Thank you very much. The thought is appreciated.

"Still, promise you'll call me? Doesn't matter what for." He gave me his card, his cell phone number written on the front.

I promise, if I need anything, I'll TEXT you. I winked at him and smiled.

He plucked his hat off his head and laughed weakly, running his big hand over his hair.

"Right. You'll text," he said, and put his hat back on, obviously embarrassed by his minor gaffe.

Promise, I wrote, and that made him smile.

CHAPTER THREE

*J*essamine

I thought they'd never leave. These poor babies are hungry. I flashed at Charlie. He laughed.

"Need help catching up on feedin' 'em all?" he asked.

Will it delay the aviary repairs by much?

"Naw. Let's get to it." We moved about the barn, comfortable in our silence, feeding our temporary charges first before I moved on to our three permanent residents.

I snacked on a granola bar from my pocket before heading outside. These birds were work, and I needed as much energy as I could get to keep up after the feeding and the cleaning...

Oh, God, the cleaning!

The pellets I stored for the local junior high school; we got enough for the kids in eighth grade to dissect for science class and had plenty left over for the next two towns over each year.

When it came to the outdoor enclosures, I had finally invested in a pressure-washer. It was easier to take the owls out and pressure-wash them clean on the regular than to scrub them by hand. That's also why the barn floor had a drain set in the center of the concrete and a slightly angled floor, so I could give it a real deep-clean a couple of times a year, in addition to the regular hand cleanings. There was only so much newspaper could do - and we went through bales and bales of that, too.

I smiled at Dawn, our resident barn owl; she was a beauty, pristine white front, back and wings frosted golden as if she'd flown too high and had been kissed by the sun. She was one that had gotten too friendly with humans and just couldn't make it out there on her own. I let live critters loose in Dawn's outdoor enclosure, which was big enough for her to fly around in, and went swiftly the other direction.

If it was dead when it got to me, no problem, but I still hated watching our charges go after live prey. Just something about watching anything be killed disturbed me.

Yep, I was one of those people that was grateful that the meat I bought in the grocery store or at the butcher didn't look like anything readily identifiable. I had tried vegetarianism, but it had made me too sickly to stick with it. Again, I needed all the energy I could muster to keep up after my pretty fly-babies.

I moved on to our other two residents.

Piper, a little northern pygmy owl that was vivacious and curious, was my first stop. She couldn't fly. Her wing had been broken and a well-meaning teenager had tried to care for her. Her wing had healed badly, and that had been the end of her flight days. Still, I loved her and kept her fat and happy. Piper was no taller than my hand from the tip of my middle finger to the lifeline of my palm. Her head was brown in color, flecked with white, round and devoid of ear tufts. Her beak was yellow, two shades lighter than her eyes. She weighed in around a hefty 2.8 ounces, fat for one of her kind. Her tummy was striped, similar to a barred owl's markings. She was pretty much an adorable little ball of feathers and she brought me great joy.

I opened her enclosure and offered up a freshly-killed, smallish mouse. She rocked from foot to foot before snatching the offering from my hand. I let her finish eating and offered another. She took that one, too, and bolted it. I smiled and put out my hand and the tiny little owl stepped up onto my outstretched fingers. Piper had been with us a while and was pretty well domesticated. I helped her up onto my shoulder. She dug her talons into my thick jacket and preened a bit. Her big yellow eyes blinked at me.

Her little toots of a call sounded on my shoulder, and I can say with utter confidence, it sounded exactly like a note from an ocarina. *Hoot hoot! Hoot hoot!* I know my smile got bigger as I moved on to our final permanent resident.

Odin was a grizzled old great horned owl with only one eye, which is how he got his name. It fit; he was a majestic beast; god of all he surveyed in his enclosure. I hung a rabbit over the end of his perch nearest the door and got the hell out of there. He could be unpredictable and a nasty old bugger when he wanted to be, and I didn't want him coming after Piper. Piper was my friend, not a snack.

I quickly closed the large outdoor enclosure and stepped back. Odin side-stepped along his perch until he reached the rabbit. He seemingly glared at me with his one orange eye and stomped a talon onto the furry little offering. He savagely tore off a strip with his sharp beak and bolted it down. Out of all my birds, he was the least shy when it came to eating.

Ungrateful wretch, I thought affectionately, with a wry twist of my lips. He continued to tear at his breakfast and I winced and left him to it. I made my way back to the barn as Charlie stuck his head out.

"Got 'em all fed except that big barred bastard." He spit on the ground. I smiled and put my fingers up for Piper, who stepped onto them. I transferred the little owl to Charlie's shoulder and wrinkled up my nose at him.

"Hun-nnn-nnnn-ter!" I said, as I passed him by.

"Decided to go with it, huh?" he asked, his brown eyes twinkling in his craggy tan face. I grinned at him and nodded. He was comfortable, in well-worn jeans and a deep forest green cowboy shirt, the kind with snaps for buttons. He had on his black mesh trucker hat that proclaimed loudly on the front that he was proud to be Native American.

When I was fifteen, I'd seen Charlie get beaned in the head, opening up quite the bleeding gash. My aunt had seen the blood and freaked out, and had called an ambulance. When the paramedics had gotten here, they asked him all the questions you were supposed to ask when dealing with a possible head injury.

I'd watched as the medic asked Charlie who the President of the United States was and Charlie had glared at the man and shouted "Who gives a shit?" The medic had taken one look at Charlie's hat, clutched in his hand, and had burst out laughing. He'd needed to go with them and get stitches, but otherwise had been okay. The point is, that was the kind of man Charlie was. Simple and direct. Given my limited communication ability, the pair of us suited each other just fine.

Charlie had worked for the Washington Department of Fish and Wildlife and was a Vietnam vet. He and my uncle were best friends despite the fact my uncle worked for Weyerhaeuser, the forestry company that had put the spotted owl on the Endangered Species list. They'd hunted together, fished together, watched baseball together, and when I showed up, had pretty much raised me together, too.

My aunt had always jokingly referred to Charlie as her brother-wife, to which Charlie objected loudly every time... that is, until my aunt put some of her cooking in front of him. Quickest way to shut ol' Charlie up, ever. I unashamedly learned every kitchen trick I could from her and used them against Charlie freely if he was in one of his moods.

When Uncle Dave and Aunt Margie had followed their retirement dreams and moved to Arizona and away from the rain, it was pretty much only on the promise that Charlie and I would take care of each other.

Easy enough; we were best friends. Charlie was the one who got me drunk off moonshine when I was eighteen. Aunt Margie had chewed him a new one for that, screeching like an angry barn owl and beating him over the head with her ever-present dishrag. Charlie was as much my family as anyone ever could be.

I went to Hunter's enclosure and opened the door. He sidled up to me and I reached in with my leather-clad hand. He blinked at me and stepped up before I could make a grab for his ankles. I made a low whistle and Charlie looked up, his eyes narrowing suspiciously.

"He loose?" he asked. I nodded, confirming it. I reached out slowly with my other gloved hand to put it on the bird's back, to keep his wings folded down, but he stretched them out. I sucked in a breath, but he gripped my hand tighter with his feet and simply fanned his wings, giving them a good stretch before folding them down. I had really expected him to try to take off! This bird's behavior got stranger and stranger the more time that went by. I was beginning to grow afraid that he was too used to humans, that he wouldn't make it out in the wild. The bird bobbed his head and blinked at me. I looked into his deep, soulful brown eyes, so deep a brown as to be black and smiled.

He was a sweet bird to me. Wary around anyone else though.

I put him in a similarly-sized enclosure so I could clean the one he'd come out of.

"You set in here, Jessamine?" Charlie asked. I nodded and he smiled.

"I'm gonna get out there, then. Call me for lunch." He ducked outside and went over to the aviary that had been damaged by a falling tree limb in the last big wind storm we'd had. I hummed to myself and cleaned the cages and enclosures, stealing looks at the barred owl as I moved around the barn. He watched me placidly, following me with slight turns of his head, as I worked.

He was just so strange...

CHAPTER FOUR

*J*essamine

Three hours later, I stepped out the side door leading inside the kitchen, the one below my bedroom's deck, and rang the old-fashioned triangle hung there to call Charlie in for lunch. He came sauntering up a few minutes later with Piper still on his shoulder. I smiled and waved.

"What's for lunch?" he asked. I put my hands up, bracketing empty air between them and brought my fingers down over my thumbs.

"Sandwiches, huh?" He smiled at me and kissed the top of my head, walking past me into the house. Piper cheeped on his shoulder. I smiled ruefully and followed them in. Aunt Margie would have a fit if she knew birds of any size were in the house. Piper couldn't do much harm, though, being the size of a sparrow *and* unable to fly.

We sat at the kitchen counter. The kitchen in this house was amazing; that, too, was Margie's doing. My aunt loved to cook, bake, can, and do anything else you could do with food in a kitchen. So, my Uncle Dave had made her kitchen a thing of both beauty and greatness.

Charlie picked up his sandwich just as the phone rang. He paused, looked at me with a wicked gleam in his eye, and sank his teeth into the thick slices of rustic bread. I gave him a look that clearly read,

Really? You're going to throw me under the bus like that? The old fart just smiled benignly at me and enjoyed his sandwich.

I went over to the phone and the answering machine picked up on the third ring. My Uncle Dave's voice floated out from the recording:

"Hi! You've reached Moonchild's Owl Haven. The owner, Jessamine Connors, is non-verbal, so, if you hear a high tone, it means 'Yes'; a low tone means 'No'. If your situation is more complicated than Yes or No answers, email might be the best way to go. If the machine gets you, well then, leave a message!" I picked up the phone before the machine got it and pressed the number 1, which gave a high tone.

"Jessamine Connors?" the woman's voice came across the line. I pressed the number 1 again.

"Er... um... Hi, I'm Janine Watkins, my dog found a snowy owl on Dungeness Spit, I think it's hurt. Can you come look?" she asked. I pressed 1, and may have held it too long. I let go and bounced on the balls of my feet excitedly. A snowy owl! I'd never gotten to care for one before.

"Do you know where Dungeness Spit is?" she asked. Again I pressed 1. Uncle Dave, Aunt Margie, Charlie, and I went picnicking there all the time.

"How long until you get here?" she asked. I pressed 0 for a low tone.

"Oh sorry! Ten to fifteen minutes?" 0, low tone.

"Thirty to forty five minutes?" 0, low tone.

"Fifteen to thirty minutes?" she asked. 1, high tone.

"Great! Great. I'll see you then!" 1, high tone, and I hung up. I jumped up-and-down over and over, excitedly.

"Calm your tits!" Charlie yelled.

I grinned and whipped out my note pad. I scribbled down '*Snowy, Dungeness Spit, NOW!*' and slapped it on the counter by his plate before I raced off to grab my emergency response supplies.

"I'll be damned! A snowy?" he called. I gave a joyful wordless whoop.

"All right, I'm comin'! I'm comin'! We'll take my truck; grab a pair of gloves for me too."

I shot out the door and took the stairs up to the hayloft two at a time. I tucked two long, thick pairs of leather gloves into the back of my waistband and went to the shelves of dog and cat carriers. I selected one of the biggest dog carriers we had, stuffed an old Army-surplus blanket inside and went back downstairs. Charlie's truck was already rumbling to life. I threw the dog kennel into the bed and checked to make sure there were ratchet straps. Spying the familiar faded yellow, I hopped into the cab. Piper cheeped from the dashboard. I gave Charlie a look.

"What? She won't leave the truck. Forgot she was even riding on my shoulder."

Now *that* I could believe. He put the old Ford in gear and the arthritic old vehicle lumbered up my driveway.

We were both grinning like fools. Snowy owls only made it down here every three to seven years and that was only if the feeding up where they were usually at, in the Arctic, was good. I'd only glimpsed one once, and I'd never gotten the opportunity to care for one. While my heart was heavy with sadness that the bird was injured, I was over-joyed at the opportunity to see one up-close, outside captivity.

I nearly vibrated with excitement.

We pulled into a lot near the New Dungeness Light Station, which was Sequim's lighthouse, and before Charlie had even come to a full stop, I was out of the truck and reaching for the carrier.

We traipsed through the sand up the Dungeness Spit, scanning for people. Soon, we spotted a woman waving and quickened our pace to reach her. She was in jeans and boots, wearing a puffy purple down parka. A German shepherd sat in the sand at her feet panting, tongue lolling out the side of his mouth. I smiled.

"Are you Jessamine?" she asked, and I gave her a thumbs-up.

"Oh, good, I'm glad you're here. I'm Janine." She held out her hand to Charlie and he shook it. I set down the carrier and stuck out my hand, and she shook it as well. Her grip was light and I tried not to grip too strongly. I was used to giving firm handshakes.

I pulled out my trusty pad from inside my coat and the pen from the loop, writing out a few basic questions: *Where is it?* and *What made you think it was hurt?*

"Oh, he's over on the ground between those logs. When 'ol Blue here was over there barking I went over to see what he had, and saw the owl. I figured something was wrong when I got close and it didn't take off. I got Blue away from him and did a search on my phone; two places came up. You answered your phone." She gave a little half-shrug, raising one shoulder and dropping it. She was an older lady, maybe in her sixties, short white hair framing a pretty face. Her blue eyes sparkled and she patted her dog. I nodded.

Please stay back, snowy owls are one of the more aggressive kinds. Charlie and I will go see what's up. I wrote and showed her.

She smiled.

"Sounds good." She stepped clear to let us do our thing.

I opened the carrier and handed Charlie one set of gloves. I had brought the kind that went all the way to our shoulders. Snowy owls had wicked sharp and long talons and this was the best thing to prevent injury. He pulled his gloves on and I extracted the old military blanket from the carrier. Thick wool, it would do just fine if we needed to use it to throw over the owl to catch him or her safely.

I made sure the thick bath sheet towel I kept in the carrier was spread in a double layer on the bottom to make way for our guest.

A mother and daughter were coming up the beach and stopped next to Janine. They were talking in low murmurs as Charlie and I approached the snag of driftwood logs. He had the blanket over his arm and was nodding at me. I signed at him in our own little language to hang back just off to my right. I climbed up onto the big log and winced at the sight below.

The owl in question was a beautiful pristine white with barely any black markings, which instantly made me think that it was indeed a he and not a she. The females tended to have more of the horizontal black edging to them than the males did. His vivid yellow eyes blinked at me and seemed to say two things: *Back off!* and *I feel like shit.* It was both pitiful and heartbreaking.

The poor baby. His feathers were filthy towards the bottom and around his feet, which told me he'd been on the ground longer than a few minutes.

I got down between the logs, and the bird put up its wings, fluttering them ineffectually. I reached out carefully and got him by his ankles, rendering his talons useless. I held on firmly, but gently, as he beat his wings and barked at me, snapping his bill. I was slightly reassured that he had some fight in him, but he abandoned the effort pretty quickly.

"Well, he's in a helluva fix, ain't he?" Charlie remarked.

I nodded and winced. I made several attempts to get him to fold his wings so I could cradle him enough to get him up and out of the snag. Finally, he cooperated. Snowy owls are supposed to weigh in around four pounds; I could already tell that this boy was severely underweight.

I handed him up to Charlie, who with long practice made the exchange quick and seamless. When I was sure he had the bird's talons in check, I let go, then scrambled over the log to the other side, and we made the exchange again so Charlie could jump down. It was the easiest way to do it, to keep the bird's already-skyrocketing stress level down.

"Straight to your hospital, then?" he asked.

I nodded vigorously, and with Charlie's help slid the poor bird into the carrier.

Our three onlookers clapped as I clasped the carrier shut. I looked in at the snowy a moment, in wonder that I would actually get to help one of these magnificent birds, but was quickly snapped out of my reverie by Charlie.

"Name him yet?" he grunted.

I shook my head.

"Can I?" the little girl asked, excitedly.

"Sure, give it a shot," Charlie said, winking at me over her head.

"Hedwig!" she cried and I died a little inside. I shook my head and surreptitiously gave the sign to Charlie that the owl was a boy.

"This owl is a boy not a girl. You can't give him a girl's name!" he cried.

"Why not?" she asked.

"Why, 'cause the other owls would beat him up!" I turned my laugh into a cough and schooled my features into all seriousness, nodding gravely at what Charlie was saying.

"Oh, then what about... Lightning! He's fast, right? When he's not hurt."

I chewed my lower lip and thought about it, nodding finally. Charlie raised an eyebrow and I shot him a look. It was his turn to laugh and turn it into a cough. Yeah, I was pretty sure the name was changing, too, but for now, it would do. I gave him an impatient signal.

"Well, okay, say goodbye to Lightning. He's gotta go see a doctor so we can make him better." The little girl's brown braids bobbed against her shoulders as she smiled sweetly up at the old man.

She ducked down in front of the carrier and looked in.

"Goodbye, Lightning!" she chirped through her missing front teeth. She waved at the bird, who looked decidedly grumpy and turned away from her. She pouted out her lower lip and returned to her mom.

"Thank you," the woman said, hugging her daughter.

I nodded and gave a wave that said not to mention it, and turned to Janine. I shook her hand and tried to give her my best grateful look.

"Thank you for coming on such short notice. I hope you're able to take care of him."

I nodded and handed her a crinkled business card out of my pocket, with the Haven's address on it. Charlie picked up the carrier and I tucked the two pair of gloves and the blanket over my arm.

Back at the truck, he carefully ratchet-strapped the carrier up against the cab.

"So what do you think you're really gonna name him?" he asked. I raised one shoulder and locked eyes with the bird. He just blinked at me and looked pitiful. I furrowed my brow and gave Charlie a sharp look.

"Keep yer panties on, kid. I'm almost done."

I frowned at him and punched him lightly in the arm. He laughed. Ornery old coot.

CHAPTER FIVE

*J*essamine

We drove to Port Angeles and the Olympic Peninsula Animal Hospital, where I did my nine-to-five. As soon as we breezed in the door, Jodi looked up from the computer monitor behind the desk.

"Uh-oh, trouble in paradise?" she asked.

I shrugged, but couldn't keep the grin off of my face.

Her eyes narrowed suspiciously.

"What have you got there, Jess?" she asked.

I hefted the carrier and let her see inside the front grate. She gasped, and I know my grin got bigger.

"Well, don't just stand there, you guys! Get him back here!" She led the way and we pushed into the back through the double hanging doors. I ducked into the first empty exam room and heard Jodi call out for Doctor Reznor, our weekend veterinarian. He hurried in a minute later.

"Jodi says you have a snowy owl?" he asked, pulling his stethoscope off from around his neck. I nodded solemnly and pulled the heavy leather gloves on, over my elbows and up to my armpits. Charlie was doing the same.

"Found out on the Dungeness Spit..." Charlie was saying, filling Doc Rez in on everything.

"Do we know what's wrong?" he asked me.

I shook my head. I hadn't felt or seen any obvious breaks, so as of right now, without any x-rays, Lightning, here, was a mystery.

I reached carefully into the carrier and gritted my teeth as I grabbed for the bird's ankles. It took a second for him to calm down enough for me to extract him. Charlie helped me get him into a position for the other vet to examine him.

"Well... wings are intact, legs seem okay. X-ray?" he asked my opinion and I nodded.

"Well, bring him back," he said, looping his stethoscope back around his neck with a gusty sigh.

Charlie pulled off his gloves.

"You have fun, princess. I'm going out to get Piper."

I nodded absently in his direction. I had the Snowy by the ankles to negate his talons and he was resting in the palm of my other hand, cradled there like a newborn, but angry, baby. I followed Doc Rez out of the room and down the hall into our radiology department. He put the plastic cone pumping knock-out gas over the snowy's head while I held him.

It wasn't long until he was out. I gently laid him down on the x-ray table. We carefully tugged his wings open and equally carefully taped them down to the table in an open position. His wingspan was massive, close to the top of their range, which was fifty-two inches. We wanted clear pictures, so we had them bent at the elbow joint so the whole wings would fit into the frame. Next, we taped around each ankle and drew the legs down so they were gently stretched, so we could get a clear image there, too.

The poor bird was flopped out on his back and, if he were a human, would likely look passed-out drunk.

I lined up the image plates and got the shadowy crosshairs where we wanted them.

X-rays taken, I left Doc Reznor to peruse the images on the computer monitor while I gave our unconscious new friend subcutaneous fluids. His keel bone stood out sharply. He was underweight, dehydrated, and just plain needed some attention.

Doc Reznor came back and let me know what was going on with him.

"He's got no broken bones, and there aren't any bullets or any other foreign objects on his x-rays. I think he's just... sick? Tired, maybe? I don't really see anything wrong."

I nodded and got to work drawing blood and running some other tests. That done, I gave the bird a push of some broad-spectrum antibiotics.

After discussion with Doc Reznor, we decided it was best for me to take him home and try to get him fed, hydrated, and to just see what happened. He would need to be quarantined from the other birds for the time being, which was easy enough. I had a set-up just for that.

I found Charlie out in the waiting room with Piper on his hand, talking with Jodi. Both of them stopped talking and traded guilty looks when I came out. I narrowed my eyes in suspicion. I raised an eyebrow at Charlie and he popped little Piper on my shoulder. He took the carrier from me and I crossed my arms over my chest.

"Now don't go and get your panties in a twist, kid," he grated out and I scowled.

"We were just saying we wish you would get out a little more, that's all." Jodi said. I searched her face. All I saw was well-meaning, so I nodded slowly and jerked my head in the direction of the truck.

"Home, then?" Charlie asked.

I gave a weary nod. I was hungry; he'd eaten most of his lunch but mine probably still sat on the counter. I waved at Jodi and she smiled.

"See you on Monday, girl."

I nodded and followed Charlie out.

The sun was shining, but it was chilly. Spring was on the move, but unfortunately, this year it seemed to be moving slower than molasses in January. We secured the poor snowy against the cab of the truck and I climbed into the passenger side. Charlie hopped in and I gave him a scowl.

I do not need to get out more! I'm doing just fine. I scratched onto my notepad.

He looked it over then turned his dark brown eyes and weathered face on me.

"You just keep telling yourself that, kid," he grumbled as his truck rumbled to life with some mild protest.

I crossed my arms and looked at Piper. She blinked her big yellow eyes at me and cheeped in what sounded like agreement with Charlie. He laughed and I scowled at the little owl and thought *Traitor* in her direction. That still didn't stop me from stroking her feathered head.

I sighed to myself. It was a long, silent ride back to the house and haven.

It was my haven as much as the owls'...

CHAPTER SIX

*J*essamine

The snowy had been put up in the house's garage, which sat on the opposite side of the house from the barn. I had the garage set up as an impromptu medical facility, with a few cages and enclosures, dependent upon the patient's needs, a stainless steel examination table, an aquarium for live food if I needed to bring some over, and a mini-fridge for medications and not-so-live food, such as liver or dead rabbits.

The rest of the garage had stainless steel shelving and a whole lot of dry-storage goods, cans of wet cat food for the owls and the pantry goods from my kitchen, predominantly. I even had a giant freezer off to the side. So, yeah. No cars in this garage; it was half pantry and storage, and half quarantine area.

I set the carrier onto the exam table, pulled on my gloves, and carefully extracted our newest patient. I put him in the largest enclosure, which was the right size to let him move around but not to fly. I put him on one of the perches. He settled with a rustle of feathers and looked pretty miserable.

I filled a water trough for him and set a bigger tray of water on the floor of the enclosure for bathing. The enclosure had been set up and waiting, so I didn't need to do any extras, like lay down newspaper or the like.

I looked him over and pulled the whiteboard off its velcro mooring. I scrawled 'Winter' across its surface, and put it back. He didn't look like a 'Lightning' to me, but as he blinked his cool and assessing yellow eyes in my direction, he definitely looked like a 'Winter', and so that was what I named him.

I pulled the towel and old Army blanket out of the carrier and went into the house through the garage door, ditching my boots just inside. I dumped the linens straight into the washer, added detergent, and set it as hot as it would go. I washed my hands thoroughly at the laundry-room sink with soap and water.

Charlie was back at the south aviary. As soon as we'd pulled in, he'd grumbled something about only having a few hours of daylight left and had headed straight for it, stopping just long enough to put Piper back in her cage.

I knew he wasn't upset with me. We were cool. I was still feeling kind of crummy, just the same. I knew that Charlie and Jodi hadn't meant anything by talking about me. They were my friends, good friends, too. I think I was feeling more discouraged with myself than anything. I mean, maybe they were right. Maybe I should get out there a little bit more. Try dating, do something...

But I was too broken for any kind of relationship, incapable of giving as much as I'd take. The last time I'd dated a man for any length of time had been Josh, three years ago, back when I'd just started at Oly Pen Hospital. We'd been together a year and I'd been happy. Comfortable, even.

He'd grown secretive and I'd grown excited, thinking he was trying to come up with a way to propose.

That excitement had turned into the bitter, broken ash of disappointment when I'd discovered him with his hand up another woman's shirt, his long fingers cupping her substantial breast, while his mouth moved over hers as if he was trying to eat her from the mouth down.

He'd never kissed me that way.

My fingers curled into fists, the knuckles going white, at the memory.

On top of that, he'd brought her to *our* place. He'd brought her to the bar we met up at regularly, after I'd get off of my shift at the animal hospital. We would grab a drink, get something to eat, listen to live music or whatever, before coming here, coming home...

I'd stood there dumbfounded at first, with no words to rail at him with. I'd wanted so badly to scream at him, to demand why, to tell him off, to tell her off, too, but all I could do was stamp my foot on the hardwood until I got his attention. Even then, he'd just looked at me, and had smiled.

Over a year of my time, a lot of my love, and a mountain of my devotion, and the bastard stood there wrapped in another woman and *smiled* at me as my heart shattered into a million pieces on the sticky barroom floor.

I couldn't stop the tears. I'd felt so many things in that fraction of a second. Heartache, pain, anger, humiliation... I think that was the worst part. The humiliation. I could see it written on all the regulars' and bar staff's faces. They knew about what he'd been doing. They had known for God knows how long.

"What'd you expect, Jess?" he'd called after me. Then he really twisted the knife as he'd shouted, loud enough for everyone to hear, "I need a woman I can talk *with,* not *at*!"

I'd cried for a week, then let the slow burn of bitterness and anger consume the rest of any of the feelings I'd ever had for him.

I couldn't yell at him. I couldn't scream at him, so I made my position clear. When he came to pick up the few things he'd left here- some clothes, DVD's, music magazines, his spare guitar- I'd handed him a shoebox of ashes from my burn barrel with a nasty smile. (The items in question I had actually donated to Goodwill.)

At any rate, the whole mess had boiled down to his words as I'd left the bar: "I need a woman I can talk *with,* not *at*!"

I chewed my lip, took off my coat and hung it on the banister just outside the kitchen, and washed my hands for a second time. I sighed, and stared down at my sandwich, laying on the counter. I looked at the clock, and wrapped it in some butcher paper and labeled it in my neatest printing with a kitchen sharpie with what it was and the date. It could be lunch for tomorrow or I might send it home with Charlie.

It would get eaten; it was just pointless eating it now, so close to dinnertime.

I took some chicken breast from the fridge and went about fixing Charlie and me supper. I peeked into the garage from time to time, checking on our new patient from across the room, satisfied when I saw him on one foot, his head tucked beneath his wing.

I made Italian, chicken Parmesan.

It was getting on toward the darker end of dusk and I looked up as Charlie came in the back door. I didn't even bother with reminding him about his boots as he tromped across the kitchen to wash up at the sink. I was feeling guilty about getting all bent out of shape at him and Jodi.

"Smells good, Jess," he commented and I smiled. It was as close as I was going to get to an apology for his talking behind my back. Even if it was well-intentioned, he knew I was sensitive about it. Still, it was best to let it go, so I just smiled, and dished him up some food.

"Should be good to go tomorrow. Finished up just in time," he grunted.

I nodded and brought my own plate over to the kitchen counter we sat at.

Old habit. It had four stools and when it was me, Uncle Dave, and Charlie, we'd always come in and sit at it like it was our own personal lunch counter, while Aunt Margie served us up from the other side.

I opened the fridge and pulled out the pitcher of sweet tea we always kept on hand. I held it up and shook it.

"Yeah," he said with his mouth full and I pulled down two tall glasses. I set them up and poured them to the brim. I knew Charlie, so I left the pitcher of tea out on the counter between our plates, shutting the fridge door behind me.

We ate in companionable silence.

Mostly because that was all I was really capable of.

CHAPTER SEVEN

*H*unter

She was somber tonight as she moved about the barn. The old man had stopped his banging and sawing outside and there had been a long stretch of quiet. Not silence; nothing was ever truly *silent,* when there was so much for my kind to hear.

She had come in after his old truck had crunched up the gravel drive, her shoulders stooped; the weight of unpleasant memories upon her. She'd set about feeding her charges.

She stopped before me, her storm-clouded eyes heavy with emotion, brimming with barely-suppressed tears, and I hated it.

I longed to be a comfort to her, to care for her the way she had, and continued to, care for me.

She sighed and, safe in her perceived solitude, spoke.

"N-n-n-o on-ne wants a broken woman they can-n-n't talk with, do they Hun-nn-ter?" she asked softly. The heartbreak on her face unmistakable.

I wanted to hurt whoever put it there, to rend their flesh with my talons sending them bloody and shrieking into the night. I blinked slowly and gazed into the storm-swept sea of her eyes, willing her to understand my thoughts, my feelings.

I thought, for a moment, something might be there, but then she turned and wandered away from me, and I felt bereft of her company. For weeks now, I had watched her move throughout this barn, this haven of hers, watched her smile, watched as she gave freely of herself to me, to my fellow winged brethren...

I shifted from foot to foot, my talons scoring the wood of my perch, and hunched my shoulders.

She made me want to be a part of her world again.

Jessamine, with her creamy skin and smattering of freckles across her nose and cheeks that reminded me of the star-scattered sky, with her low soothing voice, as broken as it was, that sighed through the barn like the wind through the trees.

I longed to touch her, comfort her, but with what I was, well, that just wasn't a kind thing to do. Though, I had never, in my long years, ever been considered kind, in any way, shape, or form.

No.

For her sake, I would leave her be. I'd finish my healing, and fly on mended wing far from her and the temptation.

It's what was best.

At least, that was what I told myself, every day I was near her.

CHAPTER EIGHT

*J*essamine

I usually worked four days on and three days off. Four, ten-to-twelve-hour days. My days off were Friday, Saturday and Sunday. I fed and medicated my little lovelies before I went to work. Charlie would arrive sometime during the day and make sure they were fed and medicated according to the instructional whiteboard on their enclosures, then the cages that needed it were cleaned and our rodent racks maintained, while I was away.

It wasn't just me and Charlie. Though it could be done by just the two of us, we had a few volunteers that would come through and do what needed doing. Never unsupervised, though. Either Charlie or I was always there to watch, teach, or consult with.

Our volunteers were usually at-risk youth working off a sentence of community service. It was my idea to go there. I knew we needed the help, the kids needed something productive to do, and Charlie and I were both tough enough to keep them in line.

If not us, then for sure the birds were.

It meant paying higher insurance premiums, but it was worth it, my way of giving back as much to the human world, as it was to the owl's world. The owls got care and feeding, and a better chance at survival.

The kids got a second chance of their own. The ones who wanted it anyway...

Some of these kids were the epitome of the old adage 'You can lead a horse to water but you can't make him drink.'

Some of them, though, took to what we did like a fish to water. It was as I arrived home that one of these kids came out of the garage with Charlie, both of them beaming.

I got out of my tired red Toyota truck and raised an eyebrow questioningly. Aaron, the kid in question, grimaced at my scrubs, which had been generously stained with blood from a dog-versus-car scenario that had not ended well.

I needed some good news.

"Guess what!" Aaron called as I drew near.

I shrugged.

"Winter is self-feeding." Charlie grinned.

I matched it.

This was the kind of news I needed to come home to.

"I believe you owe us pie!" Aaron chortled.

I dropped my jaw in mock indignation as I went past them into my garage. Winter was looking much better. I picked up the whiteboard on the exam table, rooted around for a dry-erase pen and wrote out: *How does Winter feeding himself turn into ME owing YOU pie?*

"Because, we delivered the good news and your pie is delicious, so to reward us for our efforts in bringing you said news, you," he pointed at me with both index fingers, "feel that you owe us," he pointed to himself with his thumbs, "delicious, delicious pie." He smiled his most disarming smile and I twisted my lips to keep from smiling myself.

Aaron had first come to us when he was fourteen. He'd decided to decorate portions of Sequim with graffiti. Unfortunately, neither the town nor the police had an appreciation for Aaron's artistic stylings and he was ordered to clean it up. He'd also landed himself with an order to pay restitution for the damage he'd caused and a pretty hefty community-service sentence.

We don't play out here in the sticks.

So after scrubbing off his mess and mowing lawns all summer long, he'd ended up on my doorstep after his mother had heard about us from her neighbor: Jaye Moore, director of the NW Raptor Center. Aaron had been volunteering for Jaye, but after some careful thought on the subject, she'd decided he might be a better fit here at Moonchild's Owl Haven instead.

Now seventeen, Aaron had grown into his own. Taller than Charlie and me, by like a lot, Aaron was slender. Slender did not mean weak. He carried some muscle definition on that thin frame of his and did quite a bit of heavy lifting around here that I couldn't. He wore the typical teenage uniform of worn jeans, faded tee-shirts and Chuck Taylor sneakers, his unruly mop of curly brown hair forever in his eyes, and covering the top of his ears.

His hazel eyes twinkled from under the fringe of his hair as he tossed his head to get it out of his eyes, and despite how tired I was, I gave into his wiles and agreed to make his pie.

Fine, pie it is, BUT you have to do MY chores, and let me get a shower before I set foot anywhere near my kitchen. AND you have to explain to my babies why I haven't said hello.

"Deal." He said it with a grin and they turned toward the barn.

I snapped my fingers several times until they turned around.

Wait, what am I cooking for dinner?

"Don't care, as long as there's pie," Charlie grunted.

What KIND of pie?

"Cherry," they both said at the same time and I drew back in indignation. They'd planned this all along!

Aaron held up a fist, Charlie bumped it with his own, and both of them turned around and walked for the barn. Aaron was whistling Warrant's song 'She's My Cherry Pie'. Charlie chuckled and I couldn't help it. I started cracking up.

I went into the house, still laughing, and watched them go into the barn from the kitchen window. I ducked into the laundry room and stripped out of my scrubs, dropping them into the laundry hamper. Peeking out from around the door, I checked the windows for any sign of movement. Seeing none, I bolted for the stairs and up to my room.

One hot shower and a change into some comfy sweats later, and I was ready for my kitchen. I quickly French-braided my sopping hair and went down the stairs in my thick wool house socks. I put my iPod onto the dock in the kitchen and started some music, then plucked things out of the pantry, cabinets, and fridge and set to work.

I measured out flour and sugar and took some sticks of butter out of the freezer. I used a cheese grater to grate the butter into my flour to make the pie crust. I stopped for a few moments to watch Charlie and Aaron. Charlie had gone into Hunter's enclosure, which was the newly-repaired aviary. Charlie was, essentially, chasing him from one end to the other. He would approach, Hunter would take off and fly to the other end, rinse and repeat.

It seemed mean to do, but it was an essential part of Hunter's recovery.

He needed to build up his wing and leg to full strength before he could be released.

The next step would be to take him out on a line. Much like when you'd watch horses run in circles around their human on a long lead, so too did we work with an owl, flying them out on a lead by their feet.

Hunter wouldn't be ready for that for a while, but he was recovering remarkably fast as it was. I was happy to see it, proud of him, even.

I returned to my baking. The dark cherries from my freezer were nearly thawed enough for the filling, I flopped my first crust into a heavy ceramic pie baking dish. I pressed it in against the sides and smiled as Aaron and Charlie laughed at something.

These were the days I found myself content, even happy.

Being surrounded by the birds and people I loved, doing something to make their lives better, happier... this was paradise.

I mixed my filling, poured it into the waiting pie shell, and rolled out a roof for my cherry house, smiling fondly at the memory of my aunt teaching me to bake this particular recipe. She'd gotten teary and made me promise to bake it for Charlie for every occasion, big or small. It was, after all, his favorite.

I put my pie into the oven after giving the top a sugary egg wash to turn the crust golden brown. I put my hands on my hips and turned back to the floury mess on my countertop. I shrugged and set about making my aunt's fireweed honey biscuits to go along with a dinner, even though I still had no idea what I was cooking for a main course.

Biscuits laid out on cookie sheets and ready to take up the second oven, I decided what it was I was going to make for a main course. It was going to be a giant freaking pie-fest up in here tonight, full of butter and so on. I didn't do it often, so it would be completely worth it. I started in on a savory pie crust and brought out six ramekins. I made up six individual chicken pot pies from scratch and put them in after the dessert pies came out. During the last fifteen minutes or so of the pot pies baking cycle, I slid the biscuits into the second oven.

As soon as the biscuits were done, I piled them on a plate and left out a dish of honey, black raspberry jam, and butter on our little lunch counter. The dessert pies were already on the counter by the sink to cool and I rang the boys in for supper.

When Charlie stepped inside, he gave a low whistle.

"Jess, you need to feed me like this more often!"

I snorted and pulled the whiteboard off its magnets on the fridge. I had these things stashed everywhere. *I feed you like this all the time!*

"Wow, you get to eat like this all the time?" Aaron asked.

"When she's being nice to me."

"Dude, she's nice, all the time, to everyone." Aaron said and I blushed a little that he would think so.

They both sat down and I served up the pot pies with a heaping serving of steamed broccoli on the side.

"You definitely need to feed *me* like this more often," Aaron mumbled around a mouthful of food.

Come over more often and I will. Don't talk with your mouth full. I wrote while chewing.

"Why not? You just did." He gave me an impish grin.

So NOT the same thing!

He raised a slender shoulder in a half-shrug,

"I tried," he said, after swallowing this time. Charlie snorted. I shook my head. One or the other was bad enough... put them both together and, well, yeah. Outmatched.

I smiled at the appreciative noises they were making at my cooking, wondering if they were even going to have any room left for the pie. Of course, they would... not only was Aaron still a growing boy; Charlie, I swear to God, was the proud owner of a hollow leg.

You know the rules... I wrote and flashed it at both of them.

"I got it, Charlie," Aaron said, and jumped up.

"Hell, boy, I want pie. Faster we do this, the faster she dishes it up." He got to his feet and shuffled around the counter into the kitchen.

I laughed until tears came to my eyes at the two of them moving around the kitchen getting in each other's way as they rinsed the dishes and loaded the dishwasher at warp speed.

As soon as Aaron finished wiping down the counters, I was up and dishing them each a piece of pie, and by 'piece', I mean each of them got a full quarter of that pie. I took a modest slice out of the remaining half.

The boys clanked forks, like they were glasses, said "Cheers!" and dug in.

I thought for sure they'd be too full, that some would get left behind, but damned if they didn't polish off every bite on their plates. Aaron even went so far as to lick the plate. I made an incredulous noise when Charlie, looking impressed, started in on his.

"What? I'm old. I can do whatever I want."

Which, of course, made me laugh. Truth was, I'd probably be the same way when I got to be his age.

Bad influence I wrote.

"Who, the kid? You knew that when you took him on." Charlie grinned and I stuck my tongue out at him. Aaron laughed.

I was *so* out of my league with these two.

Aaron did the dessert dishes and started the dishwasher. Now that he had his license and had bought that beat-up, old-as-dirt Datsun he was over here more and more. Denise, his mom, fretted over my feeding him, but she didn't need to. This family had never, and would never, begrudge a growing child or teen food, as long as it was eaten. Besides, Aaron more than pulled his weight, and like me, looked up to Charlie and my Uncle Dave like the surrogate fathers they were to us.

I sighed in contentment. The only thing missing out of my day was my visit with my owls. I pulled on my tired old house sweater and stuffed my feet into my boots.

"Going out there?" Charlie asked.

I nodded.

"Okay. Hey, kid, make me some coffee."

I laughed and trudged out the door making a bee line for Hunter's aviary.

He was huddled in a far corner eyeing me warily.

"Hey, Hunn-n-nnn-ter." I said softly. He behaved like a typical owl and kept his distance, which encouraged me. I smiled.

I watched him in the dim light coming from my kitchen windows for a time and sighed. Today had been a good day, despite the disaster my work-day had been. I was tired, very tired, but none the less grateful.

I checked on all my feathered charges before going inside. Little Rosie had died two days earlier, which had sort of hurt, but it wasn't all that unexpected. The poor baby had been really touch and go from the beginning. Aaron had given her a proper burial and her leaf had joined the drift at the bottom of the tree.

I knocked on the kitchen window and pointed up, indicating that I was going to bed. I had to get up early. I trudged up to the second floor and my bedroom from the outside. I ditched my boots at the door and smiled as Hunter began serenading the night from below. I closed the French doors behind me and crawled into bed.

I was dead to the world before my head even touched the pillow.

CHAPTER NINE

*H*unter

"Hey, Hunn-n-nnn-ter," she crooned at me through the fencing on the enclosure. I flew in a short burst to the back of the aviary and hunkered there as one of my brethren would. I had overheard the old man telling the boy that if I continued to behave the way I had toward Jessamine there would be cause for concern and I may not be releasable. Now was as good a time as any to play the correct role.

I had watched her from my perch, through her windows, as she'd moved about the kitchen at a leisurely pace preparing a supper for the boy and the old man.

She moved, lithe and gorgeous, from cupboard to pantry to counter. I memorized the sway of her copper hair over the back of her oversized gray tee-shirt, she had bound it up in a beautiful braid. The graceful curve of her neck and shoulder where the neckline of her tee left them bare to my sight was something to behold.

She seemed happy tonight, and when she smiled it was disarming. They had made her laugh, and though I could hear what *they* said to *her*, I had a fierce yearning to be close enough to read her answers.

Her scent was carried to me on the slight breeze, rich and sensual, lavender and vanilla, and something else. Sandalwood, perhaps. She reached up to smooth some of her copper-colored hair off of her cheek and the movement was mesmerizing.

I looked her in the eyes and I was undone.

I had to know her.

She watched me for several moments more, and then went back towards the house. When the bedroom light clicked out, I waited, calling softly. When the boy and old man left, I waited some more, and when the moon was at its highest point, I *changed*.

I had done it here once before; I'd found a pad and pen and written her the note, telling her my name. The shift was easier now than it had been then, my healing more complete.

I flexed my left arm in several directions and winced at the stiffness there. I undid the catch on the enclosure and stepped out, the pine needles soft under my bare feet. I stepped forward cautiously and nodded. My leg held, aching but bearably so.

I breathed in deeply the night air, and winced a bit. There was always a period of adjustment when it came to taking either form. My senses were sharper than an average human's in this form, but much duller than when I was an owl. After a transition, I felt as if my ears were stuffed with cotton at first, my hearing was so much less sensitive.

Each form had its advantages and disadvantages. In this one, I was stronger, denser, and much less fragile. As an owl I was breakable. But, at the same time, I healed faster as an owl than I did this way.

I crept to the base of the stairs and listened.

Satisfied that I was alone, and that she indeed slept, I climbed the stairs. I looked at her sleeping form just behind the glass, the moonlight spilling across her features turning her into something ethereal.

I wanted so badly to let myself in, to run my fingers along her petal-soft skin, but the last thing I wanted to do was frighten her. I watched her for a time, and, confident in my plan, shifted once more. I would have to be extremely careful, going back to my cache of items, hidden well in the Olympic National Park.

However, if I could return in my human form, perhaps I could convince her to take me on, to allow me to trade work with my human hands for food and board, and in doing so find a way past her careful walls.

It was a decent plan, as plans went.

Of course, the best-laid plans of mice and men often go astray.

CHAPTER TEN

Jessamine

Today was promising to be a bad day. A *really* bad day. I stood in front of the open aviary door with some mice scrabbling around in the bottom of the five-gallon bucket hanging limply from my right hand. Hunter was gone. I didn't even know how he got out!

"Fff-ffuck!" It was so worth forcing the word out. Hunter was gone. I pulled out my cell phone and called Charlie, yes, *called*. This wasn't the time for a text.

"Jess, what's wrong?" he demanded by way of greeting when he picked up.

"Hunnn-nn-nnter is gonn-nn-e, did yyy-ou or Aaro-nnn go inn-nn the aviary af-f-ff-fter I wenn-nnn- Gah!"

I dropped the bucket and punched the timber making up the aviary doorway. Why? Why couldn't I get the words out, just once!?

"Calm down, kid. I get you. No, neither one of us went to his pen after you went to bed. We finished up in the kitchen and both went straight for our trucks." I could hear Charlie moving around.

"He wasn-nn-n't ready!" I wailed. There was a long silence on the other end of the line.

"I know, Jess. I don't know how he got out, but that big bastard was pretty tough and he's out there somewhere nearby. Put out one of the kiddie pools with some of the meeces-pieces in it." I was onto him. We might not be able to catch Hunter, but we could make it easy for him to hunt.

"'Kay," I assented.

"I'm on my way. You go to work, I'll see you when you get home." He hung up without saying goodbye which was good with me.

I stuffed my phone in my pocket and went to work on his suggestion.

I pulled the empty blue wading pool out of the aviary and out into the open, and gently dumped the feeder mice from the bucket into it.

"Who let you out?" I moaned, with very little trouble. No one here to hear me, no one to judge or scream or tell me I was stupid... I sniffed back some tears and turned sharply to look in the direction of a rustle that came from the trees.

Wishful thinking. Nothing was there.

Today was going to be a bad day, and not just because of Hunter. I could feel it; like the promise of rain, the air was thick with it.

I sighed and wiped at the frustrated tears, and set about doing what needed to be done so I wasn't late to work.

As I fed and gave morning meds to the owls, I thought about Hunter and his enclosure. I stopped by the south aviary one last time on my way to my truck and double checked. Yep, the enclosure's latch was working just fine.

I was beginning to question *how* he'd gotten out. I knew it had been secure when I'd come out the night before, and if it hadn't been Charlie or Aaron...

I sighed. I guess, in the long run, it didn't really matter. He was out. I went to my truck and got in. I had to go to work.

The day progressed much the same way. When it rains it pours and I wasn't talking about the weather.

Midway through the day, Charlie called. He said that he'd come down with something awful, that he'd fed the birds, medicated the birds, and had gotten sick several times doing it, but that he'd gotten it done and was heading home, and that he'd see me when he'd gotten over whatever-it-was that was twisting up his insides.

It was busy in the hospital. We had several regular patients - and a man who came in with a half-dead cat that some boys had been shooting with a pellet gun. The poor kitty had to be euthanized.

By the end of my day I was emotionally exhausted, physically exhausted, and my stomach still churned with worry for Hunter.

I just wanted to go home.

The drive home, at least, was peaceful, uneventful. I pulled into my driveway and immediately went in to check on Winter. He was doing okay. I put out some fresh water for him and some mice in a pan they couldn't get out of. I wanted to see if he'd go after live prey. He was in an enclosure big enough to let him, so why not try?

I should have gone through the house, but I didn't. I went around and headed for the barn and let myself in.

I didn't even see it coming, but something hard connected with the back of my head and across my shoulders and I sprawled forward onto the cement floor. The heels of my hands burned where I'd put them out to break my fall, scraping them painfully on the unfinished concrete. My knees cracked painfully into the cement and I cried out.

"What have we here?" a male voice asked, from behind me.

My vision was blurry, my eyes watering fiercely from the pain in my hands and knees. My shoulders and back gave a dull aching throb.

"Oh, wow, she's kind of hot." Another one swung down from the converted hayloft, his sneakers thudding just in front of my face.

I rolled over and looked up at the one behind me, the one who'd hit me. He was a skinny man, in his early to mid-twenties. His clothes were dirty, his lank, greasy hair too long, and his face was pockmarked with sores. He grinned and his teeth were an awful grayish-blue. I cringed.

"Hey, sweetheart. Let's you, me, and Jimmy here, have some fun." The one behind me grabbed me by the back of my hair.

I reached my hands up and clawed at the fist in my ponytail. I kicked out at the one that advanced on me, my booted foot connecting with his hip. I sent him back a few paces. He looked angry and my memories flashed on another angry man's face.

I opened my mouth and screamed, and caught the back of the nameless man's hand across my mouth. I tasted blood and moaned.

"Bend her over the table, Jimmy," the one who hit me ordered. He spat on the floor and I fought.

I fought, I struggled and kicked, and I screamed, but I knew without a doubt that there was no one to hear me.

I was shoved face-down over a stainless steel table, the metal cold against the heated skin of my face. I stomped down on the sneaker-clad foot of the man who held me down and was rewarded by a shout and a curse. He lifted my head by my hair and slammed it into the table, my sinuses filled with blood.

And I continued to fight.

The owls were screeching, the cacophony of sound catching my attackers off-guard.

I struggled and tried to get up off the table, but nothing was coming of my efforts. Fingers slid into the waistband of my scrubs and began jerking them down. I screamed, long, loud, and wordless, and I kept screaming, having nothing left to do...

CHAPTER ELEVEN

*H*unter

The pack was heavy on my shoulders, an unaccustomed burden. It had taken me an hour or so to fly back to the cache of my belongings more suited to my form as a man. It had taken that much time and longer just to hike to the nearest logging road, once my belongings had been retrieved.

I'd spent the majority of my day after that retracing the tangle of terra firma and worn highways and streets back to Jessamine's road. My leg ached fiercely and several times I had paused to rest it, before pushing on.

I was just heading down her long drive when I heard her wail. I didn't bother running in this form- too slow. I abandoned my pack to the mud, my aching leg forgotten, and shifted out of my clothes, winging my way towards the barn and her cries.

I came in, low and fast, through the open door.

Two men had a hold of her. One of them had her bent, pinning her upper body against a metal table. The other was pulling her pants down her legs, his pants already half-undone in the front. His intentions were clear, but mine?

Mine were *much* more dangerous.

Anger flowed through my veins, burning me up from the inside out. I screeched my fury, adding to the wild calls of fear and warning from my brethren, and talons outstretched, I dove for the one holding her down. He cursed as they found purchase in his scalp and I rent his flesh. He let her go to cover his head, attempting to staunch the flow of blood.

I smiled on the inside, and wheeled, diving for his cohort.

He fell back, out of reach of my talons, one hand on his pants, hauling them up. I flew down and shifted, my fist flying forward in an awkward punch from where my wing had been positioned a moment before. But I landed my mark, my knuckles crashing into the side of the oaf's head, a solid box to his ear.

I kicked him square in the groin for even thinking of touching her and, my fist firmly entrenched in the front of his shirt, proceeded to knock his nasty teeth down his throat, repeatedly.

His friend, bloody, but not down for the count, hit me across my shoulders, a searing line of pain that fueled my caustic rage. I turned, his unconscious friend falling limp and forgotten to the concrete floor.

My hand snapped out and I caught the man by the throat; I bared my teeth as my fingers dug into the soft flesh below his jaw. I pulled him forward with a seething growl and bashed my forehead into his nose. I felt it give with an all-too-satisfying crunch. The younger man dropped his weapon, a broom handle by the looks of it, and covered his face with both his hands.

I buried my free fist in his solar plexus. He wheezed and would have gone to his knees, had I not had the grip I did on his throat. He made a strangled, gurgling noise and I threw him to the ground. I kicked him in the face and he stilled. I turned back to the other one, who also posed no threat anymore.

I stood amidst the human wreckage, chest heaving, eyes casting this way and that in search of Jessamine...

CHAPTER TWELVE

Jessamine

I wailed and continued my futile struggle, wrenching my body violently in their hold. One of them punched me in the back of my head and I saw stars, white flickers and flares of light at the edge of my vision.

Then one of them cursed, then screamed, and the crushing weight at my back lessened and disappeared.

I flipped over and slid to the floor, looking up in time to see brown-and-cream-streaked feathers disengage from the cretin that had been holding me down. The man pressed his hands to his bleeding scalp, and my eyes widened in shock at what I was seeing.

Hunter, I was sure it was him, I'd never seen another barred owl that big, was diving for the other man.

He missed, his talons gripping empty air. He wheeled, but before he made another attempt, his image blurred and suddenly, where the bird had been, a man stood, his arm careening forward, fist clapping the man-who-wasn't-Jimmy in the side of the head, on his ear.

Blood leaked from the orifice.

I scooted back, under the table. I stuffed my hand into my mouth to keep from crying out when Jimmy swung a broom, striking the man-who-had-been-an-owl-a-moment-before across his broad shoulders. The handle cracked, snapping audibly.

The large, bronze skinned man who had been Hunter the owl stilled for a moment, before whirling, quicker than light, quicker than sound, grasping the one called Jimmy by the throat.

I huddled back beneath the table as he laid a fist deep in the man's gut. I started as he hit the cement like a sack of rotten potatoes. I cringed as he looked helplessly in my direction, before a bare foot careened into his face. His head snapped back, blood arching across the floor, and the man went still.

My breath sawed in and out of my chest, blood and tears mingling on my face in a warm wet mess. I shook, my pants and panties still 'round my legs. I heaved in panicked breaths, watching the bare feet of the man turn as he looked for me. I bit my lips between my teeth to keep from making a sound as the muscular calves bunched and flexed beneath the man's tanned skin. He stepped forward and a knee came into view, and then two. He leaned down and looked beneath the table.

His chest and shoulders tapered down into equally-refined abdominal muscles. My eyes went lower, invited by his hip flexors, and I immediately looked elsewhere, panicked.

My eyes flicked to his face, and my breath caught.

He had high cheekbones, the hollows beneath them tapering down to a full mouth which was bracketed with deep lines of concern. His large hand was extended, palm up, fingers loose, waiting for me to make a move. My eyes went from the waiting hand to his eyes and I blinked. His eyes were dark and intense, so deep a brown as to be almost black, wall-to-wall color, just like they'd be if he were an owl. I stared as the color spiraled down, revealing whites, the irises lightening in color until a rich, lighter, and much warmer brown took their place.

I blinked again. He smiled softly at me.

I reached out, tentatively, my hand shaking. His hand was warm. It curled around mine, his grip gentle despite the bloody swelling knuckles that were proof of the violence he'd just visited upon my attackers. I swallowed and bit back a sob as I stood from under the table, looking down at the two bloody, broken men.

The man-who'd-been-an-owl pushed long light brown hair streaked with white behind his ear before he bent. He grasped the waistband around my calves and I cried out and tried to push away, but he stood hands up, palms out, and took a step back.

"I don't mean anything by it, Jessamine. I'm just trying to help you." His voice was rich and melodic, accented lightly, something almost British.

I stood still, shaking badly, and he slowly bent. I let him this time and he pulled my underwear and pants resolutely back in place. I choked on a sob and he stood.

"It's okay, love. I'm going to fly, I left my clothes and pack up on your drive. I'm going to get them and come back down here. You need to call the police. Can you do that?" he asked.

I nodded, a little too emphatically, the white sparkles returning, flitting throughout the edges of my vision. I swallowed hard and dug through my pockets. His image blurred, like it had before, and he was out the door and winging away.

I dropped where I stood, onto my ass, dumbfounded and looked down at my phone clutched loosely in my hand. I blinked and did what he'd told me. I dialed 9-1-1.

"9-1-1, what is your emergency?"

I took several deep breaths.

"H-hh-hh-elp me. Mm-mm-mmm-oon chh-ch-child Owl Hhh-hh-aven. P-p-please…"

"Ma'am, ma'am, I can't understand you. Can you tell me where you are?"

I tried, I really tried, but my words stuck in my throat, wouldn't find their way free of my battered mouth no matter how hard I tried to make them. My stutter was horrible on a good day, on a bad day the words were so mangled that barely anyone could understand me.

Tears of frustration leaked out and I wanted to scream.

I needed to do this, just once in my life I needed to be able to get across that I needed *help*, where I was located, and to please *hurry*. I sobbed into the line brokenly and prayed that just once I could open my mouth and speak like a normal human being.

Strong blunt fingers plucked the phone from my hand. I screamed and flinched.

"It's okay, love, just me. Yes, hello? Hello? Yes, my name is Hunter Grayson, I'm at Moonchild Owl Haven, there's a woman here, and she's been attacked. I dispatched the two attackers when I heard her screaming. Send ambulances and police. Yes, yes, I'll hold." He was watching me and I was watching him.

I didn't know what to do. I shook uncontrollably.

"H-h-h-h-unter." I said, through swelling lips.

"Yes?"

"W-w-w-hat are y-y-you?" I asked.

He opened his mouth, but a voice came across the line.

"Yes, yes, I'm here," he said, his eyes locked with mine.

"Okay, okay, thank you. I was passing on the road, I heard her screaming. Please hurry; she's bleeding. I think she's going into shock." He hung up the phone.

I blinked, nodding.

"S-s-s-safe." I said, and he nodded solemnly.

"You're safe with me," he said.

"N-n-no," I stammered, my body shaking to match my voice. "You. S-s-s-afe with m-m-me."

He nodded. Sirens were approaching, wailing in the distance.

"Okay, I think I get it. My secret is safe with you," he murmured.

I nodded emphatically, the stars returning to my vision, and fresh hot tears of relief coursed down my cheeks. Thank God at least *someone* understood me.

He held out his hand and helped me to my feet. I staggered against his hard body, now clad in worn blue jeans and a black tank top, with a flannel shirt in greens and blues open over it. The sleeves of the flannel shirt were rolled back over his muscular forearms, I focused on the play of muscle under his bronze-kissed skin, on the fine light brown hairs scattered there. He was solid against me and I was grateful he was there to hold me up.

His sturdy hiking boots crunched over the gravel outside the barn as he led me outside. A Sheriff's car came down the drive first, followed by an ambulance. More cars were behind them. A low moan and cough sounded from the open doorway behind us.

I startled, and Hunter's arms went around me, steadying me. Fresh tears tracked through the drying blood on my face. I sniffed. I couldn't stop crying.

"Easy, love." He helped me sink down onto my picnic table; a medic was jogging towards us.

"In the barn, the both of them," Hunter called to the Sheriff's Deputy. Ron Caruthers, the Clallam County Sheriff Deputy who'd been in my barn, was striding towards us. John Baker, from the Department of Fish and Wildlife, was running towards us from the back of the line of cars.

"Jessie! Jess!" he called.

I turned my face into Hunter and shook. The medic was trying to look me over.

"Who the hell are you?" John demanded, stopping in front of us.

"Hunter Grayson, at your service, Sir." Hunter stuck out his hand and John gave one hard look at his battered knuckles.

The medic was asking me questions. I looked at him helplessly.

"Honey, I'm gonna need you to answer me," the medic said, not unkindly.

"She can't, unless you keep it to 'Yes' and 'No'," John said.

"Do you understand me?" the medic asked.

I nodded. Hunter rose and walked a short distance away from me at the Sheriff's urging; John followed.

CHAPTER THIRTEEN

*H*unter

The Sheriff was asking me questions, but my eyes were on Jessamine. She was ghostly pale in the deepening twilight. Medics and Sheriff Deputies were moving into the barn. I heard several muffled curses and maybe some gagging. I didn't care.

The Deputy who had been in the barn a short time back stopped in front of me.

"Tell me what happened?" he asked, his mouth set in grave lines below his mustache.

"I was walking along the highway. I saw the sign for the Owl Haven and thought I would come down. I do odd jobs, work for room and board for a time, then move on. Thought there might be some work to be had. I was most of the way down the driveway there, when I heard screaming from just in there."

"What did you do?" he asked, his pen moving across his notebook page.

"I ran, went in, the skinny one, he had her bent over the table by the stairs, pinning her down. The other one was..." I coughed, my throat closing with the bitter rise of anger.

"They were fixing to rape her. So I did what any decent man would do. I beat the shit out of them." I shrugged.

The medics were leading Jessamine to a gurney. She sat on the edge and nodded to something that someone said. John clapped me on the shoulder and I made a great show of flinching, hissing out in pain. It hurt, just not *that* bad.

"One of them get you?" the Deputy asked.

"Across the back, pipe or something," I answered.

"Where are you from?" John asked quizzically.

"Wales originally, all over mostly."

"Wales, isn't that part of England?" John asked; the Deputy nodded and continued taking copious notes.

"Yes." I answered, simply.

"Long way from home, aren't you, buddy?" John asked, but he was no longer quite as hostile, at least for the time being.

I looked him in the eye when I said

"It's a good thing for her, isn't it?"

He scowled at that.

"Yes. Yes, it was" the Deputy murmured.

We turned as one; the paramedics were wheeling Jessamine past us. Her small, pale hand shot out and gripped mine.

"Hey, there." I murmured.

Her storm-clouded eyes were beseeching as she pulled me toward her.

"Do you need me, fellas?" I asked, but my eyes stayed on hers.

"You going to the hospital?" John's voice was dark, likely with envy.

Jessamine was nodding emphatically.

"I think the lady would like me to accompany her." I twined my fingers with hers and she sank back gratefully into the gurney. I looked to the medic, who nodded.

"You should probably have your back checked out. I have more questions; I'll meet you at the hospital," the Sheriff's man said to my retreating back.

"I'll have your answers there," I called back to him.

Jess was staring at me as the medic moved about her in the back of the ambulance. He shone a light in her eyes and took her vital signs. I shifted uncomfortably in my seat. I wasn't a huge fan of closed spaces. It's hard to be when you were used to the open skies and the wind in your feathers.

I wanted to go back and finish the two drug-addled idiots. Her creamy skin was marred by blood, tears, and the angry red and deepening purples of ripening bruises. Her hand still shook within my own and I wished I knew what I could do to erase the fear shining behind her eyes.

For now I simply stayed with her.

I never liked human hospitals. The smell of sickness and death was barely covered by the stench of the industrial antiseptics they used. I felt vaguely nauseated as we entered, but now was not the time for weakness.

"Sir, I'm going to have to ask you to wait here," a nurse was saying. I looked to Jessamine.

"Is that all right with you?" I asked her.

She gave a cautious, if weary, nod, and I waited for her to let go of my hand. She did, finally, and I stepped out of the curtained area.

"You can take a seat in the waiting room, it's just down the hall on the right," a friendly nurse said from behind the central desk.

I looked very politely in her direction.

"I'll wait right here, thanks."

I gave her my best smile, which, of course, she returned. I never did have any trouble with the women of this species...

CHAPTER FOURTEEN

Jessamine

The nurse pulled the curtain shut but Hunter's boots remained steadfastly rooted to the linoleum just on the other side. I closed my eyes and rested my head against the pillow. I hurt, from the roots of my abused hair to my battered face to the myriad of pulled and strained muscles in various parts of my body from my struggle with the two men.

"Okay, sweetheart, do you feel up to changing into this gown without help?" the nurse asked.

I nodded carefully and sat up, reaching for the gown. She put it into my hands and ducked out to the other side of the curtain. I was alone. I fought down the welling of fresh tears and changed quickly, leaving my scrubs in a pile on the folding chair by the bed. The only thing I kept was my notepad and pen.

I got back on the bed with some difficulty, my body protesting loudly. I pulled the thin sheet over me and hugged my knees.

The nurse came back.

"We're going to have to put your bloody clothes into bags for the police," she said gently and I nodded. She set about putting everything into brown paper sacks.

I sniffed, tears sliding down my face and wondered what was going to happen to me.

"Can I come in?" A softly accented and very masculine voice.

I nodded to the nurse and she gave him permission.

I worried my abused lower lip between my teeth. Hunter sat down on the chair and rested one hand next to me on the bed, a silent offer of support if I needed it. I tried to smile at him, but it turned into a grimace when the split in my lip pulled and began to bleed afresh.

"The doctor will be in very shortly," the nurse soothed.

"The doctor will be in now." A tall, younger man, late twenties perhaps, with sandy blonde hair just beginning to recede, stepped through the curtain. He pushed his glasses higher on his nose and looked at Hunter doubtfully.

Hunter smiled and put up his hands.

I waved mine in front of myself and then in front of Hunter, desperate for the doctor to understand that he hadn't done this to me. The doctor frowned at us both.

"What happened here, Ms. Connors?" he asked, taking a seat on the little rolling stool and wheeling it closer to the bed side.

I opened my notepad and began to write.

Hunter didn't do this, I came home and was attacked by two men. Hunter showed up just in time and saved me.

I showed the doctor the note.

"I see, and you would be Hunter?" The doctor turned to him.

"Yes, sir." Hunter fidgeted in his seat.

"Can you tell me what happened?" he asked.

Hunter recounted his side of the story, omitting the parts about being an owl. He explained to the doctor that the two men that had attacked me had appeared to be on some kind of drug.

"I see," the doctor said finally. "Can you explain to me why one of the men has what appears to be claw marks to his scalp? Did you use a knife?" he asked Hunter, frowning.

I snapped my fingers and wrote quickly. *I was attacked in my barn. I run an owl sanctuary, one of the enclosures was knocked open and one of my owls got out and attacked the man.*

"Ah, that explains it." The doctor nodded sagely and clicked the back of his pen.

"Sadie," he addressed the nurse, "I want x-rays of Ms. Connor's face, and a CT scan to rule out broken bones and any possible concussion or hematomas that may exist. Clean her wounds and..." He snapped on gloves and gently prodded the cut near my hairline, over my eye.

"Yes. No stitches, but butterfly this one." He stripped off the gloves and disposed of them.

"Why aren't you talking, Ms. Connors?" he asked me gently.

Psychogenic stutter since I was seven. Severe, this is just faster and easier.

"I see, and what was the root cause of that?" he asked. I swallowed hard and shook my head.

"Jessamine! Jess!" The shout came from out from the main hall. I'd recognize Charlie's voice anywhere. I went limp with relief and dug my little tin whistle necklace out from inside the neckline of my hospital gown. I blew a short, sharp note and the curtain jerked back.

"My God, what have they done to you?" Charlie asked and strode up.

I reached out and took his hand, fresh tears starting to fall. He hugged me and I breathed in his familiar smell of Old Spice and sage.

"What happened?" he asked, looking from the nurse, to Hunter, to the doctor.

"Right, when she's ready," the doctor said to the nurse, and strode out.

"Somebody tell me what happened right now, damn it!" Charlie was mad.

I cringed.

"Not mad at you, Jess. I wanna know who did this. I swear, I'm going to make 'em wish they were never born." He rubbed my back gently.

"I'm pretty sure I've already accomplished that." Hunter smoothly broke in.

"Who are you?" Charlie's eyes narrowed in suspicion.

"Hunter Grayson, at your service." Hunter nodded to him.

I pulled on Charlie's sleeve and showed him my first note to the doctor.

Hunter didn't do this, I came home and was attacked by two men. Hunter showed up just in time and saved me.

"Did he now?"

Charlie eyed Hunter suspiciously before sticking out his hand. Hunter grasped it firmly and they shook. I could see the wheels turning in Charlie's head. It wasn't lost on him that we had just lost an owl named Hunter, and now there was a man with the same name in front of him, a man who had conveniently been in the right place at the right time. Charlie wasn't stupid.

The nurse cleared her throat and the three of us turned.

"If you don't mind, I'd like to take Jessamine for some tests and help get her cleaned up." She smiled serenely. The two men backed away from my bedside and let her take me to parts unknown.

I felt much better, now that Charlie was here.

I just wanted to go home and check on my owls. My owls! I waved frantically at the nurse and blew three sharp blasts on my little whistle.

Charlie stepped around the corner into the hall, took one look at my face and said,

"Relax Jessa-my-girl. I've got Aaron heading out there to deal with things. Everything is gonna be fine."

I slumped back into the bed and nodded to the nurse. She resumed pushing me up the hallway.

She gave me some medicine for pain after the x-rays and scans, and admittedly, the pills made me both tired and woozy. I could tell I was going to be here a while so I tried to cooperate as much as possible to get out of there sooner.

Charlie and Hunter stayed nearby. I didn't know what to make of the man.

The three of us spent several hours sitting and waiting for news. The police came and went; I wrote a statement for them. Hunter gave his out in the hallway. No one spoke after they left.

Charlie used the restroom several times, and I remembered that he was ill. I tried in vain to get him to go home but the stubborn, bull-headed, and wonderful old man would have nothing of it. For four hours I chewed my thumbnail and tried valiantly not to be impatient. Finally, in the fifth hour, the doctor came back.

"Well, that's much better," he said, in an attempt at levity. I'd been cleaned up, but my face was both swollen and a kaleidoscope of bruising. My eyes were both ringed in deep purple, though, luckily, my nose hadn't been broken. There was a cut across the bridge and it had bled from the inside, but no permanent damage was done.

"We're going to send you home, Jessamine, but someone needs to stay with you tonight and into tomorrow. Give yourself a week off of work, and I'm going to recommend that you seek professional help in dealing with what happened to you."

I nodded wearily.

"Here is a prescription for some stronger-grade ibuprofen and for a couple of Vicodin to get you through the next couple of days. Take it slow." He handed Charlie a couple of slips of paper.

I signed the discharge paperwork and a nurse brought me some hospital scrubs to wear home.

I changed while Hunter and Charlie waited outside, and padded out into the hall in those hospital socks with the silicone grip. A nurse wheeled up a chair and I frowned at it.

"Hospital policy," she said, with a sympathetic look. I sat down and Charlie went out to get his truck. Hunter stayed with me.

"Need a lift, *Hunter?*" Charlie asked from the driver's seat, as Hunter helped me into the cab of the truck.

"I would appreciate that, sir. My pack of belongings is back at Jessamine's place." He said quietly.

He climbed up beside me, sandwiching me between the two men.

I closed my eyes and hung my head. I was just so tired. The hum of the highway beneath the old Ford's wheels was hypnotizing in my drugged state. I don't think it was long before I fell asleep, warm and safe between Charlie and Hunter.

CHAPTER FIFTEEN

*H*unter

The old Indian was suspicious. Smart, too. Jessamine slumped between us, fast asleep. She'd left her hand loose in mine and Charlie kept stealing glances at our entwined fingers then at me.

"Right place at the right time, eh?" he asked.

"That's right." I drew in a slow breath, in through my nose and out through my mouth.

"Mmm." He grunted, "Hmph."

There was a long silence between us. Finally, with another stolen glance at my hand covering hers, he cleared his throat.

"If you've something to say, Elder Man, say it," I ground out.

"Jess is a good girl," he started. "I don't want to see anything happen to her. Now I'm not sure who or what you are, but I know you ain't right-"

I cut him off.

"I am what I am, and what that is, well, it is none of your concern. The fewer people that know, the better. As for Jessamine, I was coming to meet her, properly. I wish to know her. If she wanted to get to know me back, then good; if not, then I would take my leave. Never did I think I would happen upon what I did today." I swallowed hard the bitterness of my anger.

More silence stretched between us.

"I saw what you did to those boys," Charlie said.

"And?" I asked.

"And good job, I'm impressed... Still, a feller like me has to worry. If you're capable of doing what you did to them, what would you do to anyone else that pissed you off? What would you do if you didn't like what Jess here has to say or if she did somethin' you didn't like?" He turned in the darkened cab to look at me. I stayed quiet, letting him have his say.

"Jess is all the family I've ever had," he went on. "Seein' her like this, well, I'm grateful for what'cha done."

The words left unsaid hung thick between us in the cab of his old truck.

"But?" I said.

"But! You ever *think* of layin' a hand on her like you did those boys, I'll kill you."

A short laugh escaped my lips. Not so much at his threat, though I suspected he would find me difficult to kill, but moreso that he clearly didn't know me at all. While it is true that in my long life I have committed more than my fair share of transgressions, never, and I mean *never,* was one of them laying a violent hand upon a woman.

I stared out the window into the dark, and then turned back to him.

"I'd never touch a woman that way, Elder Man."

He read the sincerity on my face and gave a slow nod.

"Glad we understand each other," he said slowly, adding "Jess is a grown woman. I'll leave it up to her. She ever tells you to get outta her life, you better do it. We clear?" He looked at me and I inclined my head.

"We are clear." I echoed him.

"I did mean what I said. Whoever you are, whatever you are... I'm grateful you were there today." He turned onto Jessamine's road.

"Me, too, Elder Man. Me, too."

He crept down the pitted gravel drive, easing his way through the washouts and potholes. I would fill them in the coming days. I had formulated a list of several things that needed to be done around here on my long hike. Charlie pulled up to the front of the house. The youth of the day before came out and hurried to the passenger door of the truck. He opened it and took a startled step back.

"Who're you?" he asked, curiosity evident in his hazel eyes.

"Hunter." I answered simply as I got out and reached into the cab behind me, lifting Jessamine out carefully. I balanced her weight in my arms with little difficulty, but I could not do it forever. I strode past the boy into the house.

"Her bedroom is on the second floor," Charlie called after me, his truck door clanging shut.

I took the stairs swiftly but gently and entered her bedroom. It was large, easily taking up half the second floor. I strode to her bed and laid her gently in it, folding the triangle of covers up over her sleeping form. I smoothed some stray hair out of her eyes and turned to go.

"Hun-nn-nter?" she murmured, sleepily.

"Yes?" I looked her over; her troubled gaze swept over me from head to toe.

"L-l-eavin-ng?" she asked.

"Not if you don't want me to." I knelt beside her bed so that we could be eye-to-eye.

She looked like she wanted to say more, but the pain medicine was dragging at her consciousness. I sighed.

"I'll be here when you wake. Is that all right?" I asked gently.

She nodded, I smiled, and her eyes drifted shut. I returned to the first floor. Charlie and Aaron were in the kitchen.

"Dude, what happened?" Aaron asked.

"Home-invasion robbery." Charlie grunted. Aaron looked around. The house, thankfully, was intact.

"She came home and went to take care of the birds. They were in the barn and attacked her. She put up a fight but it was two against one." I explained.

Aaron looked stricken.

"Well, then, who are you?" he asked.

"Hunter Grayson, I'm a nomad, saw the sign out by the highway, and came down to see of the proprietor had any work in exchange for room and board. Right place at the right time."

The boy looked me over and spied my battered knuckles. He nodded.

"Thanks. Jess is really great if you get to know her. I hope you get to stay around long enough to find out." He stuck out his hand. "I'm Aaron. I volunteer with the owls."

I shook the boy's hand and smiled at him.

"Birds been fed?" Charlie asked.

"Yeah, all taken care of. Explains the barn, it was kind of a mess when I got in there. I washed down the floor, fed everybody. We need a new broom. Got here just as the Sheriff's department was wrapping up. The Department of Fish and Wildlife guy, John, helped me out, getting everybody calmed down and fed. Nobody would tell me what exactly happened, though. I figured I'd better stay here until somebody came home." He shrugged.

"You did good, kid." Charlie patted the boy on the shoulder.

"Agreed," I added.

"You go on and get home before your mom worries, you got school in the morning. Come by tomorrow, afterwards if you want. Jess is gonna need all the help she can get around here for the next few days." Charlie sat down at the counter. He was looking a little peaked by now.

"Okay. I'll see you guys tomorrow." Aaron bumped fists with Charlie and shook my hand again. I smiled; I could see Jessamine's will all over the boy.

He turned back to me.

"You know, we had an owl named Hunter, escaped just this morning..." Aaron looked at me.

"Really?" I asked.

"Yeah. Jess named him."

"A premonition of my arrival perhaps?"

"Maybe..." he said, but looked skeptical.

"'Night, Aaron," Charlie said, giving the boy a pointed look.

"'Night, Charlie." He went out the side door, and a short time later his small pickup left the drive.

"You should rest," I said.

"Yeah. You, too. Things start early around here." He got to his feet.

"I'll take the couch," I said.

"Linens are in that closet over there." He indicated it with a wave of his hand.

"Thank you"

"Boy's right, it's an awfully big coincidence..." He raked me with his gaze.

"Coincidences happen all the time, do they not? It is why we have a word for them." I met his gaze with my own.

He searched my face for a time.

"I stand by what I said in the truck," he said.

"As do I."

"Jess know what you are?"

"Yes, for the most part."

"Okay. 'Night, Hunter." He disappeared into a guest room off the living room, looking thoughtful.

I ducked out into the yard to bring in my pack. I stopped and looked up to the moon before retreating inside completely. The old Indian and the boy might or might not be a problem. That remained, as yet, to be seen. I sighed. This was not how I planned it, but I had never been so grateful to be in exactly the right place at exactly the right time as I was now.

I knew exactly how fickle fate could be, knowing her personally. I smiled up at the moon and silently sent praise to my great grand-mother Dôn, who in her way was mother to us all. "Thank you," I breathed into the night, before slipping back inside.

It wasn't perfect. In fact, it was quite messy, but I was here and Jess was safe. I would do what I could to allay Charlie and Aaron's fears about me by doing well by Jess. It was the best I could do, given the circumstances, and hopefully that would be enough.

I made up the couch with linens from the cupboard Charlie had pointed out and sat down. I took off my boots and stretched out, staring at the ceiling.

Sleep eluded me.

CHAPTER SIXTEEN

*J*essamine

My mouth felt dryer than a desert and like it was stuffed with cotton at the same time. I lay in my bed, and had no recollection as to how I had gotten into it. Then I tried to move. The pain it caused made the whole nightmare rush in on me, like a rogue wave on the beach, crashing into my consciousness and sweeping any sense of security I had away from me.

I pushed myself up into a sitting position with a moan. Everything hurt. I was stiff and sore from head to toe, and what was worse, someone had shut off my alarm. The sun rode high in the sky; I had missed the morning feeding.

"Hey, you're up."

I looked up. Aaron was smiling at me from the doorway. I scowled at him. Wasn't he supposed to be in school? I motioned in the air like I was writing. He brought me a whiteboard and dry-erase pen.

Aren't you supposed to be in school? I flashed the sign in his direction and his eyes got really wide.

"Jess, it's after three o'clock. School lets out at two..." he said.

I covered my face with my hands and groaned, as much from the pain of moving and at how bruised my face was as at how late it was. I swung my legs over the edge of the bed and gasped.

"Hunter!" Aaron called and I heard the thud of boots on the carpeted stairs.

He appeared in the door way, the breadth of his shoulders imposing. He wore a deep green tank top today, tucked into faded and stained blue jeans. A brown leather belt with a round disc for a buckle held his pants securely to his hips. The buckle was an elaborate knotwork design. I couldn't remember the exact name of it, but I think it was Irish or something. His hair was pulled into a tangled ponytail and remained reminiscent of his feathers, a light brown shot through with streaks of white.

"What's wrong?" he asked.

I hurt everywhere and slept all day. I wrote.

Hunter's full lips quirked up on one side.

"After last night, you earned it, love." His voice was melodic and held an accent that was decidedly close to English, but not quite.

Are you British?

He laughed. "Welsh," he affirmed his nationality, then sighed. "You look a sight. Let's get you in a shower and into some of your own clothes. Aaron, help Charlie outside?" He looked to the much younger man who nodded, his eyes wide and fixed on me.

Do I look that bad?

"Yeah, and then some, Jess." Aaron answered honestly. "I'd hug you, but I don't know if I'd hurt you." He backed out of the room and I heard his cascading footsteps as he went down the stairs.

I stood up and it was a bit too quickly. I waited for the vertigo to pass and faced Hunter.

Are you some kind of were-owl or something?

He laughed again.

"Or something."

He crossed his arms over his chest and the play of muscle beneath his skin made heat curl low in my body. I closed my eyes and shambled into my bathroom slowly. He turned on the shower and asked me where the towels could be found.

Hall closet.

He returned with one, and I shooed him out with my hands and took my sweet time getting undressed and under the hot spray. I also took my time in the shower, letting the heat ease my stiff muscles. When I got out, I combed my hair and braided it, frowning at my blurry image in the mirror. I wiped away the steam and cringed at my reflection. One half of my face was water colored in every shade of bruise imaginable from hairline to chin. The other half was clear, except for a deep dark ring of bruising around the eye. The cuts didn't look like they would scar real bad, which was good. I sighed. I was a hot mess, there was no denying that.

I closed my eyes and went back in the bedroom. I pulled on a pair of straight-legged sweats and one of my most comfortable college sweatshirts. It was gray, with a purple U and W outlined in gold on it. I put on thick socks and picked up my whiteboard and pen. I erased the last messages before Charlie or Aaron could see them.

I padded downstairs and found the house was empty. Charlie was heading into the barn, Aaron was near the aviary, and Hunter? Well, he was nowhere to be seen. I felt my shoulders drop in disappointment. I sighed.

"I'm right here, love." His voice came from behind me, a soft caress against the senses. I turned around. He smirked at me, and I could see the garage door standing open behind him.

Winter...

"He's fine. Went after the live prey you left him. Should probably move him into the pen you had me in." He said the last so softly I almost didn't hear it.

Aviary.

"What?"

Aviary. Not a pen. I was trying to build up your flight muscles in your wing and your leg before I released you. I guess you couldn't wait to get out of here.

"Ah, no, you have that all wrong." He eased past me and into the kitchen, going to the stove. He pulled the lid off a pot simmering there, and a pungent odor rolled out. I covered my nose and mouth with my sleeve.

"Don't make that face, love, you and I are both about to drink this." He ladled out two mugs of the foul smelling liquid and tried to hand me one.

What is it?

"It is a restorative tea. Will help with the bruises. It tastes better than it smells." He clinked mugs with me and I choked down a swallow.

"Ugh!!" I made a face.

He laughed and took a healthy swallow.

"One cup, love; it's all I ask."

He turned back to the stove and I saw the line of bruising peeking out from around the straps of his tank. I winced, remembering the sound the broom handle had made impacting his flesh. I let out a gusty sigh. I choked down the rest of the tea obediently, and closed my eyes; my stomach roiled in protest before becoming quiescent again. Hunter turned from the stove and smiled faintly at me.

"Thank you," he said, and took the mug. I wiped my board clean.

Thank YOU. If choking down some nasty tea is all it takes to make you happy after what you did for me yesterday then pour me another cup.

He laughed.

"What would make me happy, is fixing up some things around here for you, that you and Charlie just can't do. I'll start with filling in the washouts in your driveway. That broken window in the barn could use fixing, the gutters need to be cleaned, that felled tree needs to be chopped up, and I think you have a roof leak or two?" He was searching my face and all I could do was stand there and blink at him.

It was true, some things had gotten away from me and Charlie. I just wasn't strong enough, or was kept busy by the owls or at work. I didn't want Aaron getting hurt, either. I wiped my board clean and hesitated over it with the dry-erase pen.

I can't pay you anything, money is tight as it is. I can give you room and board, a ride into town whenever you need it... I might be able to pay for supplies you need but for the most part you'll have to make do with what's around here. I don't know, it hardly seems fair.

"I learned a very long time ago that life is far from fair. You're going to need the extra help around here, at least for a few days, and I like to keep busy, so the extras are a bonus if you want to look at it that way. I like it here, Jessamine."

He took a step or two forward, closing the gap between us. In a much lower, much softer tone of voice he spoke his next words.

"I don't know what I would have done if it weren't for you, on that highway. You picked me up when countless other cars just passed me by. I wanted to come and give back. I never... I never meant for any of it to go like this. Those two were a very unwelcome surprise. I should have killed them." His fists clenched and unclenched at his sides.

I thought for a minute.

Everything happens for a reason. You would have had to lie about who, or at least __what__ you are if things hadn't happened the way they did, right?

"Probably, yes... It's what I've done for a very long time," he admitted.

Well now you don't have to lie, at least not to me. That has to be something, right? Freeing, sort of?

He smiled at me and shook his head, I think in wonderment.

"Even after all of that, you still manage to find something good?" he asked.

I erased what I had written.

Yeah, well, I guess I'm naïve that way. I couldn't keep the bitterness off my face.

"I don't think so." He tipped a finger under my chin so I'd look up.

I did, but not without flinching away from even that gentle touch. He withdrew his fingers quickly and scowled, but not at me.

"You're pure goodness, woman. A naïve person lacks experience, and is typically too trusting. I see the skepticism in your eyes. You know how things work, you willfully go against the grain and try to make a difference, a positive one, even with the odds stacked against you. You're the best kind of person there is, and I see it in you, plain as day."

I blinked several times, my eyes misting at his words. He was being too nice. He'd been nothing *but* nice and I wasn't quite sure what to do with it.

He stepped around the counter and went toward the door. "Not sure what you want to do about dinner but I can't really cook for shite, if you're not up to it, Charlie said he'd cook..."

I looked stricken and he laughed.

I'll cook. Send Aaron in, maybe he could learn a thing or two. I'll consider this cooking out of self-defense if Charlie was planning on coming in here. Canned chili over microwaved mac and cheese is about the extent of his skill level. He would have starved without my Aunt Margie around.

He came forward and took the board out of my hand and read it. He laughed and shook his head, handing it back.

"I'll send the boy in."

He slipped out the back door and I watched him go, swallowing hard. The only thing better than watching Hunter walk towards me was watching him walk away.

I huffed out a sigh. I didn't think for a minute that the feeling was mutual. I mean, who in their right mind, owl-creature-human-thing or not, would want someone like me? I shook my head and tried to clear it. I had things to do.

I set about the kitchen, moving slowly but efficiently. I pulled down the ingredients for pie and two ceramic pie baking dishes. My boys were heroes all the way around yesterday, getting the owls taken care of despite me being down for the count.

The message light on my answering machine was blinking and I hit the 'Play' button. The voices coming through, with message after message of well-wishes, made my eyes burn with happy tears of gratitude while I moved about the kitchen. One of the messages was the animal hospital telling me to take as much time as I needed, reminding me I had plenty of sick leave and vacation time. I smiled and let them play out as Aaron came in and sidled up to the counter.

"Pie? For dinner?" he asked, grinning.

You guys earned it. Go get me three boxes of hamburger-helper out of the garage pantry, pick all three the same flavor and get me three lbs of hamburger out of the freezer. I'm going easy on myself, sorry for the ghetto meal after you guys did so much out there the last couple of days. 😢

Aaron laughed and shook his head.

"Jess, you're standing right in front of me looking like hamburger yourself; you don't need to draw a sad face to tell me you feel bad. I cook hamburger-helper at my house for me and mom all the time. Let me do that, and tell me what I can do to help with the pie, so you don't kill yourself." He rolled his eyes and stood waiting for orders.

Nice try. I was born at night, not LAST night. The secret of pie stays with me grasshopper. You are not ready. Get the dinner stuff, wash your hands and get to work.

"Yes, ma'am!" He saluted me with a grin and I smiled, which turned into a slight grimace when the cut on my lip pulled.

I set to work on the pie. A few minutes later, Aaron came back into the kitchen with his arms brimming with ingredients. I pointed to where he could set up and cook, and he nodded, chatting amicably away about how my fly-babies were doing out there. I smiled at his chatter, and kept an eye on him, but what he'd said was true; he indeed knew his way around a box of hamburger-helper.

He was one-up on Charlie that was for sure! If it didn't involve open flame and time-honored tribal tradition, then Charlie was pretty much hopeless when it came to feeding himself. My aunt had spoiled him that badly.

I sighed. I wondered if Charlie had called Uncle Dave and Aunt Margie. I knew he probably had. They were probably on their way right now. At least I had a mundane explanation for Hunter's presence.

I wasn't sure about the rest, but we hadn't exactly had time to discuss things further. I was being pretty patient but I really wanted an explanation, and soon, as to what he was.

Ever since I was a little girl, I had believed in my heart-of-hearts in magic, but when I got older, that belief, like so many others, was slowly stripped away. When I was seven I had lost faith in such things; by the time I was eight I had been ready to believe again, thanks to Uncle Dave.

I put the pies in the oven and started to clean up, but Aaron shooed me away.

"I got it Jess, go sit down." He was a good kid.

I obediently heaved myself up to our little lunch-counter. Aaron cleaned up like a pro and managed to pay dutiful attention to the two pans of hamburger-helper on the stove. He set my board on the counter in front of me and I wiped it clean.

You've earned the secret of the honey biscuits, want to try?

"Yeah!" He looked eager to learn and I smiled.

Get out the flour, we're making a double batch so you'll need four cups.

I slid off the stool and got out my trusty cheese grater from the dishwasher, and set to washing it by hand in the sink.

"What else?" he asked.

Baking powder, salt, three sticks of butter from the freezer up there and the milk. Get the fireweed honey from the cupboard over there. I pointed to the freezer attached to the fridge and the cupboard with the honey in it.

We had all sorts of honey in this house, clover, creamed, blackberry, but the fireweed was our most prized. Fireweed only blooms in two-year cycles and only when the humidity is less than fifty percent. It gets its name because the fireweed plant also only blooms in areas ravaged by forest fires. The flowers only last a week, so, really, conditions have to be just right for there to be *any*. So prized is the unique flavor of this honey, bee-keepers will relocate entire hives near patches of the flowers just so their bees will produce it.

Aaron brought the jar of honey over as if it were some kind of relic out of an Indiana Jones movie and it made me chuckle.

"What now?" he asked.

Four cups of flour right here on the countertop.

"Don't you want me to put waxed paper down to save on some clean up?" he asked.

No, right on the granite, the stone keeps the butter cold and the biscuits come out flakier.

My handwriting was messier than usual; I was trying to write fast to keep the ingredients from getting warm.

"Oh! Okay. I didn't know that." He measured out four cups as I wrote the next set of instructions.

Mix in six teaspoons baking powder and two teaspoons salt with a fork. I know it sounds like a lot but remember we're making two batches here.

"Okay, on it." He measured and whisked everything together with a fork.

Grate these frozen sticks of butter on this into the flour. I handed him the cheese grater and an unwrapped stick of butter.

He grated it on top of the flour and I handed him the next, he did that one too and I showed him how to integrate it until it was all crumby. He smiled and I smiled back. I waved my hands over his in an indication to stop.

With some dough still on my hands, I wrote out

Now make a well in the center and slowly add milk until you get a cup and a half of it in there. Use one of the big mixing bowls if you're afraid of making too much of a mess.

"Uhhh..." he laughed nervously.

Just add enough milk until you can get all the dough off the counter then add the rest in the bowl.

I pointed to the top of the fridge where all my large metal mixing bowls lived. He got one down and did just fine.

I put two tablespoons of butter and two tablespoons of honey into a dish and popped it into the microwave to melt them together. I added half a tablespoon of extra honey into the dough as he kneaded it out on the counter.

I waved him off of the dough. I didn't want him to overdo it; five or six times was just fine. I indicated the rolling pin and dipped out a little flour, coating the pin's surface and sprinkling more out on the counter. I indicated about a half-inch of space between my thumb and index finger.

"Okay."

He rolled out the dough and I opened my drawer of miscellaneous kitchen gadgetry. I pulled out my round biscuit cutter and floured it as well. It was about two inches across. I smiled and he smiled back. He washed his hands and got out the cookie sheets. I was kind of tickled that he paid attention enough to know where they were.

"Oven, Jess?" he asked.

"Ff-f-four f-ff-f-fifty."

Contentment washed over me despite how battered I was. I was so lucky in so many ways. To have such an amazing and eclectic family, and such a wonderful circle of friends... I couldn't ask for much more right now, except maybe, someone to share it with. That would come in its own time, though. So long as someone was willing to settle for me.

I pushed those thoughts away as I brushed the top of each biscuit with the honey and butter mixture. Aaron popped them into the oven once it was preheated. I set my old fashioned kitchen timer to eleven minutes and I washed my hands.

We would have about two dozen biscuits when all was said and done. If they didn't all go tonight, I would make mini-sandwiches out of the rest with some Havarti cheese and Italian dry salami for a snack or lunch the next day.

I had set four places at the lunch counter when John Baker came in the side door and into my kitchen. I smiled at him and held up a plate with a questioning look.

"Jesus, Jess, look what they did to you!" He looked pained and I shrugged a shoulder inelegantly and dropped my gaze to the floor.

"Hey, man, don't make her feel bad!" Aaron exclaimed.

I set a fifth place behind the counter where I could stand and eat, without waiting for John to reply on if he was staying or not. I made myself busy by getting out the ever-ready pitcher of sweet tea from the fridge. I swear, my aunt had been a Southern belle in a former life. I smiled and put out four tall glasses at the set places and one beside my own plate, putting ice from the front of my fridge into each one before filling them with tea. John was grimacing.

"Sorry, Jess. I didn't mean anything by it," he said, taking a seat at the counter. I picked up my board.

I know. I'll heal up and it'll be like it never happened. I put on a brave smile.

It was very quiet in my kitchen all of a sudden. Everyone present knew the lie of my words. Me, most of all.

Aaron ring Charlie and Hunter in. I wrote next.

"Yes, ma'am!"

"He's still here?" John asked, his expression darkening.

Yes. Be nice. He's going to be around for the next few days to help out around here. I gave him a pointed look.

"Jesus, Jess, you don't know anything about the guy!" he hissed in a whisper-shout. The main object of our discussion was headed this way, the clanging of the triangle dying out. Watching Hunter stride across the yard made my heart give an erratic thump in my chest. He was all corded muscle that rippled with this insane grace as he moved. I swallowed, hard.

I gave John a look that plaintively said *'Be nice'* as they all came in.

"Sit down before you fall down, Jess," Charlie snarled in his typical way.

I waved him off and indicated Aaron should sit down.

He shook his head. "Guys, take your plates to the table, otherwise one of us is going to end up standing, and you know it's gonna be Jess. She's too stubborn."

I glared at him and there was some laughter but everyone did as they were told, taking their settings over to the six-person dining room table that was rarely used.

I took the first wave of biscuits out of the oven and checked the pies. They came out, too. I set them on the lunch counter to cool.

The mood was pretty harmonious as everyone pitched in to set the table, bring over glasses and the pitcher of tea, and the like. I handed John some pot-holders to put out on the table. Hunter took one of the pans of hamburger-helper over, serving some up on each plate.

I brought over jam, honey, and butter for the biscuits, which went into a basket, a dish towel over it to keep them warm.

The first pan of helper returned to the kitchen empty and clattered into the sink. The next pan went onto the potholders on the table for seconds to be served up if needed.

I took my seat at the head of the table, Hunter on my left, Charlie on my right. Charlie bowed his head and the rest of us followed suit. He gave thanks to the spirit of the animal we were about to consume and to the earth for the other bounties that it provided us. He also gave thanks to the spirits and ancestors that led Hunter to the barn the day before.

A hush descended on the table before everyone dug into their food.

You would think I would feel out of place, the only girl at a table full of men, but not so much. I was comfortable with and comforted by everyone present. Charlie broke the silence first.

"Yer Uncle Dave and Aunt Margie will be up sometime in the next couple of days," He said. I glared at him mutinously. "Don't look at me in that tone of voice! You know I had to call 'em," he grumbled.

"He's right, they're your family and they should be here," Hunter murmured.

I sighed. I knew they were right. I looked around and realized I had left my writing board over on the kitchen counter.

"I'll get it." Aaron jumped up and went over and brought it back to me without being asked. I smiled at him and gave him a thumbs-up in thanks.

I just don't want anyone to worry, or to see me like this. Especially not those two. Margie can be overprotective at the best of times. I grimaced.

"They do it because they love yah, kid."

I gave Charlie a look like *'Well, duh'* and he smirked.

"So, Hunter, Jessamine tells me you're staying around for a while," John broke in. I tucked into my food. I wanted to see how Hunter would handle this.

"That's right. There are some things around here that could use some attention," Hunter replied, taking another bite of his food.

"Well, you know, I've offered to come by and do them, so you could probably leave anytime. Say, like, tomorrow." John smiled, but it wasn't nice.

I sat up straighter in my chair, pretty incensed that he would have the nerve to say such things. Like he had any say on who did what on my property. I gave him a look that could burn the house down around his ears. Aaron had seen it a time or two; so had Charlie; they knew what it meant and both of them kind of shrank in their seats, waiting to see what would happen. I didn't get mad often, but when I did, it could be pretty spectacular.

Hunter's voice, calm with an underlying steel, gave voice to exactly what I was thinking.

"Mr. Baker, I don't believe you're in any position to tell me what I could and could not be doing when it comes to Jessamine and her property. *Especially* with her sitting right here. All due respect, you don't live here; Jessamine does, and she is a grown woman capable of making her own decisions." Hunter locked eyes with me, the warm caramel color making my center all soft and gooey.

I nodded in both agreement and thanks. Hunter nodded his head once, clearly catching the double meaning. I picked up my whiteboard.

I know you mean well, but this is MY house and MY life John. I'm the one who makes the decisions on who's in it and when. We clear?

John almost choked on his bite of food.

Charlie clapped him on the back while simultaneously laughing uproariously. "John, m'boy, I believe you just got *told*." He continued to cackle, and winked at me, his eyes shining with pride.

I smiled while wincing inwardly. I may have been too harsh, but damn it, I wasn't completely helpless.

John set down his fork and got up to go. Charlie smacked his glass onto the table.

"Sit down, boy, maybe some of Jessamine's pie will sooth your wounded pride. But, damned if you didn't have it comin'. Jess is her own person and we can all agree none of us want to see her hurt." Charlie's dark brown eyes roamed my face. "We aren't always goin' t' be able to keep it from happenin', her getting' hurt, I mean, but we damn sure can always be here to pick up the pieces when it does. Long as the spirit wills it, anyhow." He leaned back in his seat and crossed his arms, giving me a lingering look before turning his gaze on John.

My shoulders slumped and I tried not to sniff, even though my eyes were welling up again. I didn't want to ever think about a life without Charlie in it. He was my best friend and my rock despite our age difference. He was in his early seventies, though, and me, I was almost thirty, so he didn't have a lot of time left and me, I had too much. There would be a gap at some point, and I wasn't looking forward to it. Charlie put his hand over my own where it rested on the table and gave it a squeeze. I smiled at him and he smiled back.

"John, sit your ass down. Boy, make us some coffee. Hunter, you clear these dishes, and I'll get the pie."

He got up and shoved his chair in. John sat down with a stunned expression. I don't think he was used to being talked to that way and I grimaced inwardly. Charlie was rough around the edges on a good day, and I was pretty sure that, given the events of the last couple of days, today was not being considered a good one. Despite my physical appearance and injuries, my spirits were up pretty high.

He doesn't mean it like that John. That's just Charlie being Charlie I wrote out after one look at John's sour expression.

He moved into Charlie's seat.

"I'm worried about you, Jess. I'm pretty sure you've figured out by now that I like you." He covered my hand with his own and I smiled sadly and withdrew my hand from under his, both because I didn't want to be that familiar with him and because I needed it to write.

I know John, but I'm not the girl for you. I'm not in any kind of position to carry on a relationship beyond just friendship.

He scowled, and I rolled my eyes and made an exasperated noise.

That includes with Hunter I tacked on, erasing it quickly when he'd finished reading it, as the aforementioned person was walking back towards us to pick up another pair of plates.

"Okay, Jess, I can see you need some time, especially given what's happened. I'll do my best to give it to you," he said.

I closed my eyes and tried to be patient. John Baker was just *not* hearing me, but there wasn't much to be done about it right now.

Charlie set one of the pies on the table, it had been cut into pieces, but had yet to be served. Hunter came behind him with plates and forks.

"Get Jess, there, a spoon, Hunter," Charlie said.

"I got it!" Aaron called from the kitchen. He returned with a spoon for me and coffee for Charlie and John.

"What does she need a spoon for?" Hunter asked, his brow furrowed.

I smiled impishly as Charlie set a piece of pie in front of me, and dug into it with the spoon.

"It's the way she eats her pie," Charlie answered. "Has been, ever since she was a kid." He smiled down at me but I was in the little bliss-coma Aunt Margie's cherry pie brought on.

Aaron laughed at me before getting into his own pie; everyone else followed suit. I paid careful attention to Hunter. He put his fork with a generous bite into his mouth and chewed thoughtfully. He smiled at me and nodded as he chewed slowly.

"That's good, that's really good. Well done, love." He took another bite.

Soon all of us were leaned back in our seats, sighing at our full stomachs. I, for one, was glad for the elastic waistband on my sweats.

Rule here is, Aaron and I cooked, so you guys get the dishes/clean up. John, Hunter, you've never had dinner here before so you get a pass because you're guests; but you eat here once, you're pretty much furniture after that, so next time, you get to it.

I smiled sweetly at Charlie.

"That leaves me then." He smiled back in his *'I am so getting you later for this'* way.

I erased what I had written, scrawling out, *Maybe this is a lesson that you should be nicer.* And I drew a face with its tongue sticking out and stuck mine out for good measure.

"All right, kid. All right," Charlie said, getting up. Everyone else was chuckling at his expense.

"Jess, I really do hate to eat and run, but I have to get going. I've stayed too late as it is." John got to his feet. I nodded.

"I'll help you in the kitchen, Charlie." Hunter got up, too, and went after Charlie and I smiled. That might earn Hunter a few points with the old codger. We'd have to see.

John came around the table and leaned down, kissing the cheek that wasn't spangled with color, then nodded to the others. He stepped outside and donned his hat and a short time later his Jeep fired up. I sighed tiredly.

"Come on, Jess." Aaron was at my side.

I let him help me up and he took me into the living room. I sat down in my Uncle Dave's recliner and curled up in it.

"I'm gonna help out in the kitchen." He tucked the blanket from the back of the couch around me and I nodded.

"Need anything?" he asked.

I swiped my hand across my neck and he nodded at the familiar signal for 'No' before disappearing into the kitchen, where the sound of running water and low masculine voices could be heard.

I smiled at the total domestic role-reversal going on under my roof and closed my eyes. I don't remember falling asleep, but I must have dozed off for a minute or two.

CHAPTER SEVENTEEN

*H*unter

"I've got to go back to the res and put a bag together if I'm going to be staying here the next few days," Charlie said, but he looked uneasy.

"Don't like being away?" I asked.

"Naw, the res is my home. I love Jess and I love it here, but the world out here is different." He sighed and handed me another plate. I rinsed it in the sink and put it in the dishwasher.

Out of all of my kind, I was pretty much the only one that kept up with the human world and its technological advancements. To ignore them would have just set me apart as 'other', more than I already was, and that was dangerous, especially with a secret like mine. In short, I understood where Charlie was coming from, probably more than he knew.

He and I had spoken candidly earlier in the day while Jess slept and Aaron had yet to arrive. It was a risk, but one I had to take if I had any hope of staying here, with Jess. Charlie had mulled things over for far too long for comfort before finally saying, again, that he'd meant what he said: if Jess ever told me to leave, I'd better do it, or mythical creature or no, Charlie would have me stuffed and mounted. I believed him and we'd shook hands on it.

We'd also agreed that Aaron was to be kept in the dark, that my name matching with the missing owl's was just as I'd said it was, a coincidence. So far I had been lucky in that the Sheriff's Deputy and the Fish and Wildlife man hadn't recalled the owl with the same name. Perhaps that was for the best, and we should just deal with it if and when it came up.

I rinsed a dish and put it in the bottom rack of the dishwasher.

"The house here is about to become crowded," I mused out-loud.

"Yeah, I won't be stayin' once Dave and Margie get here. I was being a dick last night. There's a spare room up on the second floor. You could have taken that one." He shrugged.

"I know, I figured as much. I saw it when I carried Jessamine up. When you took the room down here, I figured you wanted me on the couch to keep an eye on me." I smiled and he grinned back.

"Here it was I thought I was being sneaky," he said. I had a moment to appreciate what Jess had said, about the truth being freeing: at least when it came to this cagy old man, it had been. Still...

"You're crafty, I'll give you that, Charlie, but really, I understand you wish to get to know me. But Jessmine is safe with me." I took the last dish, rinsed it and put it in the top rack.

"Under the sink," Charlie provided, figuring I was looking for the soap.

"You know, I believe you, Hunter. Not sure why, but I do. Probably has to do with you tellin' the truth and me comin' from where I do... I'm still stayin' here tonight, but I am gonna leave her in your care for a couple of hours. You can take the upstairs room tonight. My old knees don't like the climbing."

He dried his hands on a dishcloth and tossed it over his shoulder. I added the requisite amount of soap and started the dishwasher.

Aaron came in from outside, where we'd sent him to do a final check on the owls.

"Everything is good out there," he said and we nodded, both Charlie and I, as one. We smiled at each other. For being so suspicious of me, Jessamine's family was oddly welcoming at the same time.

"You better git, kid. You have school tomorrow."

"Yeah, about that... I kind of don't have enough gas to get home. I used the last to get here. I knew you guys needed the help..." He colored red with embarrassment, and wilted a little under Charlie's scathing look.

"Take m-mmm-my tr-r-uck," Jessamine said from the doorway.

She looked a bit sleep-tousled and had the quilt I'd used last night wrapped about her shoulders. She looked delicate, almost broken, the bruises on her face standing out in stark relief against her porcelain skin. I felt an odd mixture of anger and desire. Even as battered as she was, she was beautiful.

"Gas cann-ns too," she ordered, after he'd collected her keys.

I reached into my pocket and pulled out the last of my money and held it out. It wasn't much, with petrol prices the way they were, but in the face of so much generosity, I felt the need to be a part of things, too.

Everyone stilled, staring at the bits of green paper in my hand.

"Take it, it isn't much, but it should get you where you're going until you can make more." I shrugged a shoulder.

"I can't take your money, man," Aaron groaned.

"You can and you will. I'll pick up an odd job somewhere, same as you." I smiled a one-sided smile.

He took the money reluctantly from my hand and nodded. "I'll pay you back," he said.

"You don't have to."

"Go on, kid, the sooner you get home the less your mom will holler at you. I got a long drive ahead only to turn around and come back," Charlie grated out, and he and Aaron left the house by the kitchen side door.

Jessamine and I were finally alone, and I could tell I had some questions to answer. She picked up her little erasable board and the pen that went with it and indicated I should follow her to the living room.

I switched on the lamp standing beside the couch, the stained-glass lampshade depicting hanging wisteria blooms glowing in jewel tones of purple and green. She sat heavily on the end of the couch beneath the lamp and her pen flew across the board.

I took the end of the couch opposite her and waited patiently, memorizing the graceful line of her neck as it disappeared into her sweatshirt.

This was going to be uncomfortable for me, but she was correct in her earlier assessment. In a way, this was also going to be oddly freeing. I could count the number of times I had come clean to a human about what I was; it was a low number. Further still, I could count how many times that the consequences of my actions hadn't been disastrous, and *that* number was zero.

It had been a very long time, hundreds upon hundreds of years.

This was a different time, but still, humanity was not so very different in its attitudes now than it had been then. I was taking a very large risk in telling her anything more than she already knew. I caught her staring at me and I gritted my teeth.

I get the impression you told Charlie, now you can tell me... What are you? she asked, and immediately erased what she'd written once I'd read it.

I prayed to my great-grandmother, the mother-goddess Dôn, that I hadn't and wasn't about to commit a horrible mistake. I closed my eyes and took a leap of faith. Leveling my gaze at this woman, I told her the absolute, unabashed truth.

"I am the son of a Welsh god and a construct made for him by his uncle, the sorcerous god Gwydion."

Her eyes grew a little wide and she swallowed. "*Tell me*," she said, and relief flooded my veins.

I smiled at her momentary lack of stutter and tried to think where on earth to begin.

CHAPTER EIGHTEEN

***J**essamine*

I blinked, momentarily stunned by what he was saying. If I hadn't seen him turn from an owl into a man and back again, I would be laughing. I would think him certifiably insane and would be calling the police, but I knew what I'd seen in the barn the previous day and so, I did none of these things. Instead, I was surprised to hear the words "Tell me," escape my battered lips without as much as a quiver in my speech.

The beautiful man on the end of my couch took in a deep breath and let it out. He seemed just as surprised as I felt that I hadn't called him barking mad. I waited patiently for him to find where to begin, as I was sure this was going to be a very long story.

"Do you happen to know the old Welsh myth of Blodeuwedd?" he asked.

I know the myth has to do with a woman being cursed into the form of an owl, but that is about it I answered him honestly. Of course, the only reason I knew it was because the story had an owl in it.

He looked relieved.

"Okay, good, that's a place to start. So, uh, my father's uncle, Gwydion, was both a god and great sorcerer. He created

Blodeuwedd, my mother, from the flowers of oak, broom, and meadowsweet."

He checked to see if I was following.

"W-w-why?" I asked.

"My father, Llew Llaw Gyffes was kind of an accident, an embarrassment to his mother, the goddess Arianrhod. So she cursed him. Back then, it was a big deal for a man to have a name, to be able to take up arms, and to take a wife, so she cursed him that he would never be able to have a name unless she named him. My father's uncle, Gwydion, felt bad about it and tricked Arianrhod into naming her son. Llew Llaw Gyffes is what he got stuck with. It loosely translates to 'the fair haired boy with a good arm'.

"She was kind of angry about being tricked, and so she cursed my father again, this time that he would never be able to take up arms unless she gave them to him. Well, Gwydion figured a way around that too, which really made Arionrhod angry.

"So, she slapped my father with *another* curse, that he would never be able to take a wife of flesh."

My eyebrows went up and I tipped my head to the side, considering him. I reached out and touched the back of his arm. He felt like flesh-and-blood to me. He figured out pretty quickly what I was doing because he smiled and went on.

"So, Gwydion, that's my father's uncle, went to *his* uncle, Math, and they put their heads and magic together, along with the flowers of the oak, broom, and meadowsweet. They *created* my mother, a woman of flowers, not flesh, for my father, thus negating my grandmother's final curse. Gwydion named her Blodeuwedd which means 'flower face', and just kind of gave her over to my father."

Hunter scrubbed a hand over his face.

"My mother came into this world of magic by the magic of these two, but neither Math nor Gwydion ever bothered asking her if she *wanted* to be married to Llew. She was as sentient as you or I, and was just forced into this marriage. It was simply how things were done then. There was no such thing as justice..."

He grimaced and I folded his hand between both of my own. He took a deep breath. I could tell this was a source of embarrassment to him and I hoped he would continue, though I didn't think I could bear to make him, he had such raw pain imprinted across his features.

"Right." He pressed on, so I let him.

"So there's my mother, trapped in a loveless marriage with a man, having no say in any of it because she's a woman, and a construct to boot... Eventually she would become the goddess of spring, but during that time, she was just a beautiful maiden and the wife of Llew Llaw Gyffes. She spent as much time as she could outside my father's castle, preferring her own company to his. One day, while he was out doing whatever it was that he did, the lord of the neighboring land of Penylln, a man by the name of Gronw Pebr came riding by on a hunt. He happened upon my mother and, well, yeah... They fell in love."

He shrugged.

"There wasn't any such thing as divorce in their time, so in order for them to be together, my father had to die. It's a tricky thing killing a god, especially a Welsh one; so many ridiculous conditions have to be met. So in order to kill my father, my mother had to pretty much *ask* him how it could be done."

He sounded bitter and I squeezed his hand in sympathy.

"To make this long story a bit shorter, he told her, but it could only be done with a weapon that took an entire year to forge. Gronw got to work on it and both he and my mother stole what time they could together. Of course, she still had to fulfill her duties as a loyal wife in the meantime..."

He let out a breath and rolled his shoulders. This was an awful lot of his family's dirty laundry being aired. I swallowed, and he leveled his gaze on me again, the light caramel color of his irises growing dark with the retelling, expanding to wall-to-wall darkness with his distress.

He was looking at me with an owl's eyes in his beautiful human face and my heart began to break for him.

"She got pregnant with me," he said, his voice cracking. "She gave birth to me and there was no question about it, I was my father's son. I look just like him. She convinced my father that Heliwr was a good name for me. It means 'Hunter'," he said, but that went without saying. I smiled and nodded. It suited him and it *was* a good name.

"Anyway, she loved me. At least, I was told she did..."

This was my second indication that this story was not going to have a happy ending. My first was the obvious pain it caused him to recall the events. I waited him out patiently and he began talking again.

"Some months after my birth, Gronw had his weapon and my mother tricked my father into demonstrating just how he could be killed. Gronw used the weapon on him and struck my father a grievous injury, however before he could finish him off, my father turned into a golden eagle and flew away. His uncle, Gwydion, found him and together Gwydion and Math nursed my father back to health. With that accomplished, my father and Gwydion sought revenge on both my mother and Gronw."

Hunter pursed his lips and was lost in memory for a time.

"My father caught up with Gronw and killed him. Gwydion went after my mother, and cursed her."

He swallowed and his tone and inflection switched to that of a recitation...

"You will not dare to show your face ever again in the light of day, and that will be because of enmity between you and all other birds. It will be in their nature to harass you and despise you wherever they find you. And you will not lose your name - that will always be 'Blod-deuwedd'... And, he turned her into an owl."

He looked at me and I closed my eyes.

"He was angry, and well, I'm half my mother, so guess what?"

"H-h-h-he h-h-half-cursed y-y-you, too..."

I was vaguely proud of myself for getting the words out with only moderate difficulty, but the look of raw pain on Hunter's face squashed it. I did the only thing I could think of to do: I went up on my knees on the center couch cushion and I put my arms around his broad shoulders.

I sighed. His family sounded more dysfunctional than mine, even without the added benefit of them being gods, and magic, and things. I closed my eyes and breathed him in. He smelled crisp and fresh like the outdoors, of clean air and freshly-fallen rain, earthy, like the forest beyond the borders of my yard.

"I'm so s-s-sorry," I breathed and I meant it. I mean, I'd seen him change into an owl, I had to believe him... and I decided that I did. If all this was true, that meant that he'd been alive for a *very* long time and that was just too much for me to really wrap my head around. I mean, how *lonely*!

His arms went around me and he held me as if I would break. I liked that about him; that as big and imposing as he was, he was so gentle with me. I appreciated it. He really was too nice, and a god, or part-god-part-magical creature...

I was so confused; how did a girl like me end up with a god on my couch taking comfort from me? I was all torn up inside. I didn't know what to think or what to do. I wanted so much to tell him that I understood at least some of what he'd been through.

I drew back and smiled at him; he gave me a tentative smile in return before letting me go, to slip back to my end of the couch. We stared at each other a long time. I had so many questions, but I didn't know how to ask.

I wanted to fix it for him so badly, but I knew better. When it came to ugly family matters, there wasn't any fixing it. No one could hurt you like family. Hunter and I both sat there, living proof of that.

I was in way over my head on this one. This wasn't a broken wing, this was a broken heart and they were much, *much* harder to mend.

CHAPTER NINETEEN

*H*unter

I breathed deeply the scent of lavender, vanilla, and what I was now absolutely certain was sandalwood, as I held her soft lithe form against me. She was warm, and I longed to taste her, but I refrained. The temptation nearly finished me, though.

I was stunned that she believed me. Telling the story of my parents had always been a painful thing to me. My story was just a popular myth to most humans in Wales, so I had left the country with some of the first waves of pilgrims. Living as a man aboard a cramped ship for months had been one of the hardest things I'd ever done in my long life. In quarters that cramped, there was no opportunity to take to the air without suspicion of witchcraft or other devilry falling upon me.

Gwydion had not meant to half-curse me in his anger. Though we were not close, he had done his best to lessen the blow done to me. Through great magic, he had given me the option of shifting between my accursed form and that of a man.

My father had been much less forgiving. We knew I was his, but Llew Llaw Gyffes, lord of his lands and mighty king, would not be swayed. Convinced, in his bitterness at his wife's betrayal, that I was a product of her and Gronw's union, he had cursed me to an unhappy childhood, without a father and without a mother, left to the servants and his uncle for the raising.

I supposed that Jessamine and I were similar in that regard. Charlie had told me that she was raised by her mother's aunt and uncle. What had become of her mother and father, he would not say, just that Jessamine had come here when she was seven and had been here, with family that loved her, ever since.

Jessamine sat back at her end of the couch and smiled at me. Despite her battered appearance, she radiated warmth and understanding. My heart sighed in relief and I felt as if the burden upon it lessened some. I smiled wanly at this incredibly lovely creature, and wished fervently to lessen the burden upon her heart in the same way.

"You look tired," I commented.

I am a little. I feel like I am stiffening up again.

"Would you like me to take you to see my brethren?" I asked.

You mean the owls?

"Yes."

I thought you'd never ask! I feel weird having not seen my fly-babies today. Poor things. Sorry for asking but are there any others like you? That can change?

"No, I am the only one of my kind. Any children my mother had after she was cursed, well, there is no human-formed half to them, so they are what they are, owls only. Still, we are related to a certain extent, so I consider them brothers and sisters all... my winged brethren." I told her this as we moved down the hall to the garage door. We went into the small area and up to the owl she'd named Winter. She smiled broadly and the joy upon her face was unmistakable.

Gods above and below, she was beautiful when she smiled like that. Not even her injuries could contain it.

"H-h-hey, beautiful boy," She whispered and I smiled. She did okay, using her voice and her words around me.

"Jessamine, may I ask you something?" I ventured.

"Y-y-y-es." She looked up at me quizzically, her stormy-blue eyes alight with curiosity.

"Why did you speak to me, and the owls, as you do?"

Hurt flickered in her eyes and she cast them away from me and back to the snowy owl on the perch, just on the other side of the chicken wire.

"Y-y-you, don-nn-nnnn't judge," she said finally. "People, hummm-mman's judge. Thinn-nnk because I sss-ss-tutter, that I'm-m-m stupid." She huffed out a breath, clearly frustrated with herself for not being able to get the words out.

"You are not stupid," I said softly. "You are one of the smartest, loveliest, and bravest women I've ever met and I've been around for a very, very long time," I whispered. I was rewarded with a deep blush that swept up her delicate throat, painting her creamy skin a light shade of pink where it wasn't purple, red, or black.

"Th-th-th-thank you." She had some trouble forcing it out, but I appreciated that she tried with me. I could tell talking didn't come easy for her.

We visited the outdoor cages and pens next. She had softly-spoken words of encouragement and smiles for every one of her charges. I worried about taking her into the barn, so soon after her ordeal there, but she didn't so much as hesitate.

She did, however, pause inside the door. It was as if nothing had ever happened in here. Aaron, Charlie, and I had washed the blood from the concrete, thoroughly cleaned the cages, and had even gone so far as to move things around so it would look different in here. Jess smiled at me over her shoulder and went to the nearest enclosure with an owl in it.

About midway through her visits, we heard Charlie's old truck lumber down the drive. I stepped out of the barn and waved. He saun-tered over at a slow pace.

"She inside?" he asked.

"Visiting," I answered succinctly. He shook his head and smiled.

"Jess!" he called, "come on now! You need some rest! They'll live without you for one day." He was smiling wistfully and I let my smile join his. Jessamine poked her head out of the barn and the small smile that played on her lips and danced in her eyes made it worth bringing her out here.

She was resilient. She slowly moved in our direction and the three of us walked back toward the inviting glow of her house. She stopped at the foot of the stairs leading up to the little deck off her bedroom and I nodded, guessing her intent. She went to Charlie and hugged him.

"Aw, go on, kid. I'll see you tomorrow." He smiled and let her go and she looked like she wanted to hug me again, and oh, how I wanted her to, but then she inclined her head and gave a little wave goodnight and ascended the stairs alone.

Charlie gave me a little pat on the shoulder and we both entered the house through the kitchen.

"Lock up, I'm going to bed," he stated, and with his old military rucksack over his shoulder, he disappeared into the downstairs bedroom.

I turned out lights and locked the doors against the outside world, and with a silent mental sigh, took up my own aluminum-framed hiker's pack and ghosted up the stairs. I fought myself not to pause outside Jessamine's door and listen, and instead moved up the hall and into the second guest bedroom, leaving the door open behind me.

I was not a fan of enclosed spaces.

I dug through my pack, which was admittedly limited in clothing options, and found a pair of cotton lounge pants in the bottom. I changed into them, securing them with the drawstring at my hips. I stretched out atop the covers and cradled my head in my hands as I stared at the ceiling.

This must have been Jessamine's room as a girl. The ceiling sparkled in the diffuse light of the moon that poured through the window, giving the illusion of star-scatter. I closed my eyes, but in vain. After being mostly nocturnal for so long, I was unused to this diurnal lifestyle and found myself wide awake. So, I continued to stare at the ceiling and the insides of my eyelids until sleep finally came forth to claim me, all the while turning thoughts of Jessamine over in my head.

It was going to be one very long night.

CHAPTER TWENTY

*J*essamine

I was running late for work. I pulled on my scrubs and hastily pulled my hair into a ponytail. The birds needed to be cared for and I was pressed for time. I clattered down the porch steps from my bedroom and leapt over the last three. I didn't even break stride as I moved swiftly across the yard to the barn. I went through the door and stopped cold... This wasn't real... this couldn't be happening... The two men who'd attacked me were broken and bloody on the concrete floor. I swallowed hard, and made to take a step back but the one with the sores on his face, his hand shot out and grabbed my ankle.

He was incredibly strong, and fast as he wrenched me off-balance. I let out a little bleat of terror and tried to back away, but he was climbing my body. He grinned and blood seeped out of his mouth around his broken teeth.

"We weren't done playing with you!" he wheezed.

I screamed, long and loud, and struggled harder against his groping hands.

"Jessamine!" Light flooded the barn – and I opened my eyes to see

Hunter standing in the doorway to my bedroom, the door flush against the wall, his hand flat against the light switch.

I dragged in several breaths, and stared across the expanse of carpet between us. Hunter stood in a pair of gray pajama bottoms that hung low on his hips. His caramel-colored eyes, a bit wide, were framed by the wild tangle of his hair. He looked every bit the wild creature his other form was, and here he was, trying to take care of the poor beat-up girl with the horrible stutter.

I let myself feel the stab of self-pity and tried valiantly to let it go.

Hunter took a cautious step into the room as my eyes misted with tears. I rounded my shoulders, hunching in on myself as the first sob shook me and the careful walls I'd put up around myself in the hospital came crumbling down. I'd been able to fool myself for a while that I was okay, but I knew deep down that I wasn't. Who could be after something like that?

A low sound, like that of a tortured animal, swept through the room and it took me several seconds to realize that the sound was coming from me. The side of the bed dipped and I was pulled tight against solid warmth. Hunter's breath ruffled the hair on the crown of my head as he made quiet soothing noises.

I wept bitterly against him, his arms bracing, a protective barrier between me and all comers. We stayed like that for a long time, Hunter a rock, and me an emotional wreck upon him, until I coughed and hiccupped the last of my ugly cry.

"I-I-I'm s-ss-s-ssorry," I stammered out.

"Shhh, nothing to be sorry about. You've been through a lot in a short amount of time. This sort of thing is to be expected, love." We were quiet for a long stretch until finally he asked, "Nightmare, then?"

I nodded bleakly against his shoulder.

"Do you want to talk about it?

I resolutely shook my head. I so did not want to talk about it, or think about it, *ever*, if possible.

I began to relax in Hunter's comforting hold. I allowed my eyes to drift shut and pretended, just for a second, that this was how things could be for more than just a moment. Hunter shifted beneath me and

I grimaced slightly. I was making the man uncomfortable for the benefit of my selfish comfort.

I drew back, but he held me fast. "Just a little longer... please?"

I nodded, surprised that he'd want what we were doing to continue. I cuddled back against him and closed my eyes, listening to the rhythmic ticking of his heart. He sighed and I relaxed into him. I tried not to think too hard about how good he felt, warm and solid beneath my cheek and hand. My other arm was trapped between us, but comfortably so.

"I wish I could stay like this with you," he murmured.

I wished so too, enough so that I forced the words out.

"Mm-mm-me too."

His arms tightened around me and I could hear the smile in his voice when he teasingly asked, "Is that an invitation to stay the night, love?"

I laughed lightly and nodded. He went very still.

"Don't tease me, Jessamine," he said at last, and I drew back and looked at him, stricken.

He tilted his head to one side, and searched my face, nodding slowly at whatever he found there.

"All right, I'm sorry, love." He swallowed hard. "I believe you..." but he pulled away from me just the same and got up. I huddled down into my blankets when he switched off the light, and closed my eyes.

Of course he wouldn't want a –

My thoughts were interrupted by the lift of the covers and the return of his warmth as he slid into the bed beside me. I went to him gratefully, but at the same time apprehensively. He drew me against him, lying flat, and I couldn't help but smile at how perfectly we fit together. I rested my head against his shoulder and lay my free arm across his washboard stomach. Forget six pack, Hunter had eight... I wondered for a moment if that was even possible, but his voice stopped my random, hormone-induced, internal ramblings,

"Thank you for this," he whispered and I melted into his side even more.

How on earth could this beautiful son of two gods be thanking me for some mid-night cuddle time? Didn't he realize that he was the one doing me the favor, here? I nodded once slowly and closed my eyes, at a loss for what else to do.

I mean, what exactly could I say?

CHAPTER TWENTY-ONE

*J*essamine

I woke alone, my nose buried in a pillow that smelled of crisp fresh air and the great outdoors. Hunter's smell. I smiled, remembering the warmth and tenderness he'd held me with and my pulse gave a little flutter. I lingered a little longer, breathing in his smell before I got out of bed. I had thought I would be much stiffer than I was actually feeling and thought maybe that nasty-smelling tea of Hunter's had something to it.

I pulled on thick athletic socks first thing, and then hunted through my drawers for what I would wear that day. I went for my usual weekend-wear of blue jeans, a fitted black tee-shirt and a women's-cut flannel shirt. I buttoned the flannel most of the way and rolled back the sleeves to just below my elbows. I had picked out a purple-and-wine colored plaid pattern; I figured what the hell? I might as well match my face.

I picked up my boots from my little slate entryway and padded downstairs. I heard Charlie in the kitchen talking to someone, and so that's where I went. When I rounded the corner I was surprised to see not two, but four people there.

"Oh, my sweet baby! Look what they done to you!" My Aunt

Margie bustled forward and I dropped my boots with a hearty smack onto the hardwood, opening my arms to her. We hugged and I was struck by how we were the same height.

My Uncle Dave was standing behind the lunch counter by Charlie, his bright blue eyes swimming with tears as he watched me and his wife. I waved feebly to him behind Aunt Margie's back as she clucked and fussed over my appearance.

Hunter was at the stove looking on impassively and I grimaced inwardly, remembering our conversation the night before about how his family had treated him. I looked at him worriedly, knowing that Margie was going to cluck and fuss over me until she was satisfied, and she wouldn't quit it a moment before.

"Margie, let that girl alone!" Dave shook his head over his much-shorter wife and heaved a sigh. My Aunt Margie turned and let me go to him.

My Uncle Dave was tall and lanky, with a full head of steel-gray hair that was getting too long over his ears again. How could I tell? It was curling haphazardly out from under his old, deep-green Weyerhaeuser trucker hat. His eyebrows were big and bushy, and drawn so tightly together they almost buried his eyes as he scowled at the state of my face. He wore faded old Levi's and like Charlie, favored the old-fashioned snap-buttoned cowboy shirts. He had on a light denim-blue one on over his typical white crewneck tee-shirt. His rugged old brown forestry boots covered his feet. I frowned at the sight of his old boots on my kitchen floor. He hugged me tighter and I looked up at him and gave a tremulous smile.

I would *not* cry, damn it.

I was struck by the fact that here it was, not even two full days after my little catastrophe, and they were here. They'd just dropped everything and likely got themselves on the next plane out. My aunt and uncle were the best kind of people there were.

I looked over at Margie, who was thicker around the middle than either Dave or myself. Her hair was white and short, and her hazel eyes sparkled from behind her silver-framed glasses. She wore a white sweatshirt with gray cats on it over her old-lady jeans, the kind with no back pockets that made your butt look big. She had on her black old-lady sneakers with the Velcro closures, the ones that I always teased her about. She needed the comfortable shoes, though, on account of her diabetes.

She came up and squashed me in another hug, between me and her husband, like they always used to do when I was a kid until I started giggling and squirming. I did neither of those things now, though. I hadn't realized just how much I'd missed them.

Hunter was the one who broke the spell of our little family reunion by pulling the lid off the pot he had simmering on the stove. Aunt Margie cried out in dismay; Uncle Dave took a step back and eyed Hunter critically, but it was Charlie who made the astute observation by crying out, "Christian Christ, boy! What is that? Boiled horse piss?"

Dave laughed, Margie admonished him about his language, and I bowed my head, knowing exactly what it was before Hunter said it.

"It's a restorative tea. Will help with the bruises," and he ladled out two mugs of it.

I groaned inwardly and plastered a strained smile on my face, and took one. Hunter's caramel-colored eyes danced over the rim of his cup as we stood there letting it cool.

"Cheers, love," he said, and I took a deep breath and chugged as quickly as the hot tea would allow. I couldn't help it this morning; I gagged and choked a couple of times.

Having Margie, Dave, and Charlie watch me in horrified fascination as I put the liquid down somehow made drinking it worse than it had been yesterday.

"Easy, easy, okay, that's enough." Hunter took the cup out of my hands, even though there was a good third of the tea left in the bottom of the cup. I let him take it all too gratefully.

I looked at everyone in my kitchen and blushed and shrugged. I felt kind of bad, everyone being here like they were when really there wasn't anything anyone could do for me. I mean, I was healing up as fast as I could. Still, it was nice having them here, all the same.

"Well, Hunter, I'm glad you were and are here," Aunt Margie said finally, when the silence had gone on a little too long.

"I was, and am, glad I was in the right place at the right time too,

Madam." He gave her an award-winning smile, which made her blush, which made me grin and Uncle Dave smile, too.

"What're you boys planning to do today?" Aunt Margie asked.

I pulled the whiteboard off the front of the fridge and started writing while Hunter answered.

"Well, I was planning on taking care of the driveway today. I saw the pile of gravel out behind the barn, I assume that's what you keep it for?" He looked at Uncle Dave, who nodded. "I figured I would dig out some fill dirt, maybe create a small fish pond over there." He indicated a raw, unused patch of yard beside one of the aviaries.

"Fish pond? How do you reckon that?" Charlie asked.

"There were some materials in an old shed, looked like someone wanted to put one in at some point, but it never happened." Hunter was looking at my uncle, who was rubbing the back of his neck.

"I was planning on putting one in, yeah, supposed to be a surprise for you, Margie, but like so many other projects around here, I just never got to it." He looked a bit sheepish. Charlie was grinning at him.

I held up my long-winded sign and knocked on the counter twice to draw attention to it.

I'm glad to see you guys. Looks like Charlie already introduced you to Hunter. Hunter is going to be staying here and helping out with some of the projects Charlie and I haven't been able to get to on account that we have so many owls to take care of. Speaking of which, Uncle Dave, you need to come with me before you go play with Charlie.

I bounced a little in place with excitement.

"What is it, Jess?" Uncle Dave asked.

I waved at him to follow me and went for the garage, giving Hunter a quick hug as I went by, which raised some eyebrows. Hunter laughed and hugged me back.

Charlie called after me,

"Oh yeah, I left that for you to show 'im! He's eatin' on his own, you should move him today!" I waved over my shoulder and took Uncle Dave's hand and let him into the garage, flipping on the light.

"Holy geeze, Jessamine! Is that your first snowy in there?" he asked and I nodded excitedly, grabbed up a board, and between our personal sign language and writing it out, began the tale of Winter...

CHAPTER TWENTY-TWO

*H*unter

Spending time with just Jessamine became nigh on impossible for the next several days. There always seemed to be someone near her, whether it be her aunt, uncle, Charlie, Aaron, or John Baker, the man in the green uniform. Jessamine explained to me surreptitiously that he was with the Department of Fish and Wildlife, but that was about the only conversation she and I had in the last three days and it involved Aaron, too.

The more I saw of Jessamine in her daily life, the more determined I became to see if she would allow me to become a part of it. Dave, Charlie, and I set to work outside, clearing brush, repairing bird pens, and even building a few new ones. Jessamine and Aaron could be found with the birds, or in the kitchen with Margie, who was undisputedly queen of that particular kingdom.

At supper, the night Jessamine's family arrived, there was discussion of something called the Olympic Bird Fest, which was to happen in around a month's time. Jessamine seemed both agitated and excited by the event and I asked why.

I love being out and doing demonstrations with our permanent residents, but

I can't exactly do the talking. Sometimes I assist Jaye with her birds, but I wish Moonchild's Owl Haven could have its day too.

She bit her lush lower lip between her teeth and I bit back a groan. She had no idea just how alluring she was. I shifted in my seat, suddenly uncomfortable in my jeans and thought about it.

"Why don't I do the talking?" Aaron asked, and I smiled at the boy. *Yeah?*

"Yeah. You handle the birds, tell me what you want me to say, we can do a whole presentation." He shrugged.

"Hell, why didn't you say something before Jess? I would'a done it with you." Charlie, as ever, spoke with his mouth full.

Jessamine smiled an amused smile.

You, talk in front of an entire group of people... kids even...

He coughed. "Right, you got a point. Make the boy do it." He returned to his food, which was indeed very good.

Uncle Dave said, "That settles it, then. Hunter; you, me and Charlie will get this place into shape. Jess and Aaron will get some kind of presentation together and..."

"...I'll be in my kitchen," Margie said, getting up with her plate. Dave chuckled.

Jessamine was positively glowing with excitement in her seat and it made my heart light. She had been withdrawn to a certain extent over the last several days. I would catch her writing in a spiral notebook, but she wouldn't let any of us see what it was she was writing. Almost as many pages had been torn out, torn up, and tossed into the potbellied stove or burn barrel out back as had stayed in the book. With each sound of rending paper she had looked a combination of frustrated and stricken, and I had longed to be a comfort to her, as I was my second night here.

I couldn't forget the feeling of her warm, soft skin against my own. She had molded herself against me so fine, and had slept so soundly. She wore very little to bed, I'd belatedly discovered: a tank top and a pair of barely-there sleep shorts and that had driven me a wee bit mad with a desire to slip them down her shapely legs. One of those shapely legs had gone over my own as she'd slept and it had been a real lesson in self-control *not* to take her right then.

I wanted the woman, badly and often, but I also, more than anything, wanted her to want me, too.

Now, three nights removed from the conversation about the bird festival, we sat at supper again. Jessamine smiled shyly across the table at me and I returned the gesture easily. I honestly could not remember a time I had smiled so often. Charlie gave his customary thanks to the earth and the creatures who inhabited it before we began to eat.

"So, Hunter," Margie addressed me. "How do you like it here?" she asked and I answered her honestly.

"I like it very much. The area is beautiful." Of course, when I said 'beautiful', my eyes drifted to Jessamine. Her cuts had healed to deep dark scabs which were flaking into bright pink scars. Those would, in time, fade even further. Her bruises were that awful garish green and yellow, the darker patches gone to muddy gray-brown.

She had dutifully been drinking the tea I gave her every morning without complaint and I was glad for it.

Her bruises would heal in half the time and more importantly, so would her spirit. The tea had a calming effect, just enough to help ease her through the worst of the emotional turmoil such an attack left upon a person.

"Enough to stay around a bit longer?" Margie was asking, breaking me from my reverie.

"Now, Margie, knock it off," Dave grumbled. Jessamine was turning a deep red from her lovely throat to the roots of her coppery hair.

"What am I missing?" I asked, perplexed.

"Margie's trying to set you up with Jessamine," Charlie grunted. Jessamine rose from the table abruptly and began clearing plates. I laughed incredulously at Margie's audacity. It was the wrong thing to do. Silverware was dropped into the bottom of the sink with a clatter.

"Jessamine, wait!" I rose from my seat but she was already out the door and striding for the barn.

"You guys are dicks." Aaron was frowning at us all.

"Watch your mouth, young man!" Margie admonished.

"Margie, why can't you leave well enough alone?" Dave demanded.

I didn't care about any of it, I was out the door after Jess.

I found her in the barn. She was standing at Sadie's cage, a spotted owl with an immobilized wing she'd named after her nurse at the hospital. Her fingers were wound in the chicken wire of the front of the cage and her face was against her arm. She sniffed and my heart broke for her a little.

"Don't cry, love."

She jumped, startled and wiped at her eyes self-consciously. I sighed.

She waffled her hands back and forth in front of her and looked a little helpless.

"Talk to me," I whispered and she gave me a look that was stricken, heartbroken, and exasperated. I couldn't stand it. I went to her, stopping with barely a hair's breadth of distance between us and looked into her eyes, willing her to tell me how she was feeling. My hand came up of its own volition, my thumb grazing her jaw gently.

"I'm n-nn-not good en-nn..."

Suddenly I didn't want to hear what she had to say anymore. She *was* good enough, she was everything I wanted, and so I closed the distance between our lips, gently brushing mine over hers, sipping at her little gasp of surprise.

Her lips were warm and sensual beneath my own. I pulled her lush, lithe body tight against my own, my claiming of her mouth growing a little more insistent and she didn't disappoint me. Nothing this woman ever did *could*... Her lips parted and she let me in, kissing me back, cautiously at first before losing herself completely; ceding control to me.

She tasted like the warm air from a sun-soaked sea. Her sweet, rich, lavender scent filled my sense of smell. I let my hands wander her back, coming to rest at the small of it, where it arched in so provocatively. Her hands rested, one on my chest, the other on my bicep, and I wanted desperately for them to wind around my neck.

As if she could read my thoughts, that is exactly what she did, her gentle fingers tangling in the horse-tail of hair at the nape of my neck. She molded to the front of my body perfectly and I could have stayed that way forever, her in my arms, mouths tasting, tongues dancing...

Someone cleared their throat by the barn door and I drew back from her reluctantly. She blinked at me in surprise and slowly lowered herself back flat-footed onto the cement floor. I smiled indulgently at her before turning to see Aaron in the door.

"Awkward," He said in a sing-song voice and I saw Jessamine color out of the corner of my eye before she buried her face in my chest. I laughed, a delighted sound, and hugged her to me.

"Yeah, sorry. I just didn't want you guys thinking I was being some kind of peeping perve..." He shifted from foot to foot and looked decidedly uncomfortable.

"You'll be doing it before long yourself, lad," I reminded him. He looked stricken, and Jessamine looked up at me sharply.

"What?" I asked.

"Dude! You totally just made it sound like Jessamine and me would be making out. She's like my sister!" He and Jess traded a horrified look and the laughter left my body in one long peal. They traded conspiratorial grins and the atmosphere in the barn greatly relaxed.

"Jess, Margie's real upset and crying in the house. Dave and Charlie are being Dave and Charlie and don't know what to do with it..." Jess' shoulders slumped and she rolled her eyes.

"I don't know how she does it, either." Aaron put up his hands.

"Does what?" I asked.

"She does this kind of thing to Jess all the time. Does something to upset her, then ten minutes later is the one crying and the wronged party in need of comfort. It's totally bizarre and it's one of the reasons their relationship is so tense." Aaron lifted a lean shoulder into a shrug.

Jessamine was giving him a look that was clearly thanking him for oversharing. I smiled.

"Go, we will finish this talk eventually." I very reluctantly let her slip from my grasp. She heaved a sigh and nodded, making her way to the house.

Aaron stayed behind and was grinning. I frowned.

"What?" I asked, casually walking towards him.

"That was hot," he said. "Gross, because she's like my sister, but totally hot." I scowled at him and snapped out my arm, hooking it 'round his neck, and rubbed my knuckles against his hair.

"Argh!"

He laughed, and I laughed, and for the first time, I felt as if I truly belonged somewhere.

CHAPTER TWENTY-THREE

*J*essamine

I left the barn, my body awash in tingles from head to toe. I wondered if my lips looked as swollen as they felt and decided that they probably didn't. I was on fire inside, a desire I had never known could be this strong circulating through my system. It was a concentrated effort to make one foot go in front of the other, carrying me away from him. My core ached with wanting, and, with every step I took in the direction of the house, I resolutely told it to shut up. Excitement surged in my chest and I stopped in my tracks for a second to revel in it.

Hunter had kissed me... and, oh, my God, what a kiss it had been! I wanted to bounce up and down and squeal like a teenage girl but I resisted the urge.

I didn't know if it was possible for someone to taste like starlight and a cool night wind, but that was exactly what Hunter's mouth had been like as it moved over my own. My rapidly-beating heart slowed its pace to match my walk as I went into the house.

I loved my Aunt Margie, but she did this sometimes - well, okay, a lot of the time. It was just as Aaron had said. She would do something that upset me, embarrassed me, or what-have-you, and when I went off to collect myself, she'd start up crying and make it out like everyone was mad at her, and she would keep crying until we all came together to soothe her ruffled feathers. Uncle Dave, Charlie, and I had caught on fairly quickly when I was a teenager and the worst of it started.

I guess in some ways it was Aunt Margie's rotten luck that she got me as her charge and as her one chance at being a mother figure. I was so not a girly-girl. I mean yeah, I played with dolls and liked the color pink for a minute, when I was little, but for the most part I preferred foraging and fishing with Uncle Dave and Charlie over sewing and gardening with Aunt Margie.

A lot of things mothers took for granted with their girls, shopping for dresses to the dance, or spending an entire weekend baking, were lost on me. I did love cooking and baking with Aunt Margie, that was the one thing that held us together... pretty much the only thing. Everything else turned, one way or another, into a battle royale with her, though.

I went in the side door and into the kitchen. Charlie was at the sink rinsing dishes. I could hear Uncle Dave and Aunt Margie in the living room. She was in full wail.

Charlie winced and mouthed silently at me,

"Do something Jess, before I..." and he made a motion as if violently strangling something.

I choked back a laugh and he scowled at me. I pointed a finger at him and nodded my head once. He grimaced.

Yup, he knew Aaron had told on him. I sighed silently and moved into the living room, and fidgeted from foot to foot.

"Hey, kiddo, your Aunt Margie here thinks you're mad at her." Uncle Dave's eyes sparkled with humor at me above Margie's head, where she cried noisily into his shoulder. I gave him my sweetest smile, the one that said I'd get him later for this, and quickly whipped my expression into that of a pious little angel when Margie turned around.

I did what I always did in this particular scenario: I put out my arms and went in for the hug. After a short time, everything was right in our worlds again, and Charlie started shouting something from the kitchen about if we were done being women in there to get back in the kitchen and make some pie. Only there was some swearing, and a bunch of Uncle Dave yelling back a play-by-play, and then an amused Hunter and Aaron coming in through the back door asking if there was pie. They'd heard Charlie shout it, after all.

Pretty soon the lot of us were in the middle of fits of hysterical laughter to the point we held our sides. The laughter would start to settle, then someone would start giggling again and pretty soon we were all laughing again.

God, I loved my life, and my family, and the addition of Hunter to it, which sobered me a bit. Hunter really was an excellent addition to the people in my life. I smiled and went into the kitchen with Aunt Margie on a diplomatic baking mission. I didn't know what was happening between Hunter and me, but for once, I was cautiously optimistic about having a man in my life.

He was different, and I was hoping that kiss meant that he was for-real interested in me.

I pushed my insecurities to the side for now and concentrated on making apple pies with Aunt Margie. It was getting too dark outside to get much more accomplished today, so Charlie and Aaron made to leave for the evening, while Uncle Dave and Hunter quietly discussed the next day's plans in the living room. I smiled a little to myself and quietly retired to my bedroom as soon as the pies were out of the oven and I could politely take my leave.

Once in my room, I crept over to my bed and lifted the mattress. I pulled out the spiral notebook and held it in my hands. I stared at it, and drummed my fingers lightly on the back cover in indecision. I took a deep breath and let it out slowly, and crept back to my bedroom door. I could hear Hunter's musical voice as he spoke to Aunt Margie and Uncle Dave below. I quickly and quietly tiptoed down the hall and into Hunter's doorway. I listened for several heart-beats to ensure I had gone unnoticed, and then slipped the notebook under his pillow.

Another deep breath, some more patience, and I bounded noise-lessly back into my room, turning the knob, shutting the door and slowly easing the knob so it would latch without a sound. I let out the breath I was holding and changed swiftly into a cami and sleep shorts for bed. I lay for a long time and almost got up twice to retrieve the book, but I didn't.

I trusted Hunter. Didn't I?

Finally, I heard his tread upon the stair and I let out an explosive breath. Well, it was done. I closed my eyes and breathed out slowly.

God, I hoped I wasn't making a horrible mistake.

CHAPTER TWENTY-FOUR

*H*unter

"Good night." I nodded to Dave and Margie and ascended the stairs. Jessamine's door was closed and I had to resist the urge to go to it rather than my own. I changed for bed and sat down on the edge of the bed.

She had felt so incredibly good in my arms. I closed my eyes and let myself go back there for a moment, letting out a slow breath from where it had been pent up in my chest. I laid back and put my hands beneath the pillow to cradle my head as I usually did. Instead of meeting cool cotton sheets my hands scraped over paper, cardboard, and wire. I sat up abruptly and pulled out the spiral notebook Jessamine had spent equal time writing in and mutilating. It was much thinner than it had started out.

I opened it to see pages filled with her delicate script.

Dear Hunter,

I'm pretty sure you've seen me start this about a thousand times already. I think I've got it now. You know there's nothing wrong with my voice, and that words don't really fail me either. Getting them out is my trouble spot, not so much when it comes to writing them. At least not until now.

Sorry, I'm rambling. I guess this is me trying to say that I like you. Ew, god, no, this isn't like some elementary school note-passing thing to ask if you like me too. That's lame. This is me trying to tell you something I haven't ever told anyone else. Not Uncle Dave, not Aunt Margie, not even Charlie, and you know he's my BFF.

I came to Uncle Dave and Aunt Margie when I was seven. You see, my mom, (that's Uncle Dave's niece) met this guy when I was three. He wasn't so great. In trouble a lot and by trouble, I mean drugs and alcohol and he got my mom hooked too.

He was mean. I remember that. I mean, he was really mean. Screaming at my mom, hit her. Hit me too. Screamed at me a lot, called me names and told me I was stupid. Some kids stutter when they're young. It's a phase that most of them grow out of but my mom's boyfriend, he kind of rode me about it. A lot.

One night, my mom wouldn't wake up. I tried to ask her boyfriend Steve to help me but he told me to piss off. I started crying. I was really scared, she wouldn't wake up no matter how hard I tried and always before she would at least moan or shove me away but not this time. I tried really hard to get Steve to help me even though he scared me half to death and he just kind of snapped, I guess.

He hit me, hard, and then tried to get my mom up. Slapped her really hard but nothing. He said shit a lot then turned on me beat me to within an inch of my life. Told me this was all my fault. That my mom was dead and if I wasn't such a miserable shit that made her want to escape that she'd never have done that much dope. He left me there in the apartment with my mom's dead body.

Didn't come back either.

I was there for three or four days. It was the summer time and neighbors called the police because of the smell. They found me and took me to the hospital. I was malnourished and kind of a mess. I didn't exactly live in the cleanest environment so I was filthy, had some kind of skin infection and lice. They had to reset a couple of broken bones. I was a ward of the state for a while, until they found Uncle Dave and Aunt Margie to take me in.

Anyways, I guess I'm trying to tell you that I know how you feel. Your dad, my mom... Neglect. I know it's not really the same thing but I never knew who my real dad was. I don't think my mom did either. If it weren't for Uncle Dave and Aunt Margie I would have been bounced from foster home to foster home and who knows where or how I would have ended up.

I'm lucky I ended up here.

I'm sorry it took you so long to make it here too, but you're here now and I hope you know you can stay as long as you want. I know I'm not really good enough, being a broken girl who can't talk with people and guys want a girl they can talk with, not at... but I'm here if you need to talk. I'm a really good listener.

Anyways, that's my story. I'm here if you need it.

-Jessamine

I set the notebook off to the side and stared at the diffuse light winking in the glitter in the ceiling. I was tense with a myriad of emotion. Anger, that something so horrible could be done to a child as sweet as Jess, but not surprised. Bad things happened to good people every day. I was confused as to why she would think herself not good enough, but the answer to that was plain. She believed what her mother's boyfriend had raised her to believe and somewhere along the line, that notion had been reinforced.

I reread a line that stood out to me in the final paragraph...

Guys want a girl they can talk with, not at...

Horseshit. I wanted Jessamine with a fire that could not be contained and no one, not even Arawn of the underworld himself could stop me now.

Before I fully realized my intent I was on my feet and striding down the hallway.

CHAPTER TWENTY-FIVE

*J*essamine

I lay staring at the play of shadows across my ceiling. I had heard his footsteps as he'd moved down the hall after bidding my aunt and uncle good night. They had retired shortly after. A hush had fallen over the house, a quiet so absolute, like what it sounded like outside after it snowed... all sound muffled, the landscape as silent to the eye as it was to the ear. It had been quiet like that for a very long time, but then I heard the squeak of my door as it swung open on its hinges.

I sat up. Hunter shut the door quietly behind him and turned, blinking in the light from the windows, his expression dark and weighted with emotion.

He'd read it, all right.

I was suddenly breathless, afraid, my chest tight with anxiety. He came across the room, his footsteps muffled in the thick carpet. He stood at my bedside, hands loose at his sides.

"You are not broken," he whispered harshly, going to one knee so that he might be even with me.

"Do you hear me, Jessamine?" he asked, his pupils dilating wide, his irises darkening and spiraling out to swallow the whites of his eyes.

I swallowed, my mouth suddenly dry as he stared at me with his owl's eyes in his human face.

"Say it," he ordered.

"I-I-I h-hhh-hear you," I said.

"Good girl," he murmured, and palmed the side of my neck, stroking his thumb along my jaw. I closed my eyes as heat unfurled, painting my skin in a wash of gooseflesh that radiated out from where he touched me.

"Jess, look at me," he demanded and my eyes fluttered open.

"I don't know what slimy piece of shite convinced you that no one wanted you, but I'm here to tell you that *I* do. I want you, Jess. I've wanted you since the moment you picked me up off the road and I looked into those storm-swept eyes of yours." He placed his lips against mine in a gentle almost chaste kiss, then drew back.

I stared him in the eyes, lost in absolute wonder.

He wanted me?

This god amongst men wanted *me*?

I blinked, at a loss for words, and he smiled.

"Is that a yes, love?" he asked me, and I nodded fervently.

Hell, yes, that was a yes!

He smiled and dragged me forward, pressing my mouth to his. I opened to him and where the kiss in the barn had been slow and sweet, this one was demanding. I felt his fingers skate along my ribs to grip the hem of my camisole and I raised my arms without being asked. He stripped the thin material over my head and let it fall, bringing our lips back together in another burning kiss.

He smoothed his work-roughened palms over my exposed skin and I shivered, relishing the contact. He knelt up, keeping our mouths entwined and I heard the rustle of cotton as his pajama pants slipped to the floor. I scooted over and he put a knee to the mattress, his fingers hooking in the waistband of my sleep shorts. He pulled them down; I arched my hips off the bed, helping him. He slid them smoothly down my legs, breaking our kiss to get them down and off the last bit of the way.

His alien eyes swept over me from the crown of my head to the soles of my feet and my blood heated, simmering pleasantly in my veins. My pussy throbbed in time with my heartbeat and I felt swollen with the need for him to be inside of me. He smiled and bent to kiss me anew, and when he climbed up onto the bed with me, it was with a knee between my own.

He tasted like a summer night, warm, sultry and clean with an endless star-shot sky. His hands glided over every inch of me, gently, delicately, in a sensual touch that left me hot and aching for him to touch me so much deeper. I reached between us and wrapped a gentle hand around him and had a brief moment of anxiety. He smiled against my mouth and when I stroked him, he growled deep in the back of his throat.

I gasped at the ferocity and intensity of the sound, and he broke our kiss. He kissed along my jaw and played his lips, tongue, and teeth against the sweet-spot on the side of my neck. I arched and found a gentle, slow rhythm with my hand. He moaned and stilled for a heart-beat or two, reveling in the feeling, before resuming his ministrations. He planted a chaste kiss against the swell of my shoulder and I sighed, which turned into a gasp when he lightly nipped with his teeth.

He moved across my collarbone and across my chest, drawing the nipple on the opposite side whence he started into the heat of his mouth. He suckled it, rolling the delicate nub between his teeth, drawing it taut before letting it pop from his mouth. He repeated this a few more times, until I let out a throaty moan. Then with a devious smile curving his lush mouth, he began to kiss and lick his way across my stomach, nipping at the curve of my hip.

During his descent down my body, he had slipped himself free of my hand, and now he held both of them with his, our palms pressed together, fingers entwined. He looked up at me from between my legs, deliberately setting his tongue flat to my sex and licking, bottom to top, with one broad stroke. The tip of his tongue plunged into my folds and he used it to tease my erect clitoris until I cried out and arched my hips to meet him.

His hands slipped from mine and I buried them into the cotton, grasping the sheet by my hips, fisting the material. He pressed me down into the mattress, with one broad hand at the top of my mound, pulling gently back to give his mouth better access. His other hand disappeared momentarily, until I felt him glide a digit in the wetness at my opening. I cried out again as he slowly slid his middle finger into me, the knuckles of his remaining fingers pressed tight against my body. He stroked with his finger until he found a place inside me that caused my muscles to twitch and then, smiling an all-too-satisfied smile, he placed his mouth against that sensitive nub once more.

Hunter played me like a master plays a violin, moving his fingers and mouth, independent of one another and as one, until there was no more air left to breathe and the stars fell from the sky to flit at the edges of my vision.

I came, my pussy clenching down on his fingers, my body arching off the bed, half with orgasm, half to get away from his probing tongue, unable to take any more of its assault.

He climbed my body, much as he had going down, with soft kisses and gentle flicks of his tongue. He blew cool air against my heated skin until he was even with me, his arms braced on either side of my head, his gaze fixed upon mine. I shivered with little aftershocks beneath him and he smiled down at the beautiful mess he'd made.

CHAPTER TWENTY-SIX

*H*unter

I loved how her body continued to quiver with the pleasure I'd given her. I loved even more that I wasn't done by far with playing with her. Her wet heat caressed my shaft and I pushed forward, grinding it against her with a promise of things to come. Her hands let go of the sheets and wound their way into my hair, dragging my mouth to hers. She kissed me long, deep, and desperate, as if I were a cool drink of water on a punishing summer's eve.

I loved what I did to her, I loved what she did to me, and with a swell of emotion I let myself down against her, pressing her back into her bed. I kissed her back. She tasted like spring, like rainfall and lavender fields, cool and refreshing, tranquil and serene, and I couldn't get enough of her silken skin against my own.

Her hands roamed my back, smoothing down my sides and over my stomach and chest. Her legs went unbidden around my hips where I wanted them. She was offering herself to me, open to me, and I took the invitation.

How could I say no?

I rocked my hips, sliding myself back and forth against her wetness, teasing us both until I found the purchase I sought. The tip of me entered her wet and ready opening and she jerked in my embrace, not with hurt, but with surprise. I knew the difference. I pulled my mouth from hers and stared down into her hooded eyes.

She smiled at me and wiggled her hips provocatively in an effort to take me in further. It took considerable will on my part to draw back rather than to surge forward.

She frowned and her head dropped back into the pillow.

"Hunter please..." she moaned and I smiled.

I don't think she even realized, so caught up was she, that the words slipped free of her beautiful lips whole and unblemished.

The gods help me, to hear my name in her sweet voice nearly undid me. Jessamine would not be denied, and so I eased into her, filling her slowly, as much to draw out her pleasure as to draw out my own.

She was so beautiful, stretched beneath me as she was, the moonlight causing her skin to come alive, to almost glow from within. I slipped into her body as far as I could go and relished in the feel of my balls against her tight backside. Her breath left her in a shuddering sigh and her body squeezed gently around me. I dropped my forehead to her chest and let her milk me for a moment before, overcome, I began to move.

Her cries were clear yet soft as I took her higher with me. Her body, so soft and yielding, gripped me with surety and strength. She bit into my shoulder to muffle her cry and I cried out myself into the pillow by her throat. I thrust into her several more times, lazy strokes designed to draw out our mutual pleasure. She gave a full-body shudder beneath me and I smiled, going still. I pulled back, and looked down into the storm-swept sea of her steel-blue eyes, made soft with wonderment, and I kissed her. Reluctantly withdrawing from her wet heat.

"Wait here," I whispered, and she nodded carefully.

I stood slowly and padded across her thick carpet into her bathroom. I turned on the sink's faucet until it began to gently steam, thrusting a washcloth under the tap. I cleaned myself up quickly and efficiently before returning to her. She reached for the cloth I held, but I gave her a warning look; she dropped her hands to her sides and I proceeded to wash her gently.

She sighed and her eyes drifted shut. I went as far as the bathroom door and tossed the cloth into the sink so that I might return to her. I slid into the bed and arranged the blankets over us. She fit herself to my side and we settled.

"Are you all right?" I asked, and smiled as she nodded her head against my chest.

"Good."

I closed my eyes and drifted lazily in and out of sleep. Her breath was warm and even against my chest and I smiled. She was sunlight and sweetness personified and I was never going to let her go unless she herself sent me away.

I pressed my lips to the crown of her head and was rewarded when her leg drifted over mine. I put my hand to her knee and pulled, both her body tighter against me, and her leg higher up on my body. I felt her lips curl in a smile against my skin and felt an answering smile of my own.

"Sleep, love. I have every intention of making love to you again in the morning," I told her and she laughed and did as she was told.

She really was my sense of perfect.

CHAPTER TWENTY-SEVEN

*J*essamine

Hunter made good on his promise the next morning. I woke to him hiking the leg I had draped over him just a bit higher before he turned and buried himself deep inside me. God, it had felt amazing. What was more, he'd pulled me astride him, seating himself impossibly deep before smacking my ass and ordering me to ride him.

Oh, I'd indulged him.

It didn't bother me in the slightest that he was being bossy, either. I'd ridden him until we were both slick with my juices, and he'd flipped me on to my back and finished us.

We'd lain together, sweat-dewed and breathing heavily until our hearts had calmed and beat as one. We'd showered together and he'd slipped off to his room in search of clothes to wear, returning a short time later with his pack. He'd dumped it into a heap beside my bed and arched an eyebrow in challenge. I smiled and went to him, turning my face up for a kiss which he had freely given.

We'd gone out and cared for the birds and we were enjoying breakfast at the lunch counter. My Uncle Dave's eyes were sparkling at me knowingly behind Aunt Margie's back and I was trying to keep my face blank. Charlie came in and took the last seat and blew everything.

"Jesus, Jess, if you didn't want us all knowing you'd had sex, you should've at least one of you dried your hair." He turned to my Uncle Dave. "Let me guess, shower downstairs is dry?"

"Yep, that's how I knew." He drank some coffee. I sat there in stunned mortification. Hunter was laughing, and my aunt, in true Margie style, started beating Charlie with her dishtowel, shrieking at him not to embarrass us like that. Which, of course, hadn't been an issue when she'd done it days before.

I wanted the floor to swallow me up. *Just kill me. Kill me now.*

I got up and went outside to see Winter, to Hunter and Uncle Dave's laugh track and Charlie cussing my shrieking Aunt Margie out. I was ready to go back to work the next day. If only to get some sanity back into my life.

Normalcy would be good.

"You all right there, love?"

I smiled and turned.

"Y-yes."

Hunter smiled back.

I was almost thirty; I'd be twenty-nine in June, which was only three months away. I was pretty sure Uncle Dave, Aunt Margie, and Charlie knew I wasn't a virgin, what with Josh staying over all the time when we'd been together. Still, what had just happened in there had been pretty mortifying.

Hunter pulled me to him and I went easily into his arms. It was as if I were the missing piece to his puzzle or vice versa. Either way, we fit together perfectly.

"I want to be here with you, in every sense of the words." He sighed into my hair.

"M-mm-me too," I said.

"We have time," he murmured.

Yep, we did at that, what with him being immortal and all.

I stiffened.

Oh shit, I hadn't really thought about what it really meant for him to be a god... He didn't age, *wouldn't* age, while me, I would grow old and eventually die, leaving him behind. My heart did a barrel roll in my chest. God, how lonely his life must be. I hugged him tighter.

"Don't worry. Love, there's nothing to worry about," he soothed and for the most part he was right. We would have a few years to figure this out, before anyone would realize things were amiss. I relaxed into his hold but the little voice of panic in the back of my head screamed at me anyway.

How was this not something to worry about? I was going to age while he, he stayed the same... My throat closed as the implication washed over me. Would he still want me when I looked old enough to be his mom? Would he stay when I looked like his grandma? Of course, I was getting way ahead of myself... Who knew if we would even still be together in a year, two years...?

"I'm sure Gwydion will have an idea or two. We'll call him, after Dave and Margie go home, has to be a night of the new moon. I'm sure there is an answer to the," he coughed "age disparity, we're facing."

I snorted. 'Age disparity'. That was one way of putting it.

"Do you trust me, Jessamine?" he asked me suddenly.

Did I? With every fiber of my being.

"Yes," I said on a sigh.

"Good." He held onto me for a long time after that until peace washed back over me. Still, that seed of unease had been planted and it was taking root in my chest, squeezing my heart, weighing me down.

I was a world-class worrier.

CHAPTER TWENTY-EIGHT

*H*unter

I cursed myself and my careless words. She hadn't thought that far ahead and now I'd given her cause to worry. I had never in my long existence asked any of my family, extended or otherwise, for anything before. I would swallow my pride where they were concerned and would ask, for Jess, for at least as close to a normal life with her as I could get.

I didn't want to see her immortalized. That would be purely selfish on my part. I would much rather, at this point, grow old with her. I held her body close to mine for a long time, until the tension eased from her completely. I turned her in my arms and brought my lips to hers softly.

I breathed in Jessamine for a moment longer and smiled down at her. An answering smile lit her own delicate features, still muddy with healing bruises.

I had finished filling the depressions in her drive with dirt and had carved out a hole in the ground deep enough for the shell of the pond. Dave and I would be fitting it today. "I'm following through on the next step of your pond today. What are you doing?"

She looked in both directions and, spying all three of the others inside the house, said

"Glove t-r-r-raining w-w-with Dawn." I kissed the corner of her mouth and smiled with great appreciation at her efforts.

"Getting ready for the festival?"

"Yep."

"Good." I reluctantly let her go.

"S-s-see y-you arou-und?"

"I'll be here," I murmured.

She smiled and went off in the direction of Dawn's enclosure. The barn owl was a beauty and had a fine temperament.

I worked hard, the familiar warmth of hard labor spreading through my body. When I had found the unused pond equipment I had wanted to install it for a number of reasons, the paramount one being that Jess deserved something beautiful. The pond wasn't over-large, a decorative garden pond wasn't meant to be.

I began the laborious process of putting in the pond liner so it would hold water. Charlie and Dave joined me a short time later.

We worked on into the afternoon. Jess had disappeared into the kitchen with her aunt some time ago and it had proven very distract-ing. I kept stealing glances and looks at her through the large windows, watching her as she moved about the kitchen. When the door opened I looked up and nodded, and she waved, and I let the other two know we'd been rung in for lunch.

In the afternoon, Aaron arrived and disappeared into the house. He and Jess came out a little while later, heads bent together and made for the barn, no doubt working on their presentation for the bird festival.

Dinner was a family affair, with much laughter and storytelling, but to be honest, all I could think about was getting Jess upstairs. After dinner, we played a card game and when it was late enough, Charlie bid us goodnight, Aaron followed suit, and it was just myself, Jessamine and her aunt and uncle.

Dave finally put me out of my misery.

"Well, Jess goes back to work in the morning, and Margie and me, we need to start thinking about heading home to Arizona. Neighbors can't take care of the dogs forever." He smiled and Jess smiled too, and I could see it was a little grateful.

"You understand, don't you dear?" Margie asked apprehensively. "We'd hate to leave before you were ready."

Jess, grabbed for her pen and scribbled on her board.

I love you guys, but I understand you have a life in AZ. Charlie is here, and Aaron, and I think Hunter is going to stay a while longer. I'll be fine, I promise.

She smiled and I wondered again at how resilient this woman was. I felt my breast swell with pride for her.

"Okay, dear," Margie murmured.

"I'm proud of you, Jess." Dave echoed my sentiments.

I got up from the table murmuring my excuses, when really I just wished to give Jess some time with her family. She gave me a knowing and appreciative look as I ghosted to the stairs. I doubt anyone noticed me go into her room. If they did, no one remarked upon it.

I fetched towels from the hall closet and went into her bathroom, pulling open the glass shower door. The water made a soothing sound, drowning out the murmur of voices in the dining room below.

I disrobed, pulling the elastic from my horsetail, and stepped under the hot shower spray, closing the door behind me. The hot water felt much better on my skin as a man than the tepid, if not cold, natural water sources I frequented as a bird.

So entranced was I in relaxing under the hot fall of water, I completely missed Jessamine coming in. I started when I glimpsed her through the steam-covered glass. She opened the door and stepped into the large shower with me. It was what I appreciated about her bathroom. Not only did it have a large tub with jets, the shower was a standalone and could easily fit three people comfortably.

"H-h-hey," she said softly, crushing the front of her body to the front of mine. I was taller than she, but not overmuch, and I looked down the short distance into her upturned face.

"Hello, love," I said back, just as softly.

"Hun-n-nter, what're we goin-ng to do?" she asked, and laid her head against my chest. My arms snaked around her and I held her to me.

"I am going to contact Gwydion at the dark of the moon," I said, swaying with her, gently turning her into the water.

"Wh-wh-what w-w-ill h-he do?" she asked.

"I don't know, love. Hopefully he will give me a way. Make me mortal…"

She looked up sharply.

"Y-y-you w-w-w-ould do th-th-that?" she asked.

"Jessamine, I have lived for a very, very long time. So long, it can't be measured in centuries, but rather millennia. In all of that time, I have never encountered one such as you before, and I am fair certain I never will again. I'm tired, love. So incredibly tired. If ever there were a time to become mortal, it is now, and there is no one I would rather live out the rest of my days with than you." I looked into the storm-swept sea of her eyes and found her both touched and troubled by my words.

"Wh-wh-what if y-you get bored with me?" she asked.

I smiled thinly; I thought I was on to why she found herself not good enough…

"Who was he?" I asked gently, and she startled. I bent and kissed her lightly.

"He was a fool to pass you up, Jessamine Connors. I am terribly sorry he hurt you, but I am so very glad that he was such a fool so that I might claim you for my own. That is, if you'll have me." She was very still in my arms and I feared I may have over-stepped. I heaved a sigh and picked up her soap; turning her around gently, I soaped her back, massaging.

"I know that you hardly know me, Jess, but you must remember, I was under your care for months, I know things about you, have watched you… You really are an amazing woman. Your beauty and grace is what attracted me to you. Your strength and fighter's spirit made me desire you, but it is your compassion and acceptance that is making me fall in love with you."

I felt her shoulders tremble slightly beneath my hands, and I realized that no man had ever spoken to her in such a way; and that… that was such a shame.

I drew her back against my chest and held her as she cried.

CHAPTER TWENTY-NINE

*J*essamine

I stood in the gently rising steam under the fall of hot water, stock-still beneath Hunter's strong fingers kneading my shoulders, and listened, absolutely stunned at what he had to say. I wondered if I was dreaming, if what he was saying could possibly be true. I turned and looked him in the eyes, grateful that we were both wet and that the shower disguised the tears, though somehow I think he knew.

I searched the gentle caramel depths of his eyes and saw no subterfuge. No lies. I wanted to tell him that I thought I was falling in love with him too, but then again, I had thought what Josh and I had was love...

I thought about a life with Hunter in it. Then I took a moment to think of a life with him gone.

My mind and heart quailed at the latter and tears rose hot, fresh, and immediate. I tucked myself against his broad chest and made a pretty quick decision that had never felt more right than anything I had ever decided in my life before.

I wanted a life with Hunter in it.

I wanted it so much that I would do just about anything to attain it, even bargain with other gods, who, quite frankly, given what he'd told me about them, scared the living daylights out of me.

"S-s-s-stay wi-wi-wi-with-th m-mmm-me," I choked out.

"I have every intention," he said against my wet hair, his hands smoothing over my soap-slick skin.

The water was losing its heat and so we finished up quickly. When we got out, he wrapped me in a towel first, drying me vigorously. He dried himself and turned me around, walking me into the bedroom. He kissed across my shoulders, moving my hair out of the way to do it and I sighed in pleasure.

"Are you sore?" he asked, and I had to think about what he was asking. I blushed and nodded, a little too quickly.

He chuckled and pulled back the blankets, taking my towel from me. I got into bed and he tossed the towels into the bathroom, on the linoleum and off the carpet. He got in beside me and pulled me to him. I kissed him before he had the chance to kiss me, and I put all of my hopes, my dreams... I put everything I had into that one kiss and was rewarded by his growl of satisfaction.

I wasn't sure what was going to happen, where life was going to take us, or how we would do it, but I did know that I wanted to be a part of Hunter's life as much as he wanted to be a part of mine. It was just a matter of getting from point A to point B, and we could do that as long as we did it together, couldn't we?

I picked up my pen and notepad and asked him. He smiled and kissed my nose.

"I think that is a very good way of looking at it, love."

I cuddled to his side and closed my eyes. I wasn't exactly sure when my life had gone from the ordinary to the extraordinary, but it didn't matter.

Here I was, and I would rock it just like I'd rocked just about everything else so far.

CHAPTER THIRTY

*J*essamine

Waking the next morning with Hunter wrapped around me protectively was the most incredible sensation I have ever felt in my life. I stared at him unabashedly while he slept on, oblivious, memorizing the lines of his face, the planes and angles made softer by sleep. I traced the arch of his eyebrow, the sharp edge of his cheekbone. He stirred, and I stopped until he settled once more before I continued my exploration, my fingertips tracing down the long straight bridge of his nose. I lifted my fingers and traced the curve of his jaw, which was just square enough to keep him from looking too feminine. His full lips quirked up and I smiled.

"Are you enjoying yourself, love?" he asked, his eyes still closed.

I pushed myself up and forward and pressed my lips to his. We kissed languorously for a time, until I drew back.

"Mmmm, I love the way you taste," he murmured. His eyes flicked open and he smiled at me.

"I l-l-love the w-w-way y-you l-look at m-mm-me," I forced out.

"What way is that?" he asked, tipping his head to the side.

I closed my eyes and took a deep breath, letting it out slowly.

"L-l-like y-you adore m-m-me," I said, and opened my eyes.

"Oh, but I do," he said softly.

He kissed my lips.

"I adore your smile."

He kissed my cheeks and my nose.

"I adore your freckles."

I laughed. Truth was, I liked them too. Most people with freckles seemed to hate them, but not me. I thought they fit me perfectly.

"I adore your laugh."

He smiled and turned us so I lay on my back.

"What I really adore is that sound you make when I make you come." He smiled a slow, lascivious grin that made my breath catch in my throat.

He lowered himself on top of me, his mouth descending to my own agonizingly slowly. He kissed me, taking his time, tasting me, sucking on my lips and tongue like I was a piece of his favorite candy.

My whole body tingled, my hands cupped his face, smoothing over the light stubble there before traveling down the sides of his neck, over his shoulders. I loved the feel of him beneath my hands, the hard planes and ridges of muscle beneath the silky smoothness of his skin. I groaned as his hands traveled over my body, following the inward curve of my ribs and out again over the swell of my hip.

"My brethren need to be cared for..." he murmured, his lips against my shoulder. I groaned and laughed a little which turned into a gasp when he fit himself inside of me.

"...so I am going to make this much quicker than I'd like," he breathed into my ear.

My body ignited, his words a matchstick to start the flame. I arched beneath him and wrapped my arms around his shoulders. He drew in a long steady breath and stared me in the eyes.

I had never felt such an intense connection with anyone before, not even Josh. It was like a fine electrical current every time we touched and I couldn't get enough. I wrapped my legs around Hunter's lean hips and held him against me.

Hunter kissed me and I drowned in him completely. I couldn't fathom any place I would rather be than right here, in his arms.

I never wanted to let him go.

CHAPTER THIRTY-ONE

*H*unter

    I straightened and wiped the sweat from my brow. The fallen tree was no more. It was now neatly stacked against her house and ready for Jess to use for firewood. I closed my eyes and let the moist spring air cool my heated skin. I was waiting for Jess to come home. She would be here at any moment, and truthfully, I liked to keep as busy as possible while she was away. It seemed to make the time go by faster.

I missed her greatly while she was away at work.

Aaron would come before she came home, and Charlie was typically around. Today, though, I was alone. Dave and Margie had returned to Arizona four days ago, and though Jess missed them, she was happy.

I was happy. In fact, I could not remember a time that I was ever more at peace with my life. Jess endeavored to speak more when it was just her and me and though she didn't, I noticed marked improvement in her speech.

She and Aaron worked daily on their presentation for the upcoming bird festival, but tonight... tonight was of paramount concern. Tonight I would call upon my father's uncle to ask for some sort of resolution to Jess's and my difference in aging.

I heard her truck crunch across the fresh gravel I had laid on the drive after filling the potholes and washouts. She pulled up outside the house's garage and I strode across the drive to get her door.

"Mmm!" She made an appreciative noise as she slid to the ground. I laughed. I had taken my sweat soaked shirt off some time ago.

"Miss me, love?" I asked.

"Alw-ways." She wrapped her arms around my waist and smiled.

"Shall we take care of your charges, and have some supper?" I asked, looking her over. She looked tired, but excited. She nodded and we went to the barn hand in hand. We moved about the space independent of one another as I asked about her day. I loved hearing about what she'd done, but I loved more watching her move about the cages and enclosures, nursing her charges back to health.

Two days ago, we had released a spotted owl out near where he'd been found. Upon returning to the house, Jess had gone into a corner at the back of the barn and had carefully burned the owl's name into a wooden leaf. She had given it to me to hang upon a hook set on one of the many branches of the tree burnt into the back wall.

I had stood back and marveled at it and asked her how long she'd had it there. She had told me, since the beginning. The tree was beginning to flourish, and so I had asked her how long she'd been rescuing owls. She'd told me she was nine when she and her uncle had found their first rescue, but that Moonchild's Owl Haven hadn't come to pass until she was around thirteen. It was almost twenty years since she had begun this labor of love, if my math was correct.

With the owls fed, the feeder rodents fed and watered, and the cages cleaned, we retired to the house. I reheated left-over food from the night before while Jess showered and dressed. We were both uncharacteristically quiet tonight. I reached out and took Jessamine's hand in mine. She looked me in the eyes and smiled, but I could see she was nervous. I was too. It had been a very long time since I had spoken with any of my family. I wasn't sure how well-received I would be.

We did the dishes together and waited for fullest dark, curled together on the couch.

"What are you thinking?" I asked her.

"Wh-what if th-th-this doesn't w-work?"

"You mean what if he doesn't come?"

"No, wh-what if h-he doesn't w-want to h-h-help?" She chewed her lower lip.

"I don't know, love. It *doesn't* mean I stop looking for a solution. I want a mortal life, a normal life, with you." I rested my forehead against hers and closed my eyes.

"Y-you're sure?" she asked quietly, and I smiled.

"I've never been more certain of anything in my life, love." It was true too, but she seemed troubled by my answer.

"Y-you don-n't thin-nk we're rushing a little h-h-eadlong in-n-nto th-this?" she asked me and I raised my eyebrows in amusement.

"It may feel that way to you, love, but no. I think, for me this has been a long time coming."

I thought about it a little. Jessamine was human, and as such, limited in her experiences. I wasn't sure how to tell her that a mortal lifespan wasn't the end. That after life there was Annwn, what the Irish called Mag Mell and the Christians called Heaven.

I remained quiescent, silent on the topic, waiting for her to speak. Her troubled look remained, but finally she rested her head on my shoulder and closed her eyes. A fine wrinkle of worry remained between her brows.

"What is it?" I asked softly.

"I love you," she said suddenly, without one tremor or iota of doubt staining her voice.

"I-I'm afraid th-that you'll get bored of m-m-me and regret..." her eyes misted with tears.

"Do you trust me?" I asked gently.

"You kn-n-ow I do." She let out a gusty sigh.

"Jessamine, I love you, too, strongly. I would never regret a life spent with you." I kissed her temple.

"Y-you say th-th-that now..." she said, and I placed a finger against her lips.

"Is this about me, or about Josh?" I asked gently.

She had told me of her last romantic endeavor, and how it had ended. It was my firm opinion that this Josh character was a prat, and I had told her as much, many times over.

She frowned. I could see her thinking about it; finally her expression smoothed out in realization.

"I'm sorry," she whispered.

I smiled wryly.

"It's all right. Some scars run deeper than what is seen on the surface," I reminded her. She nodded and looked up to the clock. Her resolve had been shored up, it would seem, and I was glad of it.

I got up and held out my hand to her; she took it and I helped her up. I had told her to dress warmly, we might be outside for a bit. She had done what I asked, yet as I helped her into her rugged new jacket, I worried it would not be enough. Gwydion was notoriously fickle when it came to answering a summons or call.

We left the house, Jessamine carrying a camping lantern, and made for the edge of the wood. She was a mile or more from any neighbors and a good quarter-mile or more from the highway, which was set on the hillside above us. I nodded at her and she lit the lantern so that she could see where she was going.

The lantern hissed to life, emitting a light that glowed with the force of a captive star. I raised a hand to shield my eyes, rather impressed. We hiked into the wood together, hand-in-hand. It was much slower going than I could fly it, but I wanted Jess with me and truth be told, I don't think I would have been able to convince her to stay behind even if I'd needed her to.

We went on, our boots slipping on moss-covered logs, scrambling over moss-covered rocks, the smell of loam thick in the moist air, until we reached a suitable clearing. I shrugged out of my pack and she out of hers.

She set her lantern upon the ground and dug into the soft earth with her hands to make enough of a depression to get a fire going.

I brought out some dry wood from my pack and we set to work getting one started. As soon as it was lit, I took her hand in mine and cleared my thoughts. I nodded and she stooped, turning out the lantern, plunging us into semi-darkness.

CHAPTER THIRTY-TWO

*J*essamine

I had no idea what to expect. I stood by the fire with Hunter, my left hand in his right as we both stared into the weak flames of our fire. He reached into his pocket and threw a handful of dried herbs onto the flickering wood. Moments later a pungent, but not-unpleasant smoke roiled out. He spoke in a language I did not recognize, his voice even and clear, the words almost musical to the ear. I would call it a chant, but the words, though I did not know them, didn't seem to repeat.

I sniffed quietly, my nose running. It was a chilly early-spring night, made worse by the pervading damp. I felt as if my coat did me little good and my jeans felt like they clung to my legs. I tried not to shiver, though I was on the edge; the fire gave off more light than heat. I was tired after my long day but resolute to see this through with him.

I'd asked Hunter once what his uncle Gwydion looked like and he'd shrugged and told me it depended on which form he took. I'd asked how many forms he had and he'd looked thoughtful and told me, five that he knew of, but that he'd seen Gwydion as a myriad of different ages throughout his lifetime. It was why he'd thought of his father's uncle when it came to our particular problem. He figured if Gwydion could do it, then perhaps he could, too.

Hunter's voice ceased its praying and I studied his profile in the near-dark. His lips were pressed into a grim line and his eyes seemed far away. He shook himself, shivering as an owl would, drying its feathers, and turned his head to look at me, his owl eyes staring at me from his human face. I smiled, despite how disconcerting it was, and squeezed his hand.

"Wh-wh-what n-n-now?" I whispered, unsure if I should even speak.

"Now, we wait."

He drew me close against his side and looked around. He pulled a couple of old towels out of his pack and put them down on the ground against a fallen log, close to the fire. He added some wood and motioned for me to sit. We sat together, huddled in the dark, listening to the forest sounds and waited in silence.

I don't know how much time elapsed. In fact, I think I may have dozed off, snug against Hunter's side, because the next thing I knew, he was nudging me, a gentle prod against my side. My head snapped up and I looked across the fire, blinking to make certain what I was seeing was real.

A large stag stepped out of the wood across the fire from us, but it wasn't the right color. Rather than the tan-and-white it should have been, this majestic buck was covered in what appeared to be thick sable-black fur. Hunter and I scrambled to our feet.

"Gwydion." Hunter's voice was deep with an unidentified emotion as he greeted the stag.

The stag's image blurred and I tucked myself close into Hunter's side, holding my breath, unsure of what I was going to see.

I blinked several times. It was certainly not what I had expected at all!

Standing before us was a young man. He was taller than me, but not as tall as Hunter, and painfully thin. He wore a long-sleeved black coat that fit close to his body across the shoulders, chest, and back but flared out below the waist. Silver buttons adorned the front on either side of his trim chest and the coat dusted the ground behind his black-booted feet. The leather of his boots looked supple, climbing to his knees, silver buckles that matched the buttons on his coat gleaming along the outsides.

My eyes swept up over the boots and along his pants, which fit close to his rail-thin legs and were also black. His belt buckle, a Celtic knot-work disc, was a dark pewter, and seemed at odds with the rest of the metal adorning his clothes as a result. He wore a black sweater beneath the coat, and it, too, clung to his narrow chest. It looked soft, the loose neckline hanging scarf-like at his throat.

He had a narrow chin, his cheeks drawn beneath sharp, high cheek-bones. His nose was straight and perfect, set over a pair of almost too-familiar, full lips. His skin was ghostly pale, and had there been a moon I would have said that it glowed with its light. His hair was as inky-black as his clothes. Short in back and longer in front, it was parted on the side and a swath of it nearly covered one eye. His eyes were star-tling, as ghostly silver as the buttons on his coat, and I flushed, real-izing that, as intently as I studied him, he was studying me right back, a most peculiar expression on his face.

"Heliwr, son of my nephew, why have you called me? What's more, who is this?" he asked. Hunter palmed the back of his neck and looked decidedly uncomfortable. I wrapped my arms around his waist and hugged him, but I didn't take my eyes off of Gwydion, who was now squatting in front of our fire, his long-fingered hands outstretched to the flames. His eyes were still upon us, cool and assessing, when Hunter found his voice.

"This is Jessamine," he said finally, and the way he said it made it sound as if that should explain everything.

"P-p-p-pleased t-t-t-to m-mm-mm-meet you," I forced out in an effort to be polite. Those cool grey eyes fell upon my face and roved over me from head to toe, as if I'd done something peculiar.

"Intriguing," he said finally, then asked, "Why have you called me?" I felt dismissed, as if I were a trifle and nothing more, but it was some-thing I was used to, at least to some degree, so I didn't let it bother me. Most people heard the speech impediment and dismissed me as stupid. It's why I chose to write rather than speak most of the time. Hunter was frowning.

"I've called you because I need your help," Hunter admitted.

"Oh?" Gwydion's eyes sparkled with mirth and he stood with a smooth, liquid grace that made me blink.

"I need to know how I might age," Hunter said through gritted teeth, and Gwydion's eyes flicked back to mine, his lips spreading in a cold and predatory smile.

"D-d-don't," I said taking a step away from Hunter. Gwydion's dark eyebrows went up and he cocked his head to the side. I swallowed hard. "P-p-please, d-d-don't p-p-lay with h-him," I begged.

"Heliwr, what *is* this creature trying to say?" Gwydion asked.

"Don't. Not her, not ever." Hunter's expression turned dark and he pulled me back against him. I went willingly. Gwydion stilled and he considered us.

"You love her." It wasn't a question, so Hunter didn't answer it.

A long silence ensued.

"You called; I came. I cannot remember a time you called me, boy, so despite being in the middle of something, here I am. What is it you want, Heliwr? No games, just ask." He barely looked nineteen to Hunter's thirty, so to have him call Hunter 'boy' seemed horribly out of place and was almost too funny. I kept the observation to myself and reminded myself *what* it was versus *who* it was in front of me.

"I want to live a mortal life span with Jessamine. Age as she does... I've never asked you or anyone else in the family for anything." Hunter looked down at me and swallowed. "I'm asking now. How do I do it?"

"Did my nephew teach you nothing?" Gwydion asked, wrinkling his nose.

"You know he didn't." Hunter sighed and it was a weighted thing, full of deep sorrow. Gwydion sighed and it was an echo of Hunter's.

"Girl, come here," Gwydion said at last, after another pregnant pause. I took a step forward, but Hunter's hold on me tightened.

"I mean her no harm, Heliwr. You've just surprised me. All this time, and not once have you asked for anything of this nature. Why now? Why *this* one?" Gwydion stepped around the fire towards us when he realized that Hunter had no intention of letting me go to him. I remained still in my beloved's arms and waited for him to give me an indication of what he wanted.

"She's amazing," Hunter answered simply, as if that should explain it all.

"How so?" Gwydion pressed, and so Hunter told him everything. How we met... both times, and how he couldn't *not* love me. Gwydion looked me over, and by the end of Hunter's story was nodding absently.

"This is truly what you wish, then?" he asked after.

"Yes. With everything that I am, it is what I wish," Hunter answered.

Gwydion sighed.

"I both can and cannot help you," Gwydion said, at last. He reached out and trailed cool fingertips down my cheek. I held still, not sure what he was playing at.

"What does that mean?" Hunter asked, jerking me back out of Gwydion's reach.

"While it is true I am a sorcerer, I have no power over life and death and the natural order of things; my magic is chaotic in nature, so I cannot help you. However, I know who *does* have the power over life and death to be able to do as you ask, and I will go to him." He looked over my head at his great-nephew.

"Arawn," Hunter said tonelessly.

"Arawn," Gwydion confirmed.

Both of them were serious and both of them seemed seriously resigned. I craned my neck back and looked at Hunter, letting the question show in my eyes.

"Honestly, Heliwr, have you told her nothing?" Gwydion crossed his arms over his narrow chest.

"I've told her of you, father and mother..." he trailed off.

"Arawn is god of our underworld," Gwydion said to me and I nodded. He threw up his hands. "She doesn't get it," He put his hands on his hips.

"Of course not! How is she supposed to know when no one has ever explained it?" Hunter snapped.

"Temper, temper," Gwydion warned in a sing-song voice.

I made an exasperated noise.

"Y-y-y-you, st-st-stop being a dick!" I pointed at Gwydion.

"Y-y-you, st-st-start explaining!" That was to Hunter. I was tired, it was late, and they were talking in riddles and circles and it wasn't getting us anywhere. Gwydion looked highly amused and Hunter looked both grim and put-out.

"Arawn is..." Hunter searched for the words.

"Arawn is weak, all but forgotten. A god gets their power from those that follow them; the more that people remember them, the more power they hold onto. With as little power as Arawn has left, being all but forgotten, it is very likely that even *he* cannot help with this matter," Gwydion explained forthrightly, then muttered as an afterthought, "'Dick', indeed."

My heart sank. Gwydion considered us both.

"I like her honesty," he said to Hunter.

"I do, too."

"I will go, ask for you... Is there anything else?" He raised his eyebrows and Hunter fired off something in rapid Welsh. Gwydion responded and I looked back and forth between the two.

"It is a simple enough thing, Heliwr," The younger looking man sniffed.

"Thank you."

"Of course."

Gwydion looked at me then, and leaned forward until our noses were almost touching, capturing my eyes with his. I heard his voice, but I swear his lips never moved.

"You make him happy. Continue to do so and I will help you, but don't you *ever* call me a dick again. Read the legends and heed them well." He drew back and I cringed, huddling back into Hunter, who frowned.

"What did you do?" he demanded.

"She and I have an understanding I think," Gwydion said, eyes on me. I nodded, a little too rapidly.

"Excellent. I will see you both on the dark of the next moon, if not before." He gave us a ghost of a half-smile and put his hands behind his back. Bending at the knee, he leapt, his body blurring before taking the form of a raven and winging into the night.

I let out a breath I hadn't realized I'd been holding.

"What did he tell you?" Hunter demanded, frowning.

Not trusting my voice, I pulled out my paper and pen and wrote it for him, leaving out the very last bit about reading the legends and heeding them. I wanted to know what it meant, but it was most definitely a threat and Hunter didn't need to know about it.

He scowled in the firelight and searched my face a moment before kicking dirt on the fire. I turned on the lantern and we began the exhausting hike back to the house. I followed Hunter, sure in the knowledge that he knew where we were.

It felt like it took much less time to hike out than it did to hike in. Once in my yard, Hunter took me by the hand and went straight for the stairs leading to my bedroom's deck.

I didn't argue. I was tired.

CHAPTER THIRTY-THREE

*H*unter

The day had been too long for Jess, I could see it in the lines of exhaustion taking up residence on her fair face. Once inside the house, I helped her out of her clothes and into bed. Her skin was chill against my own and I pulled the extra blanket folded at the foot of the bed over us. She cuddled in close to me and I kissed her forehead.

I did not regret my decision, calling upon Gwydion for help. I was, however, beginning to regret taking her with me as I had. She fell into an exhausted yet troubled sleep as I held her to me and I sighed.

I was glad to be here, with her, despite the obstacles in our path. I had asked Gwydion for one other thing before he had taken his leave. Papers. A birth certificate showing that I was a man of twenty-nine years, born in the United States to an American mother and an Englishman father. I also wanted a passport showing multiple trips between America and England, from my youth until now. I wanted Jess and I to be able to marry within a reasonable period of time. Also, I wished to find employment nearby. In this day and age, having the correct papers was so much a part of that, and in order to thrive and grow into a life with Jessamine I would need such things to smooth the way.

Jessamine stirred in her sleep and I kissed her forehead again. She quieted once more and I wondered what he'd told her. It had to be more than what she had told me, to cause her to cringe as she had.

It didn't really matter.

He would hurt her over my dead body.

I closed my eyes and willed sleep to claim me. Tomorrow would be a new day, the first of the rest of our lives, even with our future uncertain.

CHAPTER THIRTY-FOUR

***J*essamine**

I didn't like to hurry up and wait, but while I was, and daily life was slow and providing no distraction, I decided to do some homework. I was sitting in my small office at the animal hospital staring at the Google search screen. I could ask Hunter what Gwydion had meant, but I still didn't think that was a good idea. I entered 'Welsh Gwydion' into the search box.

The first two returns were Wikipedia articles, which I dismissed in favor of the third, a webpage associated with Princeton College. I read the article completely, twice over. It concerned several legends associated with Gwydion. The first was about how he assisted his brother Gilfaethwy in raping a virgin woman by the name of Goewin. According to that legend, Goewin was the virgin foot-holder of Gwydion and Gilfaethwy's uncle, Math who would die without a virgin to hold his feet when he wasn't in battle. Gwydion had started a war to distract Math from Goewin, so Gilfaethwy could rape her.

Apparently, Gwydion went on to throw his own sister, Arianrhod, under the bus by suggesting she replace Goewin. Math was suspicious of Gwydion, though, so he used his magic to test Arianrhod, who gave birth to a boy on the spot, who was named Dylan. Ashamed by being called out on her lack of virginity, she took off, but not before a lump of flesh dropped from her, which Gwydion picked up and put into a chest at the foot of his bed.

I speed-read through the rest of it as it made me pretty queasy to think about, but apparently the small lump of flesh that dropped from Arianrhod became Hunter's father, Llew. And the father of Llew? Probably, he was the child of Arianrhod's rapist, who was assumed to be Gwydion.

Awesome.

So far, Gwydion started wars with trickery in order to help his brother rape his crush, had potentially raped his own sister and had offspring with her, and then went and threw her under the bus of public humiliation. I sat back and had to wonder how Hunter had turned out to be such a good and loving man after being raised by such a monster.

I was suddenly very, very glad that I hadn't asked Hunter about any of this and I paled when I read between the lines of what Gwydion had said to me. Seems in addition to being a great sorcerer and the trickster god of the Welsh, Gwydion was the poster child for rape and mayhem.

I chewed my lower lip and had a sudden aching need to hug Hunter. I thought my childhood had been messed up. Good God.

I closed out the window and got up, stretching, and went back out front. Jodi looked up from behind the front desk and smiled.

"What's up, chica?" she asked. I screwed up my face and shrugged.

"I know, it's been a while since we've been so quiet." She smiled and looked out the window past me.

I turned to see Aaron's little tan rustbucket of a truck stop in front of the bay of windows. Hunter climbed out of the passenger side and Jodi let out a low whistle of appreciation. I smiled from ear to ear. He opened the door to the lobby and stopped, a bouquet of wild flowers in his hand.

"Hey," he said softly.

"H-h-hi," I gave back tentatively, self-conscious of my coworker's stare.

"Who's this, Jess?" Jodi asked curiously.

Hunter came fully into the lobby and held the flowers out to me. I took them and smiled. He stuck his hand over the counter at Jodi.

"Hunter Grayson," he said by way of introduction.

"You're Jess's 'Hunter'?" Jodi asked blinking and I blushed.

Hunter looked at me and smiled.

"Absolutely. Yes, I am," he said.

I went to him and hugged him, sighing in contentment.

I rested my chin on his chest and looked up the short distance at him. He smiled down at me and kissed the tip of my nose.

"Wh-wh-what are y-y-you doing here?" I asked.

"Thought I would surprise you. Felt like getting away from the house for a bit; I've run out of projects. Aaron came by, we took care of the birds, and he said he would give me a ride out here. Thought I could explore a bit. Mostly, I just wanted to see you." He bent and kissed me for real then, and I smiled against his lips. I felt a touch guilty having kept him for myself these last few weeks.

"Wow, Jess..." Jodi said and I turned. She looked both happy for me and impressed.

I blushed again and Hunter laughed.

"Meet you back here in a few hours?" he asked softly and I nodded my agreement.

"See you then."

He went back out and met up with Aaron, who waved at me through the glass. I waved back, and looked down at the splash of color in my hand.

"Let's go find some water for those," Jodi said and I nodded.

We went into the back and arranged them artfully in a spare vase left in the little kitchenette portion of the break-room. I set them out at the receptionist's desk for everyone to enjoy and went on my rounds. Suddenly the day couldn't end fast enough.

It was nice to have a slow Thursday every once in a while. Thursday was my Friday, after all, but for once I could have killed to have a busy day. I checked on all of our patients, and even pitched in on some of the technician work, cleaning cages and the like. Still, it felt like the clock was mocking me. Every time I looked at it, it seemed only five to ten minutes had passed. Finally it was six, and as I was picking up my jacket and purse, I heard the lobby door chime.

"Hey, Hunter, she'll be right out," I heard Jodi say, followed by, "Jess! Hunter's here!"

I went out front and sure enough there he was, smiling, a canvas tote-bag over his shoulder. He held it out to me.

"A change of clothes. I am under orders from Charlie to take you away from the house for some fun." He smiled at me, I smiled back and traded him my jacket for the bag.

I slipped off to the bathroom and changed from my fur-laden scrubs into the jeans and blouse in the bag. It was a peasant-like blouse I usually wore in the summer, scoop-necked and embroidered with lavender sprigs along the neckline and down the long sleeves, which were gathered in a simple no-frills cuff at the wrist.

I tucked the white blouse into my jeans, grateful I had on a white camisole under my scrub shirt. The blouse would have been too see-through otherwise. I threaded my brown leather belt through the loops on my jeans and buckled it and pulled down my ponytail, running my fingers through my hair until it was as presentable as I could make it. A little lip balm and I was as good as I was going to get.

I returned out front. Jodi and Hunter were talking about the bird festival the next weekend; she was filling him in on what to expect and he listened politely, even though he'd been present for enough conversations between me and Aaron that he should know everything and then some about it.

"Ready, then?" he asked me. I nodded, and shivered internally at the way he raked his gaze over me.

"It was nice meeting you, Hunter," Jodi was saying. "You two have fun. You know where you're going to go?"

I shook my head and Hunter smiled.

"I heard about a bar playing live music tonight over in Port Townsend, I thought maybe dinner and then drinks?"

I raised my eyebrows; Charlie and Aaron must have planned this. Hunter's close-lipped smile pretty much told me what I needed to know on that front. I smirked and put my hand in his, waved to Jodi and we were out the door.

"Charlie suggested it was time to get out and have a real date." Hunter confirmed my suspicions. We climbed into my truck and I started the engine.

"I l-l-like keeping y-you to m-mm-myself." I mock-pouted. He laughed.

"I love keeping you to myself too, but at some point, we need to join the rest of the great wide world, love. Do you know where the Siren's Pub is?" he asked.

I nodded, it was in Port Townsend, nestled in the heart of old downtown on the main drag.

Port Townsend was a small Victorian town nestled on the northeastern tip of the Peninsula and was surrounded on three sides by water. To the east lay the Salish Sea; the north, the Strait of Juan de Fuca; and to the south, Port Townsend Bay. Fort Worden State Park provided a small buffer between the town and the Strait to the north, but not much of one. Siren's Pub was on the east side of Water Street, on the second floor of an old Victorian brick building.

Hunter held my hand on the hour-long drive, the radio playing softly in the cab of my truck. It was a comfortable silence, and I appreciated that he didn't feel the need to always fill it. He would raise the back of my hand to his lips every so often and plant a gentle kiss on my skin. It drove me a little crazy and it took a concentrated effort not to turn down my driveway when we passed it.

I found a spot along Water Street and parked. The sign to the Siren was visible just up the block, so we locked up the truck and I went around to the sidewalk. Hunter stood, hand outstretched for mine and I smiled, taking it. We walked up the sidewalk at a leisurely pace, looking into shop windows and just enjoying the early spring evening.

It was chilly this close to the water, with a brisk wind coming off the waves. I brushed an errant lock of hair out of my eyes and ducked into the doorway with the Siren's shingle over it. It was a long climb, up a straight and narrow flight of carpeted stairs, but it was worth it.

The atmosphere in Siren's was warm and inviting. The hardwood floors and tables were dark, rich wood. The walls were painted a deep red with just a touch of brown to them. The edges to the doorways and windows were painted hunter green, accenting the walls and giving the bar a rustic, cozy feeling. White Christmas lights crisscrossed the ceiling, providing a diffuse ambient light, enough to see by, while little crystal oil lamps flickered invitingly at each table.

We were seated at an intimate little two-person table near one of the many windows that looked out over the deck that it was still too cold to use, and beyond that, the gently-rolling waters of the small Salish Sea and Port Townsend's ferry dock. A white-and-green Washington State Ferry bobbed gently at its pier in the light of the setting sun as cars and passengers disembarked.

Hunter took my coat, hanging it gently on the back of my chair, and pushed my chair in for me. I smiled at his old-fashioned, gentlemanly ways and loved every minute of it. He took his jacket off and sat across from me. He was in his comfortable, work-worn jeans and had on a new, inky-black tee-shirt that hugged his chest and arms and made my heart skip a beat. Our waiter came and took our drink orders while the band that would be playing set up in the corner.

Self-conscious due to our very public venue, I resorted back to pointing at the menu and writing in my little leather bound notepad, glad I had plenty of paper. I think I was more reassured than anything that this was Hunter's idea, that he *wanted* to be seen with me.

Who's playing? I asked.

"An Irish folk band. Aaron assured me you liked their music." Hunter smiled, "He said if you liked Loreena McKennitt, that you would like this particular band. He said that was the music you played in your kitchen while you cooked."

He was watching me and I was smiling like a loon. I hadn't realized Aaron paid so much attention, and Hunter was turning out to be quite detail-oriented himself. It warmed me to my toes that he had planned this entire evening with me in mind.

What other surprises do you have up your sleeve? I asked.

"I have a job, and this is all paid for by me." He propped his chin in his hand and smiled across the table at me. I blinked several times, not sure I had heard him correctly.

A job? When? Where?

He laughed, his eyes sparkling.

"As of Monday. Charlie has been taking me after you've gone to work and getting me back just before you get home. It's at a hardware store in Sequim; it's not much, only a few days a week to start, but I wanted to surprise you, take you someplace nice." He grinned.

So Charlie is in on this, is Aaron too?

"Yes. They've been taking care of the owls, so I could do this." He smiled and I was filled with a mixture of joy, pride, and love for all three of them.

The waiter came back with our drinks and to get our food order, and we both laughed when we both ordered the Shepherd's Pie. He set down a Finn River Cider in front of me and some sort of amber-colored beer in front of Hunter.

The band, having completed their set-up and a short sound-check, was introducing themselves. It consisted of three men and one woman, with more instruments than people on stage. Hunter and I watched as they introduced their first song, an old English favorite, Greensleeves. I smiled, recognizing the title and we settled in to listen.

The woman sang for the most part, one man played a haunting violin, another the guitar, and the third a guitar-like instrument I had no name for. The girl played a keyboard while she sang and they were all very good. We listened, ate and drank, and I watched Hunter. At certain points his eyes shone with pride, and at others with nostalgia. The play of emotions on his beautiful face were almost more enter-taining than the music itself. From time to time he would catch me looking at him and would smile at me, and my smile would get that much bigger.

When our meals were finished, we ordered a second round of drinks and settled in to finish listening. The sun's glimmer faded completely and the water became lovely, dark and deep outside the windows, sparkling faintly with its rise and swell under the limited lights from the town.

Hunter rose and held out his hand and I took it, not quite under-standing what it was he wanted, but then he pulled me tight against his hard body, his other hand splayed at the small of my back, and with a small smile spun us out onto the tiny dance floor. I laughed and we danced sweetly to the slow lamenting song. This was simple, beautiful and perfect. I felt free, loved, and at ease with this man and for a short time I was able to push everything away.

There was no difference in age, I would not grow old while Hunter stayed young. There was no looming trial date for the two men who had attacked me, which was set for two weeks from then. There were no worries about money, or hospital bills that weren't covered by my insurance as a result of the attack. There were no concerns about having enough space to care for more owls... There were no worries about any of it right then.

Right then it was just me and Hunter, his gentle hands holding me close, the brush of his warm breath against the shell of my ear as he murmured that he loved me.

Right then, in that moment, nothing else existed except the sway of our bodies and the gentle lulling sound that encouraged us into each other's arms.

Right then, in that moment, everything was as it should be; everything was absolutely perfect.

CHAPTER THIRTY-FIVE

*H*unter

I loved that Jessamine loved her surprise, but this was a night of many and I wasn't quite through. We had a while to wait to see what Gwydion's audience with Arawn would bring, but whatever it was, I was certain of one thing. I loved Jessamine, and there was nothing in either this world or the next that would stop me from loving her.

I closed my eyes and relished the feel of her in my arms as we gently swayed from foot to foot around the small space cleared for dancing. Another couple joined us on the floor and I smiled. The way the diffuse light shone in the coppery strands of Jessamine's hair had me transfixed. The smell of her lavender, sandalwood, and vanilla soap soothed my soul as we gently rocked.

I was home when I was with her, a feeling I had never before been given the opportunity to fully appreciate. I wanted a mortal life with this woman, children with this woman, to grow old together, to travel if the fancy struck us, to learn from her and with her, to teach her, and to hold her when she cried, to laugh with her, and to be the rock she raged against when she was angry. And, oh, was she stunning when she was angry. I smiled to myself and drew back from her, spinning her and drawing her back to me. Her laugh was like high silver bells and I swelled with pride that she was here, with me, and that she wished to be.

The song ended too soon and we retook our seats. Jess was looking out the window over the water, a faraway, dreamy look in her eyes and I wondered what she was thinking about, yet at the same time didn't have the heart to ask. I didn't want to break the spell she was under, at least not yet. Instead I enjoyed the play of candlelight against her creamy skin, her straight copper locks touched with fire where they lay along her face and shoulder. The small swell of her breasts pressing against the thin material of her blouse drove me slightly mad with passion for her and I suddenly couldn't wait to get her home.

She turned and caught me looking at her, and I smiled as her eyes dilated and her supple pink lips parted. She captured the bottom one with her teeth and blushed a pretty shade of pink and I found my hand raising as I scanned the tables quickly, looking for our waiter. She was busy writing in her little notepad when I finished asking for our check.

Are you ready to go? I know I am. She gave me a delicious little smirk and I found myself shifting in my seat. I smiled, a wry twist of lips, and paid the waiter quickly and efficiently. I held her jacket for her to shrug into and let my fingertips graze the nape of her neck gently. I did not miss her little shiver, and to know that even so light a touch would garner a reaction turned me on all the more.

It was as if the air had become thinner, harder to breathe when she turned and I caught a matching naked heat in her expression. Sometimes I swore it was as if we were of one mind, one heart, and I loved her with everything I had in those moments and then some.

I held out my hand and she laced her fingers with mine and we left the little pub, descending the long staircase out to the street. The wind blew rather stiffly, and I tucked Jess into my side. We jogged up the block to her truck and she unlocked it. Once safely inside, our mouths clashed, our tongues exploring. She tasted sweet, the lingering taste of apples from her cider combining with that unique flavor that was so heady and so purely Jess.

"Drive," I growled and forced myself back to my side of the bench seat. She turned her key in the ignition and switched on her headlights.

Exhaling loudly, she pushed in the clutch and maneuvered the stick shift into first gear. The capability and grace with which she did everything captivated me.

I rode in silence the rest of the way home, just drinking in her lovely features and imagining everything I wished to do, to her and with her, in great detail.

CHAPTER THIRTY-SIX

*J*essamine

The drive back to the house seemed to take twice as long as it should have. Hunter was watching me, and I was just the tiniest bit put out that *I* had to watch the road. I finally made the turn that dipped off the highway and down the steep gravel grade that was my driveway. I wound my way down and smiled at the easy going of it. Hunter's driveway repairs were holding, and making a vast difference.

I pulled up in front of the house and killed the engine. My driveway was lonely, Charlie and Aaron's trucks absent. I turned to Hunter.

"It's just you and me tonight, love," he said softly in the dark and silence of the cab. He opened his door and I opened mine, slipping into the cool dark of my front yard. An owl or two called from the enclosures out in the yard. Hunter's warm hand closed over mine and we went into the house.

The front door clicked shut behind us and he invaded my space. I tipped my face up and his mouth pressed to mine. I sighed in contentment and he swallowed the sound with a groan. My jacket slipped from my shoulders and hit the slate entryway in a heap. I smiled against his mouth, a slow curl of lips and wound my arms around his shoulders.

He pulled my shirts from where they were tucked into my jeans, his work-calloused hands skating across the skin at my waistline before plunging beneath the denim at the small of my back. He pulled me tight up against his body and I gave a throaty moan. I could feel my pulse quicken with anticipation, the throb and beat of it spreading out through my limbs.

I toed off my boots and pulled Hunter's tee from his waistband, seeking the warmth of his skin against my hands. I ran them over his ribs and skated them gently over his ripped stomach, flattening my palms against his chest, my arms against him, just trying for as much skin-on-skin contact as I could get. He growled into my mouth and ripped his shirt off over his head, his mouth crashing back over my own as soon as the material cleared his lips. My blouse and camisole joined his shirt a moment later.

We stood, kissing fervently in the growing wreckage of our clothes and couldn't get enough of each other. I made a begging, mewling sound in my throat and distantly wondered of this wanton woman was really me.

He fumbled at his belt as I worked at my own and I giggled. We weren't anywhere close to the bedroom, but I think both of us were past caring. I stepped on the cuff of the opposing leg and dragged the pants off my leg, extracting my foot in a one-legged balancing act. Hunter's arms around me were the only thing that kept me from falling over.

He pulled the straps of my bra down my arms as I kicked free of my jeans, I stripped out of my socks much the same way I had my jeans. My hands went to his hips, pushing at the denim trapping them and he laughed against my lips. He unclipped my bra and we came up for a little air. I pulled at his waistband and his pants dropped to around his knees.

I wrapped my fingers around him and he groaned, his eyes slipping shut. I smiled and got down on my knees and replaced my hands with my mouth, licking and sucking until he threw his head back, his fingers tangled in my hair, holding it back from my face as I drew him in, my lips carefully wrapped around my teeth, until the tip of him touched the back of my throat.

"Gods above and below, Jess!" he half-gasped, half-cried and I smiled inside.

I slowly drew back off of him and let him pop from my mouth. H

He stooped, strong fingers wrapping around my upper arms as he dragged me to my feet, his mouth crushing down over my own in a demanding kiss, just this side of violent. I loved it.

My pulse fluttering in my throat with excitement, I put hands to his hips and pulled myself flush against his body. The length of him was hot and burning to the touch where it pressed between us.

He walked backwards into the living room and I followed eagerly. By then, he was nude and I was clad only in my thin cotton panties, which were soaking through. Moisture coated the insides of my thighs; I couldn't remember a time that any man had ever had such power over me. I was wild and untamed and so completely free, and I knew that shouldn't make sense, but in our world it did; it made perfect sense and I never ever wanted the feelings he evoked in me to ever go away.

I clung to him and kissed him as if he were the last drink of water and I'd just stepped out of a desert. The backs of my thighs connected with cool leather and I jumped. He'd backed me up against the back of the couch. He broke his mouth from mine and I raised my eyes from mere inches away to meet his. The color had bled again, his owl's eyes were looking back at me and it was as if the very breath was stolen from my lungs. It didn't bother me anymore; instead the sight was striking, hauntingly beautiful.

He still had me by my upper arms, and my hands were raised, pressed between us, palms flat over the smooth expanse of muscle of his upper chest. "Stop me if you need to, love. Just say the word," he murmured and spun me around.

His hand pressed between my shoulder blades and I was bent over the back of the couch. I put my hands flat against the seat cushion and gasped. Hunter was bent over me, I turned my head to the side and he kissed my cheek.

"Keep those hands where they are," he half-purred, half-growled into my ear and I shivered with anticipation.

He placed a gentle, chaste kiss where my hair began at the base of my skull, followed by another just below that, traveling in a straight line down the back of my neck. I moaned and pressed my thighs together. I felt his lips curl into a smile against my skin.

"I want you to hold still for me, love," he murmured against my skin and continued his descent, laying kiss after gentle kiss down my spine. His fingers hooked into the waistband of my panties and he gently tugged them down over my ass. His knuckles gently grazed my hips, ghosting down my outer thighs.

His lips paused at the base of my spine and lifted. "I mean it, Jess, stay put."

His breath was warm against my skin, and then his heat left me as he knelt down behind me, his hands grazing the outsides of my knees, my panties pooling at my feet in a pile of damp cotton.

I was getting a bit of a head rush, bent over the way I was, but I obediently stayed put. I trusted Hunter implicitly and I was enjoying myself, so I had no reason to not go along with what he wished.

His large hands pressed into the backs of my thighs to either side of my sex, opening me to him. "You're so fucking perfect," he murmured, his breath tickling me, and he pressed his tongue to my opening.

I arched, thrusting my hips back to meet him, and he growled in warning. I giggled and went back to my original position.

He thrust his tongue into my opening as far as he could and I gasped. It was different from this angle; not unpleasant, just the opposite. What it was, was very teasing, tantalizing, enough to set me on fire, ride that razor's edge but leave me maddeningly unfulfilled. I whimpered and writhed as much as he'd let me until finally he pulled back, standing behind me.

"Teasing you too much?" he asked.

I nodded, my vocabulary jumbled and my words all but fled. I felt heavy with need and thoroughly riled-up but I was left wanting, craving that final release. Hunter chuckled behind me and I felt him slide the head of himself up and down my slit.

"Please..." I begged, and felt a surge of triumph, both at having gotten the word out clearly and at the steady, full sensation of Hunter pressing himself inside me. I cried out, a mixture of gratitude and ecstasy, and pressed back onto him.

He stayed that way for several heartbeats, seated as deeply as he could go, simply resting there. His hands were still and warm on my hips, the sound of our heavy breathing echoed back at us.

He drew back and surged forward, sliding in my wetness, finding a pace that hit all the right places, sending quicksilver sparking through my body. His fingers dug into my hips on either side with near-bruising force, and I didn't care, I just wanted him, all of him. Our breath came in ragged pants, and I could feel that deep well begin to fill. He changed angle a few times, until I cried out, and then with a satisfied grunt drove himself deep, the head of his cock slipping over that place inside of me that had me coiling tight like a spring. He tortured that place deep inside me so sweetly, until I flew apart in his arms, collapsing over the back of the sofa, my cheek pressing against the cool leather seat, Hunter's warmth pressed over the back of me.

We came back down to earth slowly, both of us gasping. He withdrew from my body slowly, with an inarticulate cry from being over-sensitive. I knew exactly how he felt, shivering deliciously beneath him, echoing his cry with one of my own.

He robbed me of all sense when he did this to me.

His arm slid beneath my shoulders and across my chest above my breasts and he helped me upright. My wrists creaked a bit, unaccustomed to supporting me the way they had, for as long as they had, but I didn't care. He turned me and pressed the front of our bodies together. I clung to him and he to me as our pounding hearts fell out of sync, slowly returning to their normal rates.

"Was that okay?" he asked, searching my face. I nodded enthusiastically, smiling, the expression on his face causing my smile to slip momentarily until I realized why he was asking.

"Th-th-that w-was better th-than okay. That w-w-was am-m-m-azeballs!" I grinned and he threw back his head and laughed, the loudest and richest laugh I had ever heard him make, so amazing it made my toes curl, like when he kissed me.

"I love you," he said, wiping tears from the corners of his eyes.

"L-l-love you too," I murmured against his chest, and I did.

I really did.

Best.

Date.

Ever.

CHAPTER THIRTY-SEVEN

*H*unter

"Hey, Hunter?"

I looked up from what I was doing and over at Aaron. "Yes?" I asked.

"Can I ask you something?" he asked.

"I believe you just did," I said with a dry grin. He smiled back at me, almost shyly. "What is it?" I asked him, curiosity causing an itch just under my breastbone.

"You love Jess, right?" he asked.

"More than anything," I answered honestly. What was he getting at?

"When did you know?" he asked.

I set down the pliers I'd been using to mend a patch of chicken wire on one of the enclosures. They made a hollow sound on the makeshift worktable I'd set up, which was really just a sheet of plywood over two saw-horses. I crossed my arms over my chest and leaned a shoulder against one of the enclosure's supports. I leveled my gaze at Aaron. I would have to be careful here.

"The first time I laid eyes on her," I said, which was true. I think I had known we were destined to be together that moment on the highway when she'd first picked me up. Of course, Aaron didn't know that was the first time.

"Even with her all bruised and bloody like that?" he asked, his eyebrows shooting up into his hairline. Good. He still thought the first time I'd ever seen Jess had been while she was being attacked in her barn.

"Yes," I replied evenly. "I have a protective nature, so she was attractive to me even then. I wanted to heal her. Fix her hurts." True, yet untrue; how to explain that I hadn't really had a protective instinct until I met her? True still, she was attractive to me no matter what she looked like. The woman couldn't do anything at all to make herself undesirable. Just thinking about her now, like this, had my cock stirring in my pants.

"Aaron," I said, as gently as I could, "Just ask me what you want to ask me." I smiled and hoped it was encouraging.

He let out a gusty sigh.

"There's this girl…" he started.

"Ah." I jerked my head over towards Jess's picnic table. He followed me and I sat on the table, my booted feet on the seat. He copied me. I rested my forearms on my knees and waited for him to continue.

"Her name is Fallon, and she goes to my school." He palmed the back of his neck.

"Pretty, I take it?"

"Dude, you have no idea… On a scale of one-to-ten, she's a freaking twelve!" he exclaimed and I laughed.

"Okay, so Fallon's a twelve. What's the problem, lad?" I asked him.

"Have you looked at me?" he asked, holding his hands wide in front of him and leaning back, in invitation for me to assess. I raised an eyebrow and gave him a look.

"Okay, fair point, well made," I said, but I said it with a smile.

His eyes clouded and he scowled.

"Boy, I don't find males attractive as a general rule, but as far as lads go, if I were a female…" I looked at him critically. "Eh, you'd hold your own. So, what is the problem?"

"She's kind of dating this douchebag." He bit his bottom lip and closed one eye, looking at me out of the other.

"I see. Has she noticed you yet?" I asked.

"I don't know... I think so?" He chewed his lip and looked so very young. I gave an inward sigh.

"Does she talk to you?" I asked.

"Oh, yeah, all the time! We like the same music and some of the same movies. She thinks what I do out here is cool, and said she wants to come out some time. She promised to be at the bird festival to watch me and Jess present. She wants to meet you all." He was smiling and I laughed.

"Aaron, she's noticed you," I said flatly.

His face crumpled. "Then why is she with that dickbag Jordan?" he asked.

"Girls your age can be complicated-" I began, stopping at the crunch of gravel beneath booted feet. Jess was coming across the yard with a pitcher and some of those red plastic Solo cups popular at modern American parties. She poured us each some cold sweet tea and brought out one of her white writing boards from beneath her arm.

What are we talking about? she inquired.

I looked to Aaron for silent permission. He gave a gusty sigh.

"Girls," he answered, flatly.

Jess raised her eyebrows, and with a wicked gleam in her eye, pulled out her whistle.

"No! That's okay, don't call Charlie. I asked Hunter 'cause we're closer in age..."

And you were afraid Charlie would give you a bad time? She held up her sign after he trailed off.

He blushed.

Don't worry, your secret is safe with me. I love Charlie to death but dating advice from a 70 something year old man... outdated much? Hunter was a good choice.

Aaron smiled and held out his fist. Jess bumped it with her own and sat down on the bench between us. With us on the table top it put her lower and made it easy for us to read what she was writing.

Recap, I missed most of this.

"Okay, so there's this girl at my school named Fallon. Same grade, even a few of the same classes." He took a drink of tea.

"I really like her, and Hunter asked if she'd noticed me, and I was saying we're friends, but she has this boyfriend who is like this total douche named Jordan."

Jess began writing.

What makes Jordan a douche?

"Okay, okay, okay!" Aaron scrambled off the table and took four gigantic leaps out into the yard, putting distance between us.

"So, picture this blonde-haired, blue-eyed kid, about this tall," he held his hand up to indicate his shoulder height, which was respectable enough, given how tall Aaron was. "Wearin' a white tee-shirt that's three sizes too big, crotch of his pants around down here." He leaned down and waved his hand between his knees, then straightened.

"Now, this is how he walks." Aaron leaned back and thrust his hips forward, brushing his thumb against the side of his nose.

Jess began laughing, and I had to admit that the sight was a bit funny; then he walked, with a slouching, rolling gait, towards us and I had to laugh, too.

Aaron straightened and held out his hands. "As if that isn't bad enough, he has on this big silver chain around his neck, and talks like this..." and he immediately launched into an over-the-top, nonsensical accent I had heard some inner city youths use. Jess and I laughed.

She wrote *Okay I'd say he's a bit misguided, what makes him a douche though?* She looked at Aaron critically.

"He's all acting like he's hard when he's not! This is Sequim, not Seattle, and I don't even think Seattle has a 'hood like the bigger cities. It's not like we're freaking L.A. or whatever!" Aaron leapt back up onto the bench and dropped down onto the table top beside me.

"What's worse is he deals drugs, weed mostly, and calls girls 'bitches' and 'hoes', like it's cool. Fallon is a *nice* girl, sweet and pretty, and we'll be talking or whatever and he'll come by and be all like 'Yo, you's my bitch, stop talkin' to that fool!' and she's always apologizing for him and goes after him and it kind of drives me nuts." Aaron looked a little hopeless.

I couldn't see Jessamine's expression from this angle, bowed as her head was, over her writing board.

I can't speak for all womenkind here, or your friend, but I remember what it was like when I was that age.

"Any insight is better than no insight at this point," Aaron remarked dryly, and I thought it was a very grown-up thing to say.

This is a lot to write so bear with me...

"'Kay," he said.

When I was in college, so, older than you guys by like two or three years, I dated, but not much. Pretty self-conscious, you know? There were some nice guys and some not so nice guys.

"'Kay," he acknowledged.

She erased what she wrote and went on. *I fell in with someone that, in retrospect, wasn't so nice my graduating year...*

"Josh?" Aaron asked, wrinkling his nose.

Yes, Josh. I can't remember if you'd ever met him.

"I've been around three years, you got rid of him two years ago. So yeah, in that year I met him a few times. I always thought he was kind of a douchecanoe. He was never really interested in anything you were doing. Let you do all the work while he just sat inside the house and played his stupid guitar. I never figured out what you saw in him. Charlie bitched about him all the time behind your back. Said you could and should be doing much better than the likes of him." Aaron grinned.

Okay, hold up... Charlie never bitched about Josh behind my back, that's not Charlie's style, you know it and I know it. He told me to my face that Josh wasn't good enough for me and he was right. YOU DON'T TELL HIM I SAID THAT. I would never hear the end of it.

We both laughed and she erased what she wrote and looked around, as if Charlie would pounce out of the shadows at any moment.

My point is, now that I'm a year or two away from Josh and have Hunter here to compare to, I get what Charlie was trying to say. It guess it's no secret I have pretty low self-esteem. She shrugged and looked decidedly uncomfortable.

I wanted to comfort her but I waited, letting her have her say.

That's the difference between Josh and Hunter. Josh saw my low self-worth and exploited it to his own end. Hunter sees me struggle and tells me I'm beautiful and perfect.

"You are," I remarked.

You follow me?

"I think so... you're saying Josh is Jordan in this situation... That maybe Fallon doesn't think she deserves better treatment?" Aaron looked at Jess who nodded emphatically, put a finger to her nose and with the other hand pointed to Aaron. Her whiteboard slipped off her lap and landed in the gravel at her feet.

She picked it up and wiped it clean with her sleeve and continued writing.

Right, even though Charlie kept saying I deserved better, my low opinion of myself kept me from seeing it. I mean, Charlie, Uncle Dave and Aunt Margie pretty much raised me, they had to love me, right?

I was quiet.

"Er..." Aaron looked off-kilter.

Rhetorical question, you aren't supposed to answer that. Sorry.

Anyway, that was my line of thinking. I didn't think I deserved better and Josh fostered that illusion. It's a form of control. Josh never hit me, never laid a hand on me, but he didn't love me, and the way he treated me was a form of abuse in a way. I know that now. I know what being loved is better than any notion I had before.

She smiled up at me and my heart squeezed in my chest, crushed under the weight of my pride in her. She cleaned off the board and went on.

Admittedly I don't know the entire relationship dynamic going on between Fallon and Jordan, but from what little you've told me it sounds like Fallon is young and doesn't know any better about how a woman is supposed to be treated by a man.

Aaron nodded and she erased and went on.

She gravitates to you because you're doing it right and it feels nice to be around you, but girls and boys are raised to believe that when you love someone, or when you think you do, you stick it out through thick and thin. We're a monogamous culture, you stick with your mate/boyfriend/husband.

"Right," Aaron said, agreeing.

How long have Fallon and Jordan been dating?

Aaron looked up at the sky and blew out an explosive breath while he thought about it.

"We're all juniors in high school, coming up on senior year. I've seen them together a lot since... seventh grade? Maybe eighth?" he nodded.

That's four or five years, Aaron. Hell, even for adults that's a long time! She's comfortable... Jess stopped and frowned at what she'd written and erased *'She's comfortable'* and replaced it with *'It's familiar'*

Letting go of what is familiar for the unknown can be anxiety-inducing. Really anxiety-inducing, but it can also be really freeing. Exhilarating.

"So, what should I do?" he asked.

Be her friend. Be patient with her, she'll figure it out, and when she does, just be there for her. But it has to be her decision.

"Well, lad, I agree with everything Jess has said to a point," I said smiling. "I would suggest that her agreeing to see you present with Jess is a good indication she's interested in spending time with you. Ask her to dinner after, here at the house. That way it doesn't feel like a date, just a gathering of friends. No pressure." I leaned back and Jess beamed at me.

Really good idea. Yes. Do that. Don't be disappointed if she says she can't, just be patient and available until that isn't feasible anymore. Don't wait for her forever, that isn't fair to you.

"Yeah, I get that." He looked at the dirty white rubber toes of his well-worn purple canvas sneakers.

Just keep being you, Aaron. You're a good kid, best pseudo-little brother a girl could ask for. Jessamine laughed and got up, giving him a one-armed hug. She kissed me, a quick, chaste, press of lips and took her cup and pitcher back into the house.

"I hope we helped," I said, shrugging, though honestly, I hadn't done much.

"No, yeah! You guys are great! I just have a lot to think about..." he said.

"What do you know about Fallon's home life?" I asked, struck by a sudden moment of insight.

"Single mom like me. Dad took off when she was young." He gave a one-shoulder shrug and I nodded.

"So she had no man in her life to show her how a woman should be treated," I mused.

Aaron frowned. "Jess had Dave and Charlie, they're both stand-up guys... So how did she end up with Josh?" He raised his eyebrows.

"You'd have to ask Jessamine that, just remember, she had a life *before* Dave and Charlie came into it." I drained the iced tea from my cup in one long draught.

"Dude, I don't think I *want* to know what happened to her before she came here, then."

I stared at her as she stood in her kitchen, phone pressed to her ear, pressing a button here and there to answer whoever was on the other end of the line.

"You don't, you really don't," I said, strolling over to the enclosure and resuming my work.

CHAPTER THIRTY-EIGHT

*J*essamine

I hung up the phone and sighed. John had a rescue for me, a little saw-whet owl that had flown into his window around dawn this morning. He said he'd brought him in to recover, but that the little guy must have been more rattled than he'd thought, because he just wasn't coming out of it like he should. I'd stuttered out to bring the little guy in and had invited him to stay for lunch. We hadn't really spoken since the night he'd been to dinner and I'd chewed him out. I liked John well enough as a friend, not to mention he could give us all kinds of trouble when our permits came up time to renew, even if it was only every three years we needed to renew them.

Charlie came out of the bathroom and looked me over.

"You look like you've swallowed a lemon," he commented.

I shrugged. *Rescue coming in. John Baker with a window strike. Saw-whet.*

"He still butt-hurt about the other night?"

Don't know. Invited him to stay for lunch.

"Oh? What's for lunch?" Leave it to Charlie. Still didn't know how he managed to stay thin with as much food as he packed away. He should have been the size of a grizzly.

Was going to make something, I don't know what yet. What do you want?

"You got any of that flat bread stuff to make them pocket sammiches?" he asked.

I went to the pantry to check and came back with a pack of pita bread.

"Pocket sammiches it is, then! How about some of that pasta salad?" he asked.

I nodded and set to work building a do-it-yourself sandwich buffet and crafting the Italian pasta salad and a green salad. As soon as I heard tires on the gravel drive, I went into the garage and hit the 'Open' switch.

Wiping my hands on my dishcloth, I ducked out into the spring sunshine.

"Hey Jess," John said and opened up his passenger door. He withdrew a cardboard box, the kind that typically held copy-paper reams and I jerked my head towards the garage. Aaron jogged up.

"Got an intake?" he asked.

I nodded and he went into the garage and pulled down a clipboard with the beginnings of a new patient chart on it. I smiled.

"What kind of patient?" he asked.

"Saw-whet!" John answered for me and I smiled at him.

"Found him on my back deck this morning. I heard a thump against the slider, I figure it must have been him," he said as we walked into the garage. He gently set the box on the stainless steel exam table.

I pulled on some gloves that went just above the wrist. Saw-whet owls were about a palm-full, slightly bigger than northern pygmies, and oh, my god, were they adorable! With a round head devoid of ear tufts, big yellow eyes that took up the majority of their face, and tiny beaks, they looked like they were straight out of a cartoon.

John lifted the lid off the box and the little bird looked up, blinking. This one had eyes leaning more towards amber than yellow. Its tiny cat-like face, set on its oversized head, held an expression that looked pitiful.

"You p-p-oor baby!" I crooned softly, without thinking about it as I reached into the box. The little owl was far too docile, which was in line with it being concussed. I lifted it out carefully; its little head swiveled and it blinked again. I could feel the rapid flutter of its heart even through the leather of my gloves and it broke my heart a little.

Predominantly brown, the little bird's head was spotted with cream; the feathers of the body were streaked and mottled, a mixture of the two colors blending together. Aaron put an old towel into the bottom of one of the smaller kennels and went about filling water and the like. I pulled a penlight out of my breast pocket after setting the little owl down.

John was just watching me do my thing, his tee-shirt straining over his big shoulders as he crossed his arms over his chest. I hadn't even realized he wasn't in uniform. I hardly ever saw him in street clothes.

I shined the light into the little owl's eyes and watched for reaction. Its pupils were equal and reactive. The weight was good, the talons had the expected amount of wear for a wild owl. Over all, the little girl, for it was indeed a girl, was in good shape, but given her behavior, obviously concussed pretty well. We would keep her a few days, maybe through the week, and let her go as part of the festival. I didn't want to keep her too long, but I didn't want to let her go too soon, either.

I placed her into the kennel Aaron had prepared to let her rest and wrote out my diagnosis for the boys to see.

"Good! I'm glad she's okay." John was smiling.

"Can we name her Fallon?" Aaron asked suddenly and I suppressed a smile and nodded.

"Thanks, Jess." He pulled out his cell phone and took a picture of her, and went out of the garage, texting away.

"Girl he's trying to impress?" John asked. I nodded.

"Here it was, I was beginning to think that boy might be gay," he muttered and I made an incredulous noise. "What? Not that there's anything wrong with that!" He ran his hand through his hair and asked, "Is there?" like he wasn't sure which way I swayed.

I rolled my eyes and shook my head. No, there wouldn't be anything wrong with that! I loved Aaron for Aaron, he was a great kid. Gay, straight, or a purple people eater from Mars, it made no difference to me.

John grimaced and at least had the grace to look embarrassed. I huffed out a sigh; it really wasn't his fault. I mean, we were raised out here in the sticks and a lot of people still had a lot of prejudiced attitudes out here. I was damned lucky I was raised by Uncle Dave, Aunt Margie, and Charlie. They held no such notions and were as progressive as they come.

I pulled off my gloves and motioned for John to follow me. I left the garage door open to get some fresh air in for the little owl and went into the house from the side door. John followed me in and down the hall.

"So, uh, how is Hunter? Still here?" he asked and I nodded. I washed my hands at the kitchen sink and motioned for him to do the same. It was always a good practice when handling animals, wild or domestic, before eating or, really, doing anything else.

I picked up my whiteboard and pen.

Yes, he's outside repairing one of the outdoor enclosures.

John grimaced and took a deep breath.

"Listen, Jess, you know I've had my eye on you for a long time now..."

I stilled and set the pitcher of tea I'd pulled out of the fridge on the counter. I nodded carefully. John sighed.

"He beat me to it didn't he?" he asked.

I think my face fell. I had never had an interest in John beyond friendship. I just wasn't attracted to him in that way. How the hell do you tell someone that though!?

"Never had a chance did I?" he asked, reading the war of emotions on my face.

I shook my head miserably. I hated letting him down, he was a genuinely nice guy...

"Don't feel bad, Jess," He said and my heart broke a little for him.

How can I not? I don't want YOU to feel bad. You're a great guy John, just not the guy for me...

He winced a little and took a seat at the lunch counter.

"Can we forget my dumbassery and stay friends?" he asked, meekly.

You are not a dumbass and of course we can.

"Charlie might argue with you on that one," he said with a smile.

Charlie used to be Dept. of Fish and Wildlife before he went Tribal Affairs.

"No shit?" he asked and looked impressed.

Not kidding. Charlie is just an ornery old coot that had a bone to pick with the government. Bet he'll be nice to you today. No uniform. I smiled and he did too.

"Think I'll wander out there and see if anyone needs a hand if it's okay with you," he said, but really I think he just wanted to talk with Hunter.

I nodded.

I'll ring everybody in for lunch as soon as I finish a few odds and ends I promised. *I figured we could eat outside. It's nice.*

"Yeah, that sounds good." He smiled at me and I went around and hugged him. He hugged me back, awkwardly at first, and then, nodding, went out the side door and into the side yard where Hunter, Aaron, and Charlie were standing near the enclosure they were mending.

I smiled and went to work brewing some more tea to replenish the low amount in the pitcher. Aaron came in a moment later and asked what he could do to help. I told him to set the picnic table and threw him a vinyl table cloth from one of my bottom kitchen drawers. He grinned and went to it.

He came back in and I flashed a sign at him.

They talking about me?

Aaron looked aggrieved. I stuck my tongue out at him.

Fine I won't make you break some precious bro code you've got going on with them but you have to realize it sucks being outnumbered like I am!

He laughed and I wrote out...

Ring them in. Fix plates in here and eat out there.

"Yes, Ma'am!" He saluted and went out to ring the triangle.

It was good to be surrounded by friends and family.

CHAPTER THIRTY-NINE

*H*unter

"John! Civilian life look good on you boy. Should do it more often," Charlie grunted and I turned to see Jess' Department of Fish and Wildlife friend approaching. I painted a pleasant smile on my face. I knew this man harbored feelings for Jessamine, but she was, and always would be, mine now.

"Uh, thanks Charlie, I'll try to do that." John smiled.

I nodded.

"Mr. Baker." I held out my hand and he shook it.

"Please, call me John," he said.

I nodded and an uncomfortable silence descended on us.

"I'm gonna go help Jess," Aaron said and jogged off towards the house.

"So, uh, what're you guys up to these days?" John asked, and Charlie spit on the ground. I chuckled and decided to throw the chap a bone.

"Well, we put in the garden pond, over there," I pointed.

John gave a low whistle. "Looks nice. Good habitat for a turtle or two," he nodded absently.

"...and we were just discussing building some new enclosures around back. Since Margie left, the garden around the back of the house isn't being used for anything. Jess doesn't garden, nor does Charlie here." I left off the fact that I didn't garden either. There was no use in saying so. I didn't wish to antagonize the man. He must have been thinking it anyway though, with what he said next.

"You don't garden either?" he asked me, his smile a bit rueful.

"No," I said, succinctly.

"I think it's a good idea, as long as you're staying on to help her." He looked me over and I blinked, surprised.

"I am..." I said, cautiously.

Charlie looked from one to the other of us and wandered off without a word, to help Aaron wrestle a table cloth onto the picnic table.

"Jess is a good woman," John said.

"The best," I intoned.

He chuckled.

"I've had a crush on her since junior high," he confessed. "Been chasing her ever since she off loaded that last asshat. I guess it just isn't there for her." He shrugged a little and I wish I could say I felt for him, but I didn't really understand. I'd never been there. Then I thought about what it would be like to have Jess tell me no, that she didn't feel anything for me, and I winced.

"I'm sorry, mate," I said, and I was.

"Still friends." He forced a smile, "If nothing else at least I still have that."

I clapped him on the shoulder. Good man.

"So," I said, "I was thinking about a large enclosure, to house multiple birds at once. A space to rear fledglings; Jess said she sometimes got them but usually had to make do with using one of the aviaries." The problem, she'd said, was that it sometimes pushed other birds recoveries back because she didn't have a place to keep them where they could fly on their own, slowing down their rate of recovery.

"A space like that, out back, would be ideal since no one spends all that much time back there. Less human traffic means less likelihood that any of them would get too used to humans and imprint."

John was nodding.

"What do you think you'd need, materials-wise? I have some old lumber out back that's still good so long as it gets used," he commented.

"I could get some other materials together out of what the hardware store will be getting rid of," I mused aloud.

"Did you tell the hardware store that Moonchild's is a five-oh-one-C-three?" he asked.

"What's that?" I asked, scowling.

"A nonprofit organization. They donate, Jess can cut them a receipt for the worth of the goods and they can submit it with their taxes for a tax break," he said.

"I didn't know that." I was completely lost. "I'll mention it to them."

"Might help," he said.

"Thanks."

"Don't mention it." He smiled and I returned the gesture.

"Hey, guys!" Aaron called. "Come and get it! Jess says to dish up in the house, we'll eat out here." He disappeared back into the kitchen.

John and I exchanged looks and went into the house together. I was cautiously optimistic that perhaps a friendship could be had with the man. Whatever Jess had said or done, the woman was as much magic as I or Gwydion. I smiled to myself and followed John through the make-shift buffet line.

CHAPTER FORTY

*J*essamine

I was a little nervous. Okay, I was a lot nervous. We were at Railroad Bridge Park in Sequim. The park was home to the Dungeness Audubon Center and it was sunny, and epically beautiful – and *way* more crowded than I had expected it to be.

Piper cheeped from my shoulder, and I took in a deep breath and exhaled slowly. Hunter rounded the corner and stopped when he saw my face. His expression softened and he dragged me into his arms.

"You'll do fine," he murmured into my hair. I nodded a little too stiffly against his shoulder and he chuckled. His voice took on a soothing, almost hypnotic tone. "Aaron's going to do all the talking, it's just you and my brethren. Just you and the owls." He kissed me and I relaxed against him.

It was going to be okay. I knew that. I swallowed hard and took a step back. He held out a finger to Piper and she stepped up. I nodded and went to the dog carrier that held Dawn, our barn owl and most fit flier. I pulled on my glove and extracted her, making sure her jesses were secure around her ankles. She flapped her wings in a bit of indignation before settling comfortably on my gloved hand.

I took her out from behind the Audubon society's building and to the perch we had designated for her. I set her on it and secured her jesses, and stepped back. Hunter put Piper into a little cage that Aaron had found at a garage sale. It was as big as one of the dog carriers and made from an ornate brass-like metal. It reminded me of something out of the Victorian era with its three sweeping domes, surmounted by another to create a tower as wide as it was tall.

We'd cleaned it thoroughly and had decided that it would be perfect for little Piper to be part of the lecture. Northern pygmy owls weren't caught very often and were even more rarely seen in the wild. Same with the saw-whet.

We had little Fallon with us too. We had decided that she was fit for release and that it would make a good finish to the day out here today. We could talk about saw-whets, she could meet her namesake, and when the lecture was through, we would drive over to John's and let her go. In celebration, John had a barbeque planned for us.

It was shaping up to be a really busy day.

I looked around for Aaron and saw him striding towards me and Hunter, a pretty, athletic blonde girl striding alongside him. I nudged Hunter who looked up and smiled.

"Not as pretty as my girl by half," he murmured and I laughed.

"Hey, Hunter! Hey, Jess!" Aaron called when they drew close.

I waved, smiling brightly.

"Fallon, this is Jessamine Connors and Hunter Grayson. Jess runs the owl haven where I volunteer," Aaron said, by way of explanation.

"Hi!" Fallon greeted and shook my hand. I waved enthusiastically with the other.

"Hello, Fallon, nice to meet you." Hunter shook her hand.

"Aaron's told me all about you guys." She laughed.

I brought out my notepad.

If Charlie were here, he would ask you what lies Aaron has been telling.

She read the note and laughed.

"Where is Charlie?" Aaron asked.

Taking care of the birds back at the house. He'll meet us here before people start milling around and drive over to John's after this for the BBQ. Fallon's coming right? I asked.

"Uh..." she sounded uncertain and Aaron smiled.

"If she wants to," he said.

"Yeah," she finally agreed, smiling. "Thanks, that'd be really great!" Up-close, she was even prettier. Tall and willowy, with fair hair and sparkling blue eyes, she looked like she belonged on the cover of a magazine, not here in Railroad Bridge Park. I liked her instantly.

She was quiet and shy, and didn't really seem to rely on her looks. She was a very down-to-earth girl, in her manner of dress. While most teen girls dressed more to impress the opposite sex, Fallon wore jeans, sturdy sneakers, and her high school's hooded sweatshirt which was purple with yellow lettering. It had the school's mascot, a wolf, on the front and I saw that the back read 'Lead, follow, or get out of the way!' when she turned to get a good look at Piper.

I gave a low whistle to get Aaron's attention. He turned and I jerked my head toward the truck.

"Sorry!" he said sheepishly and went in that direction. Hunter laughed and put his hands on my shoulders, massaging. Fallon was still looking at little Piper, then moved on to look up at Dawn on her perch. She was about to get a little too close when Hunter spoke up from behind me.

"I wouldn't get too close," he said kindly and she was about to ask why when Dawn opened her wings and ruffled her feathers.

Fallon jumped back with a yelp.

"She was so still! I didn't think she was real!" she exclaimed.

Aaron was coming up with the carrier that held Fallon the little saw-whet and the carrier that held Odin. I looked up at Hunter and he let me go. I smiled. He really did know me.

I went forward and pulled on my gloves and took Odin's carrier. I brought out the crotchety old man and secured him to his perch by his jesses. There was no way he'd be coming off it, glove training hadn't really been his thing. In fact, four orange traffic cones went around his perch, establishing a decent perimeter. They were the tall tube kind with the black rubber base and the loop at the top. Through the loops we strung caution tape and made a diamond around the bird, a very clear indication to stay back, and to look but to go no closer.

Aaron was telling Fallon about the little Fallon and Hunter and I exchanged smiles at the delighted sound that came from the girl as she peered into the front grate on the carrier. Aaron was proudly pulling on a pair of gloves to transfer the little rescue owl into another birdcage that looked like it should be an antique but really was a find at a local pet store. It was little Piper's old cage, for when we used to loan her to Jaye to take on her school lectures.

Jaye was setting up on the opposite end of the field. Rows of moveable aluminum bleachers on wheels had been set up to one side with an expanse of grass between us for the lecture and demonstrations to take place. I could make out Jaye's slight form moving between her hawks', falcons', and eagles' perches and portable enclosures.

Hunter and Charlie would be building a collapsible enclosure for Odin for these events. For now, the traffic cones, caution tape, and Charlie standing sentry would have to do. People were starting to arrive, so I made an effort to get a move on and get the rest of what we had to offer out.

We had two tables, one with general information on the owl haven, what to do if people found an injured owl, and a place to receive donations.

The other table was all Aaron's baby. He had it set up to help people dissect their own owl pellet. We had two five-gallon buckets of them standing by, a couple boxes of surgical gloves and the other trappings to get the job done, and several giant trash cans lined up, complete with trash bags, for cleanup.

Hunter, Aaron, Charlie, and I all wore black tee-shirts with a lifelike three-quarter's full moon on the back, an owl silhouetted against it on open wings. Bold white letters proclaimed 'Moonchild's Owl Haven' across the back, and smaller, where the pocket would be on the breast. They looked good and had been a gift from my animal hospital for the occasion.

I looked around nervously for Charlie as I brought down the last carrier, a barred owl named Butterfinger.

Not my idea. Barred owls were the most common owl found out here, next to the barn owl, except right now Moonchild's didn't have any. Butterfinger was on loan from Jaye and the Northwest Raptor center. He was a mild-mannered bird and went on the final perch between Dawn and Odin.

We had briefly toyed with the idea of having Hunter fill in, but had dismissed it as being folly *and* dangerous. Too many people would miss Hunter-the-human and wonder why he wasn't present, seeing as we had been inseparable since his 'arrival.' I asked him if he ever missed flying or his owl form, and he had confessed to me that he sometimes went out on a short flight while I was sleeping. At first, I didn't quite know how to feel about that, but had decided that it was something that was Hunter's and Hunter's alone, that we all needed a little alone time and that it wasn't something I could share in anyway, so why shouldn't that be his?

We finished setting up and when we were done we had the two cages, one set higher than the other, on two round tables that were garage-sale finds. So we had Piper the northern pygmy, Fallon the saw-whet, then Dawn our barn owl, Butterfinger the barred owl, Odin our great horned owl, and, in the only collapsible enclosure we'd managed to build in time, Winter the snowy owl, looked pretty pissed off and disgruntled.

I grinned; we'd reasoned that Odin was used to people, even if he was grumpy and bit, but Winter was wild and due for release in the next week or two. So Winter got the enclosure and Odin got Charlie. Odin was on the losing end of that deal.

Charlie was striding across the grass at a good clip and I smiled. People were in their seats, and Jaye was taking to the field to introduce. Hunter called to Aaron, who came up even with me. I glimpsed Fallon's blonde head as she took a front-row seat and I smiled at Aaron. He winked at me, and we headed for the field so Jaye could introduce us. Success or failure, we were here, and in it to win it. I took in a deep breath and with a smile plastered to my face, I turned and waved at the crowd.

Jaye went first with her falcons and then it was up to me and Aaron. I pulled on my glove, took Dawn to hand and we strode out. I hadn't needed to worry. Aaron was a natural crowd-pleaser.

Aaron had devised a demonstration a long time ago with Dawn, putting clickers inaudible to the human ear out in the grass for her, to demonstrate an owl's exceptional hearing. We put Dawn through her paces and my pretty girl didn't disappoint. There was 'Oh'ing and

'Aw'ing and applause, and we returned to our end of the small field. Aaron did all the talking, I did all of the handling, and everything worked out perfectly, far better than I expected. I was suddenly excited about future opportunities to teach. The fake smile I'd plastered on in the beginning morphed into a genuine one within a matter of minutes.

Jaye went out again, and we traded off between us for the better part of two hours, educating and demonstrating, telling our specific bird's stories, and about conservation efforts in general. Finally, when we returned to our respective ends of the field, and with our birds safe, fed, calm, and secure, people started wandering over for a question-and-answer session.

I had my whiteboard at the ready and Charlie stood near Odin and fielded questions about him like a pro. He was extremely patient when it came to the kids, and I was surprised at how patient he was with the adults. Hunter answered questions about Butterfinger and Dawn, while Fallon stood between Piper and Fallon with a clipboard of information Aaron had given her. Aaron was elbow-deep in curious kids and teens dissecting pellets and explaining about owl feeding habits while I manned the information table. Very little talking needed to be done there, with all the literature we had available.

The day wore on.

John had shown up and was helping keep an eye on the birds, looking for any signs of stress and making sure people kept their distance, and I appreciated it. When all was said and done, Charlie would be taking the residents back to the haven while the furniture and Fallon, our release bird, went with us to John's.

Jaye came back to collect Butterfinger and tried to thank us for coming when it should be us thanking her for allowing us to come. She had, after all, arranged the whole thing with the park and Audubon society. I expressed my gratitude, we hugged, and with waves and smiles parted ways. She had her own fly-babies to get home and settled.

Hunter kissed me and said he was headed to the house with Charlie to help get everyone cared for. I kissed him back and nodded, grateful. We packed everything up, discarded our trash correctly and tried to leave our space better than we'd found it.

It had been a long and very successful day for the owl haven. We'd raised two hundred dollars in donations, which was enough to buy the materials we couldn't have donated for the aviary project in the back that Hunter and Charlie wanted to undertake.

I got in my truck, kissed Hunter a final time through the window, and with Aaron and Fallon behind me, followed John's Jeep to his house.

CHAPTER FORTY-ONE

*J*essamine

I carried little Fallon in her cat carrier around the back of the house and onto John's big back deck. Aaron and Fallon followed, carrying a cooler full of food I'd prepared for the occasion. John was in charge of the meat. I had spent a chunk of last night fixing a pasta salad, a potato salad, a fruit platter or two, and three cherry pies to bring.

John fired up the gas grill and let it sit to get hot.

Aaron and Fallon immediately set to work setting up the food on a side table while I set little Fallon on the porch railing, far away from all the human activity, to settle. John handed me a bottle of Finn River cider and clinked the neck of his bottle against my own.

"You did good out there today, Jess. Take a load off and relax." He gave me a crooked grin and I smiled in return.

I dropped into one of the eight seats round his huge back patio table gratefully. The sun was going down and he went around the perimeter of the deck lighting citronella tiki torches. He then lit three citronella candles in the center of his table. Fallon and Aaron came over and sat down and we all let out a comfortable sigh at once, then laughed.

"I think we did good, Jess. What about you?" Aaron asked.

I beamed at him and nodded.

Fallon's phone made a sound like crickets in her pocket and she pulled it out. She frowned at the screen.

"Something wrong?" John asked.

She grimaced. "No, it's fine." She put the phone away after tapping out a short message.

It chirped before she even got it into her pocket. It chirped four more times in the next two minutes.

Parents? I wrote.

"Boyfriend." She scowled. "He always wants to know where I'm at." She heaved a sigh and pulled out her phone, coloring in embarrassment at whatever was there.

Aaron was as stone-faced as I'd ever seen him, I smiled at him, tremulously proud of his self-control, and put pen to whiteboard.

Sounds pretty controlling. Are you okay?

Fallon opened her mouth but her phone started ringing. John's eyebrows went up.

"Sorry, I, uh, I should probably take this." She answered the phone with a meek "Hello?" and an angry male voice came through the speaker by her ear. She got up abruptly to go around the side of the house and Aaron made to stand, too. I put out my hand and gestured for him to sit down. Fallon hadn't seen and was stepping off the deck.

When she'd passed me I'd heard swearing coming from the phone. I frowned. *Not that I didn't believe you, but from what I just heard coming from that phone, it's confirmed. Fallon's boyfriend is a dickweed.*

John laughed at my sign directed toward Aaron, and Aaron scowled.

"So what are we going to do about it?" he asked.

"Hey, now wait a minute," John said, putting down his cider. "What makes you think you two should be getting involved?" John asked.

John, when you were seventeen, would you call your girlfriend a "fucking bitch" and threaten to "slap her like the nasty ho she is"? Because that is what I just heard come out of that phone, in that lovely girl's direction.

I scowled at him and he swore.

"Son of a bitch, what're parents teaching kids these days?" He looked at Aaron.

"Don't look at me, I wasn't exactly a model citizen until Charlie and Jess got a hold of me. My mom didn't raise me to be a punk; she couldn't help that she had to hold two jobs at the time to make ends meet." He sniffed. "I blame my deadbeat dad. I don't know what Jordan's excuse is."

It doesn't matter. What does matter is that Fallon is better than that. What we need to do is make her understand that she is beautiful and smart and lovely and deserves so much better than what he's offering.

Both boy and man looked thoughtful for a while.

I erased my message just as I heard Fallon's soft tread coming up behind me. I turned to see her come up on the deck, Hunter and Charlie behind her. Hunter had her phone in his hand and I smiled at that. I looked at Fallon and got up, tucked her under my arm, and whisked her into the house and into the bathroom.

Okay. I'm only going to say one thing on this matter...

"Okay," she said tremulously. She quailed as I ran the tap.

Your boyfriend isn't much of a boyfriend. No man should talk to a woman the way I heard him talk to you through that phone. You deserve better than that and he doesn't deserve to breathe the same air as you.

"He's not always like that–" she started and I raised my hand, palm out, to halt her.

I said I was only going to say one thing and I did, and now I want you to think about this, I mean really think about this: Where do you see yourself in five years?

"Graduating college," she said without missing a beat.

Okay, now I have to ask, do you see Jordan graduating college with you?

She chewed her bottom lip.

"No," she admitted, finally.

I gave her my most solemn look and her shoulders slumped.

Wash your face, sweetie, dry those tears. We're going back out there, we're not letting this ruin the night. You're going to set little Fallon free and we're all going to celebrate.

She smiled and did as she was told. I handed her a towel and she dried her face and hands.

"Aaron said you were tough," she said. I smiled and held out my arm. She laughed and linked arms with me and we went out onto the back deck to a bunch of sour faces that lightened and smiled when we came outside.

Aaron, I think Fallon should do the honors of setting little Fallon free don't you?

It was getting darker and he had to squint to read my sign. He grinned broadly and nodded.

"C'mere, Fallon, put these on," he said, and I went to Hunter who still wore a dark expression. John and Charlie had their heads together. Hunter drew me to him and kissed the top of my head.

"Planted some seeds, did you?" he asked and I nodded, watching the two teenagers.

"Charlie and I found her crying at the end of the drive on her phone, begging for the boy on the other end of the line to stop yelling at her. I took it away, told the boy he was a prat, and shut the phone off, but not before calling her mother and giving her your number in case she wished to reach Fallon."

He kissed the top of my head again absently. The girl in question had the gloves on and was listening to Aaron's careful instructions on how to catch the bird in the carrier.

"Her mother was concerned, she's had her suspicions about the nature of her daughter's relationship with the boy. She said she was glad I put a stop to this episode and that she has tried speaking to Fallon before, but perhaps if Fallon will not listen to her, she may listen to us."

I nodded and smiled, jerking my chin in the direction of the girl who had the little saw-whet carefully clutched between her gloved hands.

Hunter pulled me back into the warmth of his chest and rocked me a bit. He kissed the top of my head and I smiled, he couldn't seem to stop doing it.

I asked him, *Still have her phone?*

"Yes."

Good, don't give it back until she's ready to go home. She's earned a douche-canoe-free night.

Hunter laughed softly. We watched Fallon open her hands. The bird got up on her feet and blinked, but made no move to fly just yet.

"Hold still, she'll go when she's ready," Aaron urged.

Fallon laughed nervously and I more than half-hoped that Aaron would win the girl. They made a cute couple.

"Uh, Aaron, she's not flying away..." Fallon said, but just as she opened her mouth to say more, little Fallon fluttered her wings and took off into the trees.

I blinked back tears.

"You been doing this twenty years now, Jess, ever since you was nine, and you still cry every time!" Charlie remarked and there was laughter. I dashed at my eyes and sniffed and waved a hand at him to bugger off. He chuckled.

"Got a beer for this ol' Indian?" Charlie asked John.

John got one out of the cooler next to the grill and handed it to Charlie who looked over the bottle with admiration.

"Good boy," He said and cracked it open with his bottle-opening key chain.

"I'm not a dog, Charlie. Hunter, you want a beer?" He turned and Hunter smiled.

"Have any warm?" he asked.

"Warm beer?" John asked.

It's an English thing... I wrote. Hunter and I had had this conversation a while ago. I still declared him disgusting for it.

"Sorry, man, I put it all in the cooler." He pulled out two and handed them to Hunter.

"I only drink one at a time," Hunter laughed.

"Yeah, but at least your second one can be warm." John made a face.

"Appreciated."

"Jess, you make pie?" Charlie asked. I held up three fingers.

"Good woman, just like your aunt Margie except without the drama," He grunted and took a pull off his beer. I slapped his shoulder. He loved Aunt Margie as much as me and Uncle Dave, but he had a point, too.

Steaks sizzled as John threw them on the grill and the smell of cooking meat wafted through the air. I smiled and cuddled back into Hunter. Fallon was smiling and listening to Aaron, all traces of sadness gone.

It was a good day.

CHAPTER FORTY-TWO

*H*unter

I smiled and left Fallon, Jess, and Aaron in the barn. It had been a week since Aaron and Jess had performed and lectured for the Bird Festival, and Fallon had been here nearly every day with Aaron since. Her mother had even come on Wednesday night to meet us and say thank you. Jess insisted they stay for supper. Fallon had broken things off with her ne'er-do-well boyfriend and had been much happier since volunteering at the owl haven. Her mother was even more impressed that Fallon's volunteer work at the haven could go onto her high school transcripts and might help her chances of getting into University.

The last week with Jessamine had been pure bliss. The woman was a balm to my soul, soothing in so many ways, her calm and gentle nature my addiction, if addictions could be a healthy thing.

I was putting the tools I'd been using away when I heard the exhaust and bass emanating from a car coming down the drive. I came around the side of the barn and watched the black Honda hatchback roll to a stop. A boy matching the description Aaron had given us got out of the idling car, gangster rap spilling out 'round him, dirtying the pristine atmosphere around it. I came forward.

"Yo, I'm lookin' for my girl Fallon," he said, jerking his chin sharply into the air.

"I don't believe she wishes to be found by the likes of you," I stated simply.

"I don't care what the bitch wants. She's mine and I'm here for my property, you feel me?" he asked.

"Leave now, before I call the authorities." I pursed my lips. Fool child.

"I said get my mutha-fuckin' girl out here, fool!" He jabbed his hands in my direction.

"Little boy," I began, "leave now. The girl is not and has never been 'yours'. She doesn't want you here, and you are not welcome."

"Yo, you disrespectin' me?" he demanded.

I smirked. "From where I am standing, I see nothing to disrespect." I turned to walk away.

It was the wrong thing to do.

CHAPTER FORTY-THREE

*J*essamine

    Pop pop pop! The sounds were sharp and immediate, followed by a slamming car door and the wash and ping of gravel as the car outside peeled out. My heart clouded over with dread. Aaron, Fallon, and I traded looks and dashed down the stairs from the old hayloft. I was the first out the barn's door and what I saw stopped me in my tracks.

Hunter lay face down on the drive, the back of his white tank top flowering crimson.

I screamed, a wordless broken wail and scrambled to my knees beside him. I didn't know what to do! I screamed and screamed and prayed and Charlie came out of the house.

"Jess? Jess, what is it? Were those...? Son of a bitch!" He landed on bended knee beside me and started doing things. I vaguely remembered that he had been a medic in Vietnam, surely Charlie would know what to do. I looked around: Aaron was on his phone, a glazed look in his eyes, speaking mechanically into the line. Fallon stood to the side, shaking.

"Jess, Jessamine!" Charlie barked. I looked at him. "Hold pressure here!" He pressed my hands down and blood welled between my fingers hot and slick. I moaned and sobbed.

Please God, let him be okay. Let him be okay, let him be okay. Gwydion, please hear me, please help me, I don't know what to do! I thought furiously and tried to do what Charlie told me to do. I was shaking and fighting the rising swell of panic inflating like a balloon in my chest, expanding painfully, squeezing everything else out of its way.

Arawn, that's the name of his death-god... I remembered faintly, then savagely wrestled that thought to the ground. No. Hunter was not going to die. No. No. No. No. No!

You keep your damned hands off him, you hear me, Arawn! Not yet, not yet, not yet! You can't have him yet! I prayed furiously, tears dripped off the end of my nose and splashed onto the back of my hand.

Sirens wailed in the distance, too far in the distance.

Not yet, Arawn, do you hear me! Not! Yet!

CHAPTER FORTY-FOUR

*H*unter

I lay on my back, the sun warming my face, painting the insides of my eyelids with fire. I dragged my hand off the grass and put it up over my face to block the searing light. I tried to remember what happened and couldn't come up with...

The boy. I turned around, a loud noise and searing pain, falling into the void...

I sat up sharply and looked around. I was in a meadow, jewel-like butterflies flitting from flower to flower, glowing brightly in the too-white sunlight. Fruit trees rustled in the slight summer wind. It was comfortably warm, a perfect day. I looked down at my tunic and breeches and groaned.

"No!" I roared furiously.

"That is not the reaction we are accustomed to." An amused, musical, female voice said from my right. She spoke in the old tongue and I blinked.

A copper-haired lovely woman in a white homespun gown lounged upon a stone, bare toes peeking from beneath her gown, a crown of flowers upon her brow. Fierce green eyes raked over me.

"Bébinn?" I asked.

"Well met, Heliwr." She smiled and grief axed me in my chest, cleaving me in two. Her smile turned into a frown.

"So I have passed beyond the veil, then?" I asked.

"Not quite. You are in the spring meadow; the summer fields of Annwn yet await. You fight, cling to the mortal coil. I would know why." She crossed her arms and raised a brow.

"Please, Bébinn, I would speak with Arawn, I beg you!" I reached out a hand, beseeching.

Bébinn laughed, a high sweet sound that was bitter broken glass to my ear.

"Why ever would you wish to speak with my husband?" She was baffled and I tried valiantly to collect my scattered thoughts, pressing a hand to my brow.

"I beg of you!"

"Not until you tell me why, Heliwr!" She had a stubborn set to her chin and I sighed.

"I cannot leave the mortal plane," I said.

"Why ever not?" she asked.

"There is a woman there..." I said, and I told her of Jessamine.

"She is to me as the moon is to the stars, she is my one. I cannot contemplate an existence without her. She saved me, and I, in turn, saved her. Together we are two halves of the same whole." I looked up to her, pleadingly, not even bothering to disguise the tears in my eyes. Bébinn's expression softened.

"We do not always get what we want, Heliwr," she reminded me gently.

"Do you not think I know that!?" I asked. I pounded a fist savagely against my chest. "I am the only-born son of Llew Llaw Gyffes! You know my story..." I challenged her then, pointing a finger in her direction, the anger and bitterness rising in my throat like so much bile. "... and in knowing my tale, have you known me to have *ever* gotten what I wanted?" I asked quietly.

"Perhaps not what you wanted, but what you needed?" she said back.

"I need Jess," I said with absolute certainty.

Bébinn cocked her head to the side and considered me with a sweep of her gaze.

"What do you want from me, Heliwr?" she asked, her tone gentled.

"Persuade your husband to hear me out. Just listen to what I have to say..." I pleaded.

She nodded finally, and transformed into a white dove, taking wing across the meadow and out of sight. I closed my eyes and prayed to every god and goddess I could think of that Jess was safe, that she was well, and that I might see her once more.

CHAPTER FORTY-FIVE

Jessamine

They had taken Hunter by ambulance to a nearby field and had airlifted him to Harborview Hospital in Seattle. I hadn't been allowed to go with him. Instead I had agonized through the almost-two-hour drive from Sequim to Seattle. John had driven us, and by 'us', I mean me and Charlie. Aaron and Fallon had been taken into protective custody. Fallon had said it was Jordan's car speeding up my drive while I had stood in numb shock.

I had paced in the hospital's waiting room for a further four hours while Hunter had been in surgery, and then recovery. Now I sat mutely, a dried-out husk, at his bedside and waited. The doctors had said that he had lost a lot of blood and sustained some pretty horrible injuries to his insides. His heart was okay, but one of his lungs had taken a bullet.

Hunter was in a coma while they waited to see if he would make it.

It was a big IF.

I hadn't moved from his bedside, and I wouldn't until he woke up. I wiped errant tears away while Charlie and John talked behind me in hushed tones about what to do. Hunter's blood was still on me, my clothes, and under my fingernails.

John tried first.

"Jess?"

I raised my chin to acknowledge that I'd heard him but my eyes were glued to the tubes taped to Hunter's face.

"Jess, come on, let's get you cleaned up." He gripped my elbow and tried to get me to stand.

"No!" I ripped my arm savagely from his grasp.

"Jess, come on now." He tried again.

"No! I'm not leaving him," I sobbed and he stilled. Charlie too. I hadn't even noticed the words had come out clear.

"Jess." Charlie, this time.

"Jess, come on, you need a change of clothes, a shower, something to eat. The hospital will call us if anything changes."

I huddled in on myself miserably, refusing to budge.

"Let's give her a minute," Charlie said over my head. John grunted, in agreement or distaste or what-have-you, what, I couldn't tell you. I didn't care.

I couldn't even muster a care for my owls back home. For that I felt a small pang of guilt, and a laugh bubbled in my throat and burst upon my lips in a fresh sob.

"Please, don't leave me," I whispered and squeezed Hunter's hand. It was warm in mine, but his color was off. His usual sun-kissed bronze wasn't warm and alive like usual. Instead his tan just sort of sat on his skin, which was marred by a waxy pallor.

I sniffed and wiped at my tears with my other hand.

Please, don't take him away from me... I prayed at Arawn.

"Gwydion, where the hell are you?" I muttered.

"Right behind you." Hs lyrical voice answered me coldly.

I put my feet to the floor and stood, turning so I could see him. He looked as he had in the wood, young and clad in the same black outfit. I sniffed, my eyes welling with tears that spilled hot and fresh down my cheeks, and the cold silver of his eyes softened a little around the edges.

"H-how could this h-happen," I hiccupped.

"I am not wise to the ways of men. I haven't been for a long time," he said softly.

"Save him?" I asked gravely.

"I cannot. He is in the spring meadow, on the edge of Annwn. He is in Arawn's hands now."

He sighed. I sobbed.

I turned to look at Hunter and my legs turned to jelly, spilling me back into the chair at his bedside. Gwydion's hand gripped my shoulder and I took Hunter's hand between my own.

"H-he has to live..." I said, my voice brittle.

"It will be what it will be," Gwydion murmured and stayed behind me. I laid my head on the bed, my lips pressed to Hunter's hand and murmured my prayers to Arawn, a god I did not know, for mercy...

CHAPTER FORTY-SIX

*H*unter

I did as Bébinn asked and waited. The sun did not move in the sky, the temperature never grew too warm or too cold, the breeze was never anything but pleasant. I sat upon the rock, eyes closed, head bowed, and willed Jessamine to be all right. I prayed to my family to look after her. A shadow passed over me, and when it did not immediately move, I looked up.

Arawn was ever a cutting figure; he wore neither white nor black, though his long hair and trim beard were black and his skin a pale marble-white. His eyes were golden and deep, grave where they rested upon me.

"You are neither here nor there, Heliwr. Why do you resist my final call?" His voice was bass and deep and held the belling of the hounds in full hunt.

"Her name is Jessamine," I said, and Arawn's chin rose a notch, his nostrils flared and he breathed in deeply through his nose.

"Long has it been since I have been prayed to," he said, "yet here, you are and a woman's voice invades my waking dream. At first, she demanded, then she asked, and still, now, she pleads." He looked down his nose at me.

"She is a good woman. When I first saw her, I thought her to be your wife, Bébinn, come to fetch me here." I smiled wanly.

"You wish me to spare you?" Arawn asked.

"I wish for more than just that," I looked up at him, "I wish for a life with her," I said.

Arawn's eyebrows rose.

"I asked my father's uncle, Gwydion fab Don–" Arawn spat on the ground and I winced, but pressed on, "to ask a boon on my behalf."

Arawn threw back his head and laughed.

"A worse emissary you could not choose!" He crossed his arms and I blinked in confusion. "There is no love lost between Gwydion and myself. Long has he vexed me, boy."

"That's Gwydion for you, he vexes everyone," I said dryly.

"What of this boon?" Arawn asked, curiosity shading his tone.

"I was going to ask you make me mortal. I wished to age as Jessamine does, have a life with her, grow old with her, die with her..." I stared at my hands.

"There are few of us old ones left," Arawn drawled.

"I am aware," I said.

"What you ask of me, it requires great power." Our eyes met and I could see his indecision.

"Less now, I would think." I held out my hands so that he might take in our surroundings.

"Your father's blessing and I might do this." He nodded judiciously and my heart sank.

"I..."

"That is my condition, Heliwr fab Don."

I closed my eyes and let out a breath. I nodded, finally.

"I will summon him, then." He turned, and I wondered just how I would do this.

CHAPTER FORTY-SEVEN

*J*essamine

I slept. I don't remember falling asleep, but I did, and when I woke it was in a meadow, bright and full of sun, wildflowers swaying gently in the breeze. I blinked and sat up, confused.

"There you are." Gwydion stood, his arms crossed over his narrow chest.

"Am I dreaming?" I asked.

"Yes. It was the best I could do. If you want to say goodbye, then you'd best stand up quickly and follow me." He snapped his fingers at me impatiently and I got to my feet and looked down at what I was wearing, confused.

I must be dreaming, I wouldn't wear something like this in a million years. It was a dress, for one, and I just didn't do dresses... It was a cream color that made my skin seem even paler, and looked like something out of a medieval fantasy movie with long heavy skirts and long belled sleeves, the top of the gown off the shoulders. It looked like a cream-and-white version of the Sleeping Beauty Disney princess dress.

"Come on!" Gwydion said impatiently, and began striding away from me across the meadow towards the trees at the far end. I gathered up the cumbersome skirts and ran after him, the tall grasses and wild flowers thrashing in our wake. Butterflies in impossible jewel tones fluttered and scattered in front of us, fleeing from our path, re-collecting in our wake.

"What is this place?" I asked.

"The spring fields of Annwn. My nephew has been summoned, he told me, presumably to speak with his son. Some mortals reach this plane in sleep; a little bit of guidance and here you are. Your body is where it should be, beside that of Heliwr's in his hospital room." He looked sideways at me.

"Thank you," I said, then, in a stroke of inspiration, asked, "Is it because I'm dreaming that my words aren't mangled?"

"Your words haven't been mangled since the first time I saw you." He looked at me, puzzled. "You spoke just fine in your human hospital."

I stopped and thought about it. I had, hadn't I? I resumed pushing through the long sweet meadow grass and flowers, almost crashing into Gwydion's back when he stopped short.

I peered around his shoulder and saw another man's back. His hair was just as raven-dark as Gwydion's, and curled over the collar of his gray cloak. He was speaking to someone I couldn't see.

"I understand, but this is your modern-day way of thinking. I am of the old ways. Humor me, Heliwr."

An exasperated sigh.

"My father hates me, he would never agree to this, just to see me..."

"Hunter!" I made a break around Gwydion and shot past the man in gray, stopping short. Hunter was sitting on a rock in old-fashioned clothes like me, like, really old-fashioned, his hair loose about his shoulders.

His eyes widened and filled with horror.

"No, Jess, you shouldn't be here!" he cried, yet opened his arms all the same. I went into them and held close to him.

I should be crying, but the tears just weren't there. I felt odd and disconnected but I was here, and Hunter was here and I took it for what it was– a chance to say the things that most people never got to say to their loved ones.

"I don't want this to be the end," I said.

"I know, love, I know," he murmured against my shoulder, but I had no feeling here.

It really *was* as a dream. Simply images, sounds, but no sense of touch. I breathed deeply and was assailed by the antiseptic hospital smell; things began to fray; and then Gwydion was beside us and things drew back together.

"Thank you," I whispered to him and he nodded.

"Quickly. I cannot do this forever," he stated.

"Gwydion?" Hunter asked.

"She's dreaming; it was the best I could do, son of my nephew," and he stepped away from us, solemn. The man in gray looked furious but not at us, his malice was directed solely at Gwydion.

"Jess," Hunter began, but I interrupted him.

"I'm here, with you at the hospital," I rushed. "I love you so much, I'm not ready to let you go, so please, please fight, don't leave me, Hunter, because you have all of me, if you leave me there won't be anything left for Aaron, for Charlie, for Uncle Dave and Aunt Margie. I won't make it without you. You're my other half, I can't go back to being a half a person without you. So please, please, don't go."

Hunter looked over my head at the man in gray and I turned.

"Please, don't take him away from me, Arawn," I said.

"She is bright," the man in gray stated flatly.

"I told you she was."

"I can also see why you mistook her for my wife," Arawn remarked.

Hunter opened his mouth to reply, when a shadow passed over our little group. I looked up into the too-bright sky. A dark shape plummeted in my direction and I turned and pulled myself tighter against Hunter and wished that I could feel his warmth, that I could carry the memory of my last moments with him as fully as I would the feel of his hand beneath mine against the standard hospital sheets.

The large flying shape resolved itself into that of a man and I blinked, shocked. He was the spitting image of Hunter in all things, except eyes and hair. Whereas Hunter's eyes were a rich dark caramel, this man's eyes were a clear, light blue. The man's hair was fair, so blonde as to be white, while Hunter's was more reminiscent of his owl's form, brown with the white streaks that could be a man in his early thirties going prematurely gray or a really good dye job, depending on who you asked.

I swallowed hard.

The man contemplated us and then asked in Hunter's lovely voice,

"Heliwr, son of my wife, why are you here? Arawn, what is the meaning of this?"

Gwydion stepped forward and took me by the elbow.

"Time to go, Jessamine," he said softly.

"Please, no..." I moaned brokenly.

"Jess, it's okay," Hunter said, but his eyes held only sorrow, the loss that was already hollowing me out reflected in his eyes.

"It's not okay!" I screeched.

Gwydion took me from Hunter and I crumpled, both inside and out.

"Llew, hear the boy out," Gwydion said and I screamed my frustration and heartbreak to the empty, too-bright sky until the light dimmed and I woke with a gentle start.

Alone.

The sheets beside Hunter's too-still hand were damp with my tears, the IV taped to the back of his hand was pressing into my temple. I stood up with a start and looked him over. He still had his color, which hadn't really changed. I waited, holding my breath, and let it out slowly when I saw his chest rise then fall in steady rhythm. He was still alive, still in there somewhere, but not.

I sat back down heavily and watched him sleep. I was tired of these gods and their rules and games, keeping Hunter a prisoner of their will. I sniffed and wiped my nose on my bloodstained sleeve, not caring. I closed my eyes and went back to praying.

I knew they could hear me.

I just hoped it would be enough.

CHAPTER FORTY-EIGHT

*H*unter

I fisted my hands in my hair and emitted an inarticulate cry that encompassed my anger, my frustration, and a myriad of other feelings that all led up to just how helpless I felt in this situation. Gwydion was gone, and with him, Jess, her words echoing in my consciousness.

I won't make it without you... I can't go back to being a half a person without you...

I rounded on my father, who stood coolly appraising me.

"You." I pointed at him and he raised his eyebrows.

"You selfish, spoiled son of a bitch!"

I spat on the ground.

Llew threw up his hands and turned to Arawn.

"I did not come here for this, I won't stand here and–"

"All you have to do is give your blessing on this, and you can be rid of me forever," I grated out.

"Blessing for what?" Llew asked, suspicion clouding his eyes.

"Your son wishes to live a–" Arawn began.

Llew barked out a laugh.

"You don't need my blessing for that." Llew crossed his brawny arms across his chest.

"As I was saying, your son wishes to live a mortal lifespan with his woman, age and die as a human man." Arawn leveled his golden gaze on him.

My father was still, so very still, for long minutes, the only movement where the breeze ruffled his hair or the fur edging on his cloak.

"Why should I grant you this?" he asked me.

"How long are you going to hold yours and mother's mistakes against me?" I demanded in return.

"*My* mistakes?" he bellowed.

"Yes! Yours!" I stabbed a finger in his direction.

"Tell me, boy, what mistakes were mine?" He was coloring red with rage but I didn't care. Too long had I held this at bay.

The words flooded out of me in a torrent of malice.

"You, who had your wife created for you, a being with her own free will, tell me, did you even try to know her feelings? Did you even try to court her, treat her with respect, or did you simply treat her as your God-given right? As your property?"

He was silent and so I went on.

"Does it really surprise you that she would choose another?" I demanded.

"You were not there!" he choked out, nearly apoplectic with anger.

"I *was* there! *I* was the one to take the punishment you could not visit upon my mother! Raised without a father by *your* uncle!" I screamed.

"You are not my son!" he screamed back.

I got inches from his face. The heat of my anger was an inferno in my chest and I screamed back at him,

"Look at me! I am a mirror image of you! How can you deny I am your son when I look just like you!?" We stood, squared off, our chests heaving, Arawn standing somberly to one side.

I broke away first, and paced in a direction that was simply *away* from the man responsible for half of my creation.

"You would choose a life among them?" Llew asked finally.

"No. I choose a life with Jessamine," I said back.

"Do what you want, Heliwr. You are your own man. Never darken my door again." Llew turned to Arawn.

"He is not my son. He is a man with no father. I killed that man centuries ago. Let him do what he wants." And with that he shifted into his form of a great golden eagle and took to wing.

"Will that suffice?" I asked.

Arawn looked troubled and yet almost sheepish. He grimaced.

"I did not realize your relationship to be so... contentious." He finally settled on the word. It wasn't the best fit, but it was diplomatic. I let him have it.

"It is as it has ever been," I sighed.

"Do you love this woman?" he asked, suddenly.

"With everything that I am." I closed my eyes.

He sighed and seemed torn.

"Long is the day, and long is the night..." he murmured.

I finished for him.

"And long is the waiting of Arawn."

I smiled, and he did, too.

"I believe I can wait a little longer for you; a human life is not so very long for one such as us." He crossed his arms and leveled a stern gaze at me.

"You must understand the choice you are making. If I do this thing for you, you will be stripped of all that makes you 'other'. You will grow sick, you will grow old, you will be susceptible to all that can ail you as a simple human man – and no longer would you fly..."

I raised my hand.

"As I told my father, I tell you... I choose Jess."

He nodded.

"This will be painful, do you wish to stay a little longer? Allow your body further time to heal?" he asked.

"No. I want to get back to Jess. She thinks me lost. I don't wish for her suffering to continue."

"Very well. Close your eyes, this will not be a simple thing."

I did as Arawn bid. I had thought I was prepared; little did I know it was impossible to prepare for such a thing.

CHAPTER FORTY-NINE

Jessamine

For three days it was touch-and-go. I didn't shower, I didn't eat, and for the most part, they let me be. Charlie stayed with me, and John came around often, making the long drive from the Peninsula almost every day. On the third day Charlie had enough.

"Jess, come on now. You're taking a shower, changing out of those clothes ain't going to make no nevermind! You think Hunter's gonna wanna wake up to you like this? Come off it now!" He crossed his arms and looked pretty damned heated, but I didn't budge. Not until I heard it.

Hunter coughed.

I turned around and his eyes were open, he was scowling, and it was as if the heavens opened with rain after a long drought. I fell to my knees beside the bed and I cried. Taking his hand that reached for me between my own, I kissed the backs of his fingers. Charlie was out in the hall, calling for a nurse, and the tiny hospital room filled with men and women in scrubs, bustling about Hunter's bed, forcing me back and away from him. I was suddenly no more than a leaf caught in an eddy in the sudden stream of humanity pouring into his room.

Charlie had me by the shoulders, gently but firmly holding me back while they asked Hunter questions and worked to calm him down, administer pain medicine and finally, to extract the tube that had been helping him breathe, now that he was breathing on his own.

That had been horribly painful to watch.

He had choked, sputtered, and coughed until finally, in a raw and hoarse voice he had said, "Jess, I love you. Listen to Charlie, go shower."

I had dissolved into tears and a kindly nurse had told me to use the bathroom in his room. Charlie had a bag of clothes that John had fetched from the house and had thrust it into my hands. I'd done as Hunter asked at warp speed, and by the time I was through, it was just Charlie and him in the room. Charlie got up and pressed me into the seat by the bed.

"I'll leave you two alone a minute," he'd said and disappeared out into the hall. The door clicked shut behind him.

"How?" I asked. I hadn't had trouble with my words since the realistic dream that hadn't been a dream. I think it was Gwydion's gift to me... although it may have been the trauma of seeing Hunter shot, I just didn't know. I didn't care. He was here and I would have traded what little speaking ability I had left for him in a heartbeat.

"Arawn," he rasped.

I smiled a little sadly.

"Are you..?" I asked, and he nodded.

"I chose you, Jess. I *choose* you." He pulled me, weak as he was, and his arms went loosely around me. I kept myself off of him, mindful of his injuries, and we kissed, softly, a press of lips, wholesome and sweet, and I felt a like whole person again.

Thank you, Arawn, Gwydion... Thank you, so much.

CHAPTER FIFTY

*J*essamine

Hunter had to stay in the hospital for close to two months. I took as much time as I could off work to stay with him, but in the final two weeks, I was limited to visiting on just the weekends.

We spoke of my dream that wasn't a dream, and Hunter told me what he had given up for me. I had cried and he'd told me to stop, that in his eyes, while feeling physically free as an owl, he had been locked in a lonely emotional prison while in that form. It took me time to come to grips with that but I had never seen him so at ease before. He worked hard to get better and he would have months of therapy to go, but *today*, today he was coming home!

I pulled my truck up to the hospital's main entrance and rushed around to open the passenger door. I bounced on the balls of my feet, waiting for the nurse to wheel him out. It was a little disheartening how much weight he'd lost, but when I'd said something, he'd told me my cooking would put it back on in no time and the muscle definition would come back in time, too.

After two months of artificial hospital lighting, Hunter put his hand up to block out the sun when they finally brought him out to me.

He got into the truck with only minor difficulty, they smiled and waved and he waved back and we drove away, heading for I-5 and the James Street on-ramp.

"What became of the boy?" he asked me as we pulled onto the freeway.

I put the truck in its final gear and he linked fingers with mine immediately. We always touched when we could.

"Convicted, attempted murder, tried as an adult... He's going to prison for a very long time," I said.

"A shame," he said, and I could hear he meant it.

I was glad Jordan was going to prison for what he'd done, but I still couldn't help but feel bad for him just a little bit, too. No one had tried to stop him, no one had cared enough to keep him from going that far. I was sure Fallon had tried but that was a lot for one lone seventeen-year-old girl.

We spoke of plans for Hunter to get back on his feet, and of finances as well; a victims' advocacy group had reached out to see what could be done to help with Hunter's medical bills, which were in the hundreds of thousands of dollars.

We spoke of what he wanted me to fix for him when he got home. He celebrated that he would have to eat no more hospital food. When we got to the ferry terminal, he reveled in his first experience of driving onto a ferry. We took the Edmonds-to-Kingston run across the water, a short thirty-minute voyage and about fifteen minutes into the almost-hour drive home from the Kingston ferry dock, he was fast asleep, my hand clutched in his lap.

He woke when we pulled into the driveway.

Balloons and a big 'Welcome Home Hunter' banner hung on the barn. Aaron, Fallon, Charlie, John, Jodi, Jaye, and a small phalanx of her volunteers were all there to greet him.

Jaye had risen to the occasion, and along with John and Charlie had managed both her sanctuary, and Moonchild's Owl Haven since Hunter was hurt and I lost my mind for a while. Now that I wasn't divided between Seattle and home, I would be able to take better care of my fly-babies. I was forever indebted to Jaye and her kindness though, with no way I could ever repay her.

We had let Winter go two weeks after Hunter went into the hospital. I felt bad he couldn't be there, but Fallon had taken video with her cellphone and uploaded it to YouTube so he could see. She was very technologically talented, and was building Moonchild's a better website.

People began cheering when Hunter got out of the truck and he waved at them before we helped him inside. Charlie had dragged one of the recliners into the kitchen for him and he sat gratefully while I cooked and everyone laughed and drank and was merry. It was quite the welcome-home party.

My favorite part though?

When everyone was gone and it was just Hunter and me alone in our bed. Carefully and slowly we made up for the last two months, and conceived our first child.

EPILOGUE

SIX MONTHS LATER...

*H*unter

I stood, and for the first time I could ever remember, I was nervous about seeing Jessamine. Family, friends, all were gathered under the protection of the barn. Lights had been installed, the bird enclosures moved upstairs, carefully ringing the rails, so not only did the humans bear witness, but so did the owls.

The railings and pillars dripped with ribbons and lavender, perfuming the air lightly as everyone directed their attention to the barn's massive door.

I stood in front of the altar which we had placed at the foot of the tree burned into the back wall, the wooden leaves fluttering on their hooks. Charlie was my best man, John and Aaron my groomsmen. Jessamine had Jaye, Jodi, and Fallon as her matron of honor and bridesmaids.

Dave and Margie were bringing her up the aisle, and for a moment I forgot what it was to breathe.

She wore a long sleeved gown, the sleeves sheer; the satin bodice hugging her delicate curves in a fall to the floor that left her silhouette both sensual and alluring. The swell of her pregnant stomach did not seem out of place in the dress, but rather made her more beautiful to me, my one and only love, the mother of my son who was growing inside her...

Dave and Margie gave me the hand of their great-niece and adoptive daughter, and we stood before our friends, our family, and our owls and made the most solemn of pledges, the strongest of vows we could muster from the depths of our hearts.

I married my wife, the other half to my whole, and made our union one of forever before the gods.

Never had I been happier in the choice that I made.

I chose Jess, for now and forever.

My love.

My wife.

My heart.

AUTHOR'S NOTES

Some very special people and organizations made this book happen and they deserve some special recognition.

First of all, Jaye Moore is a real person, a real, special person that run a very real and special 501c3 Nonprofit by the name of the NW Raptor Center. Yep, it's real folks. Jaye and her troupe of volunteers are out there on the Northern Olympic Peninsula of Washington State living the life of Jessamine Connors and I'm here to say they could use your help!

Without Jaye's knowledge and input I never would have been able to understand the commitment and methods behind wildlife rescue. I wanted to make sure I made Jessamine's world as believable as possible.

If you are interested in helping with the cause, please visit Jaye and NW Raptor Center's home on the web at: http://nwraptorhttp:I'm not sure why this is deleted. I didbn[t delete it, and I can't seem to put it back. and remember, all donations are tax deductible and not only go to the rescue of the owls of the Oly Peninsula, but also a myriad of other wildlife including hawks, eagles, falcons, deer and more!

If you find sick or injured wildlife, do not try to help them yourselves! You need to get on the web and find the number of a professional like Jaye to come to the rescue.

I know folks mean well but...

It is vitally important to call in the professionals when it comes to this kind of thing, not only for your safety, but for the animal's safety as well.

If you want to do more than just throw money at one of these organizations, take the time to volunteer and learn to do it the correct way. There are a lot of operations out there that could benefit from your help and if the first one you call can't, they are usually more than happy to direct you to one who can!

Finally, my medical go-to guy, and childhood friend, Josh Grant. Without his knowledge and input on how to help and care for the humans, I would have been woefully underprepared in dealing with our hero, Hunter's, injuries. Josh is a real-life hero, serving as a medic in the U.S. Army, and in case you missed it, yep, that's right! You knew you recognized that name, he's the real-life inspiration for another army medic, Grant Mason in my book Lyrical Hearts!

Thank you, Josh. You, sir, are the awesome!

As always, dear readers, thank *you* for picking up my book and reading. I hope I've entertained you again, and as long as you are out there reading, I'll be in here writing.

ALSO BY TIMBER PHILIPS

Hallowed Be Thy Light

Hunter's Choice

Love in Purgatory

ABOUT THE AUTHOR

Timber Philips hails from a land filled with beauty and steeped in magic; the Pacific Northwest. She swears you can see fairies and goblins, magic and promise around every tree and in every drop of water and she shares that magic whenever she can. She loves welcoming everyone to her worlds of romance rooted in fable and fantasy.

Stalker Information:
www.timberphilips.com

Facebook Group
https://www.facebook.com/groups/timberswolves

facebook.com/authortimberphilips

bookbub.com/authors/timber-philips

instagram.com/authortimberphilips

twitter.com/timberphilips

www.ingramcontent.com/pod-product-compliance
Lightning Source LLC
Chambersburg PA
CBHW070632170726

48291CB00003B/984